SOARING SPARROW PRESS
presents
a comic novel

by the author of *The Champion of Reason*

The Geographer

Jim Riva

ISBN: 1-891262-01-7

First published in 1998 by Soaring Sparrow Press

Cover design and interior design by Satoshi Uegaki

Printed in the U.S.A.

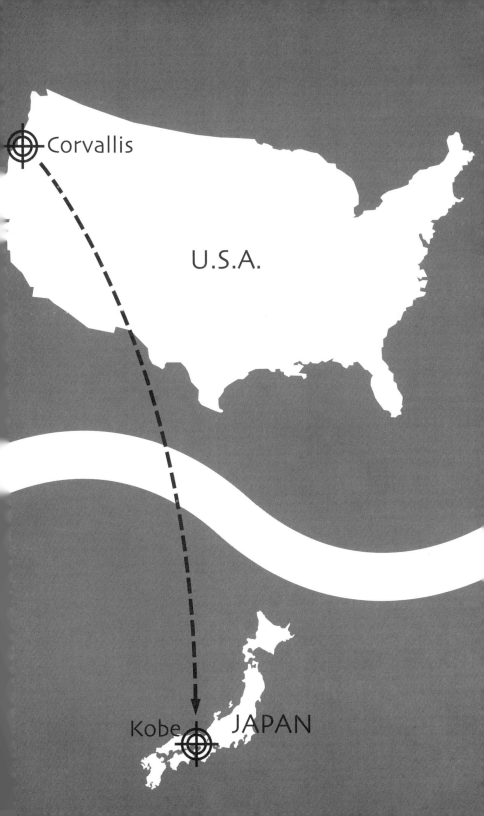

Corvallis

U.S.A.

Kobe JAPAN

Note from the author:

Macrons appear over some vowels, such as the first 'o' in Kyōto, to denote the long vowel sound that occurs in many Japanese words and 'Japanized' English words. Vowel sounds in Japanese are the same as they are in Spanish and Italian. Definitions/explanations of Japanese words are footnoted at the bottom of the page on which the words first appear. Some characters in this book speak in Japanese, but translations appear in parentheses so that they can be read like subtitles in a foreign film. Translations, which are also underlined, have been made non-literally in some cases in order to capture the real meanings. For example, the real meaning of the Japanese proverb 'Sanshō wa kotsubu de piriri to karai' probably wouldn't be understood in a literal translation (Japanese peppers are small but spicy hot) but could be perfectly understood by translating it as 'Good things come in small packages.' The Japanese characters in this book who speak in Japanese do so in conversational Japanese and, as the story is set in Kōbe, most of them speak in Kansai Dialect.

P.S. This book is a work of fiction, pure and simple. More specifically, it is a historical novel, and it was written with no intention whatsoever to defame anyone in any way. Although the book has its critical side, it would be totally inaccurate to accuse me of being a Japan basher. I wouldn't have lived in Japan for the better part of 14 years if I didn't enjoy the country. I met many, very many, wonderful people there. I'm happily married to one of them.

Acknowledgment:

I did my best in writing this book, but my best would not have been good enough without all of the help I received from my wife, Sawako.

May 8th, 1994

Winston Baldry had been away for far too long. Two days away from his hometown of Corvallis, Oregon were more than one day too many, but the proximity of the International Geographers' Convention in Seattle, Washington gave him the gentle nudge and the swift kick in the rear to set foot outside the state of Oregon for the first time in his 41-year-old life. Returning by bus because he did not own, and had never owned, a car, he gazed out the window and stroked his beard. The hair on his head was completely black, but his beard was completely white. Without it, he would have looked too young to be taken seriously as a professor. As being taken ridiculously was as unwanted as being taken seriously was wanted, he negated the visual contradiction in public by wearing a hat. With his hat on, he appeared to be in his late 50s. Perhaps his beard was prematurely white because his biological clock was overcompensating to display the real time on a face that had remained boyishly youthful from never having accumulated stress that would have naturally come from venturing out of his shell and into the unknown. 'Unknown' isn't quite the right word because Winston knew anything and everything about world geography. He could amaze you (and bore you to death) with facts and figures. With the whole wide world in his head, he was respected by many, although some of his students referred to him disrespectfully as Whitebeard the Hermit.

Winston's wife, Wallis, who he met while working on his Ph.D. at Oregon State University in Corvallis and married soon after getting hired at the same university, didn't want Winston to be without his beard, because without it, he looked much younger than her. Wallis by no means looked old; she simply looked her age, also 41. She had been spared any wear and tear that might have come with childbearing because Winston's sperm seemed to be as averse to traveling as *he* was. They had tried everything and nothing had been successful. Still relatively young, Wallis had that look in her eyes that older people do when they feel it's too late for them to do what they really wanted to do. What Wallis really wanted to do was travel, and that want, a burning desire, was refueled every day at Let's Go Travel in downtown Corvallis, where she worked as a travel agent. Her problem was that her husband would not travel anywhere and she didn't feel right traveling without him. They didn't even go on a honeymoon. They were married a few weeks after Winston got hired in 1981, and he said that he needed to devote all of his time, if not all of his energy, to preparing for his upcoming classes. He promised her that they would go on a honeymoon soon, but that promise was made again and again over the years until the countless pre-attached excuses left it empty. She had an inkling early on that she wasn't going to be visiting other countries. Twelve years before, while visiting her sister at the coastal town of Newport, she threw a wine bottle into the Pacific Ocean with a message in it that said: "This is a chain-message in a bottle, started on July 22nd, 1982 by Wallis Baldry of 633 Sunnyside Street in Corvallis, Oregon, USA, wishing whosoever may find it happiness. If you wish to participate, please contact the last person on the list and also the person on the list who lives farthest away from where you live. Then add your name to the list, put it back into the bottle, being sure that the cork seals it well, and throw it back into the sea." For three months, the bottle kept getting washed up just fifty miles south at Coos Bay, but then a fellow who had found it four straight times on the beach outside his cabin wrote to Wallis for the second time and said that he would soon be vacationing in Acapulco and would take it with him and throw it into the sea down there. That's when things started getting interesting. Four months later, Wallis received a letter from a woman in Esmeraldas, Equador, who wrote in Spanish that the cork was in such bad condition that she had to push what was left of it down into the bottle but there was no need to worry because she found a bottle cap that fit perfectly. Wallis was really looking forward to her next letter, but it was a long time coming–so long, in fact, that she had almost given up hope. It was in December of 1993, ten years after the letter from Equador, that she received a postcard from Fiji from a New Zealander who said that she was on holiday in Fiji and one of the local fishermen caught a shark and found the chain-message in the bottle when he gutted it. The woman went on to say that the bottle cap was so damaged by oxidation and the acids in the shark's stomach that it broke off when the fisherman took it off but that she could rest assured that her chain-message would keep on going because she cleaned the mouth of the bottle and put an aluminum cap on it that would stand up better against the elements. Wallis was angry at that darn shark but found renewed hope. Winston told her that ocean currents would carry it due west and that it might wash up on the shores of eastern Australia or some island on the way, such as New Caledonia. She hoped that it would wash up on New Caledonia. What a wonderful follow-up that would be after such an exotic place as Fiji!

Looking out the bus window and stroking his white beard, Winston thought about the many exotic places that his friends the Pipers had been. Having just returned from a three-week trip to Egypt, Turkey, and Greece, they were coming to his house that evening for dinner and would have a lot to talk about. They certainly would have fit in a whole lot better than he did during the dinner-scene the evening before at the Seattle Convention Center. 400 geographers were there, some with names like Mapp, Rivers, Forrest, and Lake. They were seated for dinner in the convention hall when one of them, a fellow who had just returned from a field season in the Amazon, asked a waitress about a particular dish and was told that it was Yorkshire pudding, which prompted a National Geographic Society explorer of the Arctic to say, "I had Yorkshire pudding in Yorkshire," which prompted a map maker to shout out, "I had Peking duck in Peking," which set the ball to start rolling with shouts from over here and way over there: "I had Belgian waffles in Belgium," "I had a hamburger in Hamburg," "I had a Singapore Sling in Singapore," "I had Swiss cheese in Switzerland," and so on. People shouted from their seats ("I had Hungarian goulash in Hungary," "I had a Spanish omelette in Spain," "I had Swedish meatballs in Sweden," . . .) until a National Geographic photographer who had been to 137 countries stood up to shout, "I had Parmesan cheese in Parma," which got people to start standing up to make themselves heard with shouts like, "I had Welsh rabbit in Wales," "I had Bristol Cream in

Bristol," "I had Sole Florentine in Florence," and "I had Dijon mustard in Dijon." There were shouts by people who let it be known that they had taken a bath in Bath, had bad wind in Bad Windsheim, had the worms in Worms, used a French tickler in France, had the Hong Kong flu in Hong Kong, read the *Canterbury Tales* in Canterbury, bought a Manila envelope in Manila, etc. until reactions of disapproval by self-appointed leaders created an implicit rule that their personal experiences be confined to what they had eaten or drunk, making 'I smoked a Cuban cigar in Cuba' definitely unacceptable but 'I ate a Cuban cigar in Cuba' possibly acceptable. There were shouts from people who had eaten Brussels sprouts in Brussels or a frankfurter in Frankfurt or French fries in France or Hollandaise sauce in Holland or German potato salad in Germany, or had drunk Scotch whiskey in Scotland or Irish coffee in Ireland or Darjeeling tea in Darjeeling or Cognac in Cognac or Bordeaux in Bordeaux, and so internationally on and so gastronomically forth. Winston sat experientially all alone. Tillamook cheese was not known outside of Oregon, and he didn't dare shout out on American soil that he had eaten American fries in America. No doubt about it, the Pipers would have fit in better.

George and Adele Piper were at the home of the Baldrys when Winston got back. They were showing Wallis some of the many photographs they had of one or both of them standing in front of this place or that place. Adele always wore high heels, except when she had a very bad backache from always wearing high heels. She also wore a lot of accessories, and bright, red Estee Lauder lipstick could often be seen on her two front teeth by people who went to the registry office, where she worked. The smell of Nina Ricci stayed behind wherever she had been, and wherever she had been was a comfortable place to be because, like her husband, she liked being comfortable. The group tours they went on were first class all the way. As for George, he always wore a suit in public. The only person who had ever seen him in his adult life without a suit on was Adele. (She was also the only person who had ever seen him in the adult diapers he wore out of necessity.) He was very particular about his appearance, especially his shoes. He shined his shoes every night and judged other men by their shoes and how well their shoes were shined. Even when seeing a good friend again like Winston, the first thing he did, after saying hello, was look down at his shoes. That's what you might expect from a conscientious shoe salesman who started at the bottom and worked himself up to branch manager and then to the owner of his own shoe store, where he had a lot more cushion. He met Adele for the first time when she came in to buy new shoes and asked her out while getting excited pressing her big toe inside the high heel she was trying on.

Winston welcomed them back, asked them how they were, thanked them for the postcards, told them he was looking forward to seeing their pictures and hearing all about their trip, and said that he was hungry. They all sat and talked for a while in the living room before moving to the dining room for dinner and a continuation of the conversation.

WALLIS: *(to George and Adele)* I wanted to have a special meal in your honor with some condiments typical of the places you've been on this trip. I couldn't find any figs, of course, so I bought Fig Newtons. I also bought a jar of green olives. I hope you like the Greek salad. I couldn't find any feta cheese, so I used white cheddar. I hope it's a suitable substitute.

GEORGE: I'm sure it is. The olives over there weren't green, were they, Adele? They were black, or sort of a purplish black.

ADELE: Yes, and they didn't have pimentos in them.

GEORGE: But they were good nevertheless.

WALLIS: How was the food in general?

ADELE: Oh, the food at the hotels was excellent, as you would expect at four-star hotels. Even the continental breakfasts were quite good.

GEORGE: And we were very pleasantly surprised to find a McDonald's almost everywhere we went.

ADELE: But sometimes they weren't so easy to find. I think we spent half the day trying to find one near our hotel in Cairo.

GEORGE: *(to Adele)* That's when you broke one of your high heels. *(To Wallis and Winston)* What a disaster *that* was.

ADELE: *(to George)* Don't remind me.

GEORGE: She broke another one while we were walking around in Rhodes and—

ADELE: Oh, that's the worst place for walking around. All of those confusing, little cobblestone streets! They should pave those streets. I spent the rest of our time there back at the hotel.

GEORGE: But the hotels were great. The one I liked best was the Hilton in Istanbul. The service was top-notch. They even pressed my suits.

ADELE: And the view we had of that big river was wonderful!

WINSTON: That must have been the Bosphorous, which separates the Sea of Marmasis and the Black Sea. Turkey is fascinating. In addition to the Mediterranean to the south, the Aegean Sea to the west, and the Black Sea to the north, it shares borders with Greece, Bulgaria, Georgia, Armenia, Azerbaijan, Iran, Iraq, and Syria. It's a little larger than Texas, with diverse physical features. Judging from the way you went, up along the Aegean, I guess you saw a lot of fertile, rolling steppeland.

GEORGE: I think that 'lush' is the best word to describe it.

ADELE: Yes, lush, very lush.

WALLIS: Oh, you've seen and done so much!

GEORGE: Well, we believe in living life to its fullest. You know, you only live once.

WALLIS: On this trip, what impressed you the most?

ADELE: Without a doubt, the Pyramids.

GEORGE: Especially the Great Pyramid. It ranks right up there with the Great Wall of China in my opinion.

WALLIS: Did you go inside it?

GEORGE: No, it was much too hot that day to be out of the tour bus for long. We just got out long enough to take some pictures.

WINSTON: You were thirty degrees north of the equator, about the same latitude as northern Florida, but it must have been very hot out there in the sand of Giza.

ADELE: You can say *that* again.

WINSTON: You mentioned in the postcard from Egypt that you took a cruise on the Nile.

GEORGE: Yes, we took a wonderful half-day cruise on a luxury boat that had a nice, big bar and even had a couple of jacuzzis on it.

WINSTON: Did you get up as far as Lake Nasser?

GEORGE: How far up did we go, Adele?

ADELE: I don't know, but we went pretty far.

WINSTON: The Nile is 4,145 miles long. Seventy percent of the water of the Nile comes from the Blue Nile, which starts in Ethiopia. The White Nile starts in Khartoum, in the Sudan. I know you didn't go up *that* far, of course, but I was just wondering if you made it north of Lake Nasser to Aswan High Dam, where the Nile is 1,800 feet wide.

ADELE: Well, the Nile certainly is wide, and it was very special and very mysterious to be *on* it. I felt a little like Katharine Hepburn in *The African Queen*. Unfortunately, George doesn't look at all like Humphrey Bogart.

GEORGE: *(to Adele)* Well, you're not exactly the spitting image of Katharine Hepburn, you know.

ADELE: *(to George)* Oh, now don't get angry, George.

WALLIS: You've had so many wonderful experiences!

GEORGE: We also went on a luxury cruise to a couple of Greek islands.

WALLIS: The postcard you sent us from San-something—

GEORGE: Santorini.

WALLIS: —was absolutely gorgeous. I'm going to laminate it and put it on the bathroom wall next to my postcard from Fiji and the beautiful postcard you sent us a few years ago of Kinkakuji Temple in Japan. That's where I'd like my ashes to be thrown when I die. Remember that, Winston—Kinkakuji Temple.

WINSTON: Santorini is the remains of a volcanic eruption. It must be quite impressive.

GEORGE: It's spectacular.

ADELE: Idyllic. But so up and down. And you have to be careful walking because of all of the donkey poop. It was really treacherous.

GEORGE: *(to Wallis and Winston)* She broke another one of her high heels there.

WALLIS: How many high heels did you break on this trip, Adele?

ADELE: Four. It's a good thing George is in the shoe business.

GEORGE: *(to Adele)* Well, I won't be in business for long if you keep going at this rate. I keep telling you that what you need is a nice pair of low-heel shoes with good, firm support.

ADELE: Oh, George is just upset because his black suit was ruined in Turkey when a camel slobbered on it while he was posing with it.

Everyone laughed except George, especially Wallis. She laughed and laughed and continued laughing after Adele and Winston were laughing only because she couldn't stop laughing, and she kept on laughing even after her laughter became very strange and her face went white and her eyes filled with fear and everyone became very alarmed.

August 12th, 1994 (three months later)

" . . . To unfasten the seat belt, pull the buckle. Should there be a sudden drop in air pressure, oxygen masks will drop within reach. People with small children should put on their own mask first and then assist their children. Life vests are under your seat for use in case of an emergency water landing. The life vests can also be inflated by blowing on these tubes. The aircraft has four exits. . . . " Winston Baldry was the only person on board listening attentively to the safety instructions given on this Northwest Airlines flight bound for Ōsaka as the plane rolled out to the runway at Seattle's Sea-Tac Airport. He could have conveniently taken a flight up from Portland and caught a connecting flight to Ōsaka but, no, he inconveniently came up by train and took a bus to the airport in order to put off, for as long as possible, his very first flight. He still had his hat on because he didn't want it to get bent out of shape in the overhead bin, where he had barely managed to fit in a knapsack containing a Folgers coffee can, inside of which, wrapped in bubble wrap, was an urn. Having requested meals without nuts because he was very allergic to them, there was a note on the overhead bin above him. There was a note there too about the fellow seated next to him, Joe Haywood, who had requested meals without meat. So there they sat, below the notes: '57B, Joe Haywood, No Meat' and '57C, Winston Baldry, No Nuts'.

Joe Haywood had Karel van Wolferen's book *The Enigma of Japanese Power* on his lap and was looking at the back page of an airline copy of the *Seattle Times*. "The baseball strike starts today. The season's probably over," he said to Winston, then folded the paper up and put it behind the air-sickness bag in the pocket of the seat in front of him. "Please return your seat to the upright position for take-off," a flight attendant told Joe before telling Winston, "Sir, it's better for people seated behind you who want to watch our in-flight entertainment that you not wear your hat during the flight. I can put it in the cabin-storage compartment for you." Winston gave the flight attendant his hat, and Joe did a double-take of the man seated next to him with the black hair and the white beard.

"So, business or pleasure?"

"Mostly business."

"Are you all right?"

"Just a little tense. This is my first flight."

"You're kidding."

"I'll be teaching world geography for two terms at a high school in Kōbe. Holy moly, I could use a drink."

"Well, you're not going to get one until we're up in the air and the seat-belt signs have been turned off. But it's a long flight, so you'll have time to drown your anxiety."

"It's part of a Japanese Ministry of Education program to promote internationalization."

"I'm all for internationalization. I'm in international sales. Car tires. Goodyear. Business picked up for a little while after George Bush went over with the car-making bigwigs and threw up all over then Prime Minister Miyazawa. But now I'm back to flying Economy Class instead of Business Class. Maybe Bill Clinton ought to go over in the same spirit and throw up all over Prime Minister Murayama. So, are you going to Japan alone?"

"No. Yes. I mean–I don't know what I mean."

"Relax. I've flown thousands of times. There's nothing to it."

"I've got my wife's ashes with me. She passed away three months ago of a stroke brought on by a brain tumor we didn't even know she had."

"Sorry."

"I know it's strange to say, but this is our first trip together."

"At least you're saving money on airfare."

"Money was never the issue."

"What was?"

"On the day she died, she said she would like to have her ashes scattered at Kinkakuji Temple in Kyōto. So that's what I'm going to do."

"Very romantic. I had an uncle who specified in his will that his ashes be packed with gun powder into a fireworks and shot off during a barbecue held in his honor. But the guy who shot off the fireworks, my cousin Gregory, didn't shoot it off right, and it went straight into a convertible that a guy happened to be driving by in with the top down. It set off a very impressive display before causing one hell of a fire. We all got in trouble with the police, except my uncle, who got off scot-free."

"Staff, prepare for take-off," the pilot said, and the flight attendants sat down on their flipdown seats. The engines opened up, and the 747 started moving and picking up speed until it was racing on the runway at 190 miles per hour. Regretting his decision to accept the offer to teach world geography in Japan in place of another world-geography teacher who was killed by a Chihuahua that jumped from the tenth floor of an apartment building, Winston held on tight to his armrests and said, "Holy moly!"

"They're going to show the movie *Backbeat* about the early Beatles," Joe said while calmly looking at the entertainment guide of the inflight magazine as the plane lifted off and rose quickly over the Puget Sound, carrying a very tense Winston Baldry, a stick just out of the mud, closer and closer to the coastal border and international waters.

The next day, at Ōsaka International Airport

Winston disembarked with his hat back on as a very disoriented 'alien' at 4:00 p.m. Japan Time and went with the flow of people following signs for IMMIGRATION/BAGGAGE CLAIM. With dark circles under bloodshot eyes from not having slept a wink for the past thirty hours and very little in the past week of high anxiety, he walked for what seemed like a very long time with his carry-on shoulder bag on his shoulder and his passport, entry card, and customs-declaration form in hand until he finally came to PASSPORT CONTROL. People were standing in many different lines, most for JAPANESE RESIDENTS, a few for ALIENS. The lines of aliens were moving much more slowly because immigration officials there were asking questions and checking their computers.

It was a Saturday, on the weekend marking the end of the Bon*
holidays, when the traditional thing for Japanese to do was return to
their ancestral hometowns. On the following day, the country's expressways, railways, and airports would be a congested mess with people
returning to make it back for work on Monday. Many untraditional people
who did not take overseas vacations escaped the intense heat by heading for popular cool places like Karuizawa, Kamikōchi, and Hokkaidō,
while senior politicians were busy wondering whether or not they should
pay a controversial visit to Yasukuni Shrine† on the 15th, the anniversary of the end of World War Two, to pay tribute to the war dead. It was a
brutally hot August. A few little children had died of dehydration in
parked cars while their mothers were busy playing pachinko.‡ The heat
had made beer the top-selling chugen,§ and Asahi Super Dry was
outselling perennial best-selling Kirin Lager. Some people may have
been thinking about washing their cars with beer, as the monsoon-
month of June was very dry and Japan was experiencing a drought of
such severity that water was being rationed in some parts of the country
and efforts were being made to bring rain by 'seeding' clouds. The
drought would have adverse effects on the rice harvest, which would
make it two bad years in a row, as the relative coolness of the previous
summer brought about such a bad harvest that rice needed to be
imported, dealing a big blow to the Japanese ego that had been getting
battered since the burst of the bubble economy in early 1990 and the
subsequent and ongoing recession that replaced optimism with pessi-
mism. The Japan that Winston had come to was a country with the wind
out of its sails. People didn't feel like jumping for joy while doing their
Bon Odori.** The American dollar broke the psychological ¥100 barrier in
early June, causing the biggest shock to the yen/dollar relationship
since 1971 when Richard Nixon took the dollar off the gold standard and
ended the fixed exchange-rate of ¥360 to the dollar. Companies relying
on export were setting up factories abroad if they hadn't done so
already. Lifetime employment was a thing of the past; restructuring was
a thing of the present. Unemployment was up higher than the official
figure of 3%, and that meant that *pachinko*-playing was also up. What
little excitement there was didn't stop with *pachinko*, though. J.League
soccer, which began a year before, was still spawning soccermania.
There was also dinosaurmania because of the blockbuster movie
Jurassic Park, which happened to be running concurrently with the 21st

---

* summer festival, traditionally from July 13th to July 15th, welcoming the return of
deceased ancestors' spirits.

† Among the war dead are convicted war criminals, with General Hideki Tōjō topping
the list.

‡ vertical pinball. 70% of the pachinko parlors in Japan are run by ethnic Koreans.

§ traditional mid-year gifts.

** traditional Bon dance, performed around a special pillar-platform to traditional, local
music.

sequel of the original *Godzilla* (this one titled *Godzilla vs. Space-Godzilla*) and had so much more 'teeth' in it that anyone could plainly see that the Japanese film industy was not going to help the country out of its economic woes by penentrating foreign markets any more than its execrable music industry was. Winston Baldry wasn't going to be seeing many, if any, of Japan's economic woes because they seemed to exist only on paper. To people who didn't have their perceptions affected by gloomy economic reports, Japan still seemed to have the bustle in its hustle, and the money flow was still astounding.

Winston finally made it to the front of the ALIEN line. He handed the official his entry card and his brand-new passport containing a one-year visa for 'specialist in humanities' that he received from the Japanese Consulate in Seattle. The official looked at Winston's strange-looking photo in the passport, then up at strange-looking Winston in person. After looking at the visa and running a computer check, he asked Winston where he would be staying. Winston showed him a letter from his contact person, Mrs. Junko Teratani, that gave the address of a person named Shingo Tsujimoto in Kōbe. The official wrote down the address on Winston's entry card, stamped his passport, and gave him a card informing him that he had to go to the local ward office within ninety days to receive an Alien Registration Card. Winston thanked him and walked down the stairs to BAGGAGE CLAIM, where the checked-in baggage was already going around on the carousel. Joe Haywood pushed his way in and grabbed his suitcase. Seeing Winston, he wished him good luck.

"Oh, by the way, a very polite way of greeting people in Japanese that you should know is 'Watashi wa kichigai desu'. Try it. Watashi wa."

"Watashi wa."

"Kichigai desu."

"Kichigai desu."

"Watashi wa kichigai desu."

"Watashi wa kichigai desu."

"Good. Be sure to use it. Sayōnara."

Winston repeated the expression a few more times to commit it to memory as Joe headed for CUSTOMS CONTROL, snickering from the thought of that stressed-out guy with the white beard and black hair innocently greeting people with a taboo word (kichigai) in an expression that really meant 'I am a lunatic'. Winston's two brand-new Samsonite suitcases finally came around. He took them off, put them on a cart, and pushed the cart to CUSTOMS CONTROL, where he greeted a stone-faced customs official with "Watashi wa kichigai desu".

"Nihongo ga hanaseru no?"

"Pardon?"

"Can you speak Japanese?"

"No."

"Pasupōto." (Passport.)

"Here you are."

"Anything to declare?"

"No."

With his white beard that looked like it might be fake because of his otherwise youthful-looking face, Winston aroused the custom official's suspicious nature. He opened Winston's suitcases and felt around,

then asked him to open his knapsack. He took the top off the Folgers coffee can, removed the bubble wrap and, finding an urn, removed the top to see what was inside.
"What is this?"
"Ashes."
"Eehh! Hashish?"
"Yes."
It was a common case of double misunderstanding between two speakers of different languages, but it had very bad consequences for Winston. Two customs officers took him to the Kansai airport bureau of the Ōsaka District Customs Office and stood him before their seated superintendent, Hisao Muramatsu. Superintendent Muramatsu put out his Mild Seven cigarette after listening to the details. Then he looked up at Winston and pointed at the jar in question.
"Sa."
"Watashi wa kichigai desu."
"This is hashish?"
"Yes. It's my wife's ashes."
"Your wife's hashish?"
"Yes."
"Your wife wa, where is he?"
"He?!"
"She."
"She's gone."
(To the other policemen): "Kare no iu tōri kichigai nanda na. Yome-san ga ita ka dō ka shirabedase. Kono jā o kanshiki ni mawase. Furiizu-dorai no hashish kamoshirenai. Atarashi teguchi dana. Dōisho o yōi shirō." (He might be crazy like he says. Find out if his wife was on the flight with him. Take the jar to the lab for analysis. It might be freeze-dried hashish. That would be a new one. And get a confession ready for this guy to sign.)
Junko Teratani, Winston's contact person, waited in the arrival area with a sign that read WINSTON BALDRY for a very long time after the plane he was supposed to be on arrived. Then she checked with a person at the Northwest Airlines counter and was told that Winston Baldry was indeed on that flight. Afraid that he might have passed by her without seeing the sign, she had him paged, but without success. She made an inquiry at Airport Security and learned that he was being detained on suspicion of possessing an illegal drug. So she called the United States Consulate General in Ōsaka. The consulate was closed and would remain closed, according to a recorded message, until the following Monday because of *Bon,* but the mobile-phone number of an embassy minister in Tōkyō to call in case of an emergency was given. She made the call and spoke with the minister, Marshall George, while he was putting on makeup in full drag at a place in Roppongi that catered to men who liked to secretly dress up in ladies' clothes and spend a couple of relaxing hours conversing with other 'ladies' at the establishment. Known to other transvestites there as Queen Marsha or Madame George, Marshall George got back to business the next morning. He had higher rights-protecting priorities to attend to than this matter of another American who had apparently tried to smuggle narcotics into

the country, such as the matter of a long-term resident American priest in Sendai who faced deportation for refusing to be fingerprinted for his new Alien Registration Card, and the litigation matter of a resident American hemophiliac who contracted AIDS from tainted American blood that the Japanese Blue Cross scandalously didn't treat with heat. He finally got around to the matter of this Winston Baldry after lunch and was finally given permission to speak to him over the phone late in the afternoon. Fluent in Japanese, Marshall proceeded to inform Superintendent Muramatsu that the jar in question contained nothing more than the cremated remains of the man's deceased wife and explained the mistake he made in English that led to the unfortunate misunderstanding. Muramatsu didn't want to admit that the problem was his imperfect English because he was very sensitive about his English. He got up early every morning to catch NHK's 20-minute *English Conversation* program, he subscribed to the English newspaper *Mainichi Weekly,* and he took lessons for many years at Bilingual language school in Ōsaka. (He would still have been going there once a week to receive lessons from a blue-eyed bleached blonde with silicone implants if Bilingual, which he joined because they advertised that they hired only good-looking teachers, had not gone bankrupt two years before.) So he told the embassy minister what he then told the Drug Enforcement Agency and the National Police Agency: It looked like freeze-dried hashish in the urn and that's why it was sent to the lab, but above and beyond that, there was reason to believe, based upon the suspicious way the suspect gulped during questioning, that he swallowed an illegal drug, and that was the real reason he was being detained.

Muramatsu didn't mind making things difficult for the detained American because he blamed the American for having made things difficult for *him.* He moved the American to a more detaining detention room and forced him to sit on a portable toilet under constant surveillance until he had taken a big shit. Winston tried to cooperate with all his might—It's a good thing his face didn't freeze in some of the ways it was contorted—but unfortunately for him, and much more unfortunately for Muramatsu, as it would turn out, Winston was constipated from having gone from jet laggy to jet laggier.

That evening, there was a special dinner at the Hotel Ōkura in Tōkyō attended by the United States' Ambassador to Japan (Walter Mondale), the deputy director general of Japan's Foreign Ministry's Cultural Affairs Department, a senior editor for the *Japan Times,* a foreign correspondent for the *Los Angeles Times,* and many others, including Marshall George, who was now wearing a suit and certainly not telling anyone to please call him Queen Marsha or Madame George. Marshall told the story about the hapless American man and the vindictive police captain over dessert, and in the morning of the same day in west-coast America because of Japan Time being 15 hours ahead of Pacific Time, the story appeared on page three of the *Los Angeles Times* under the headline ASHES TO HASHISH, DUST TO BUST. Right away, the story generated interest. The American man's desire to grant his wife's wish of having her ashes scattered in Japan at Kyōto's Golden Temple, Kinkakuji, re-warmed the hearts of people whose hearts had been warmed by the final scene of the recent box-office smash *The Bridges of Madison County.*

That afternoon, a high-ranking member of Amnesty International, who cried during the famous final scene of *The Bridges of Madison County*, issued a statement lambasting Muramatsu for "not being man enough to admit his mistake in English and subjecting Mr. Baldry to degrading cruel-and-unusual punishment just out of spite". That evening, the House Majority Leader, Richard Gephardt, was on *News Hour* with Jim Lehrer to discuss, among other things, the American trade deficit with Japan, and he happened to mention the Winston Baldry incident as being "a perfect example of Japan's lack of fair play with America". That was all it took to wind up the Japan bashers, for whom Winston Baldry immediately became a sitting symbol standing for protectionism and the need to impose trade sanctions under the Super 301 clause of the U.S. Trade Act.

The humorous side of the story was not forgotten. The ordeal of the American man forced to sit on a toilet in detention until he had taken a good, healthy shit gave plenty of ammunition to jokesters. On the night of the very same day, Jay Leno cracked a joke about it on the *Tonight Show* and David Letterman poked fun of it on *David Letterman*. In Las Vegas, a bookmaker started taking bets on the exact time and day that Winston Baldry would, as the media were putting it, "move his bowels". A man in Macon, Georgia, Frank Frank by name, bet $1.00 against 100,000,000 to one odds that Winston Baldry would move his bowels more than four months later at the stroke of midnight signaling New Year's Day. "Go big or stay home," Frank was quoted as saying in *USA Today*.

Nobody was looking forward to Winston Baldry's bowel movement more than Winston Baldry was. On the other buttock, nobody was looking forward to it less than Superintendent Muramatsu, for he knew how things were going to come out, so to speak, meaning that he didn't have shit on the American, so to speak, meaning that his chances of getting promoted were going to go down the toilet with Winston's shit, so to speak. He thought about tying some cocaine up in a couple of condoms and making the American swallow it like small-time drug smugglers often do. He still had access to cocaine from a seizure made three days before on a Columbian freighter. What he didn't have access to was American-made condoms, and he had no idea where to get some or even if they were available in the protected market. With Japanese-made condoms, it would have been an obvious frame-up. Muramatsu didn't want to get nailed for planting evidence against an American because America was capable of making such a big stink about things like the big stink they were making about this incident. It would have been so much easier if the fellow were not American.

Newsworthiness in America made the story newsworthy in Japan. The *Japan Times* ran the ashes/hashish story and called it the biggest mistake in English since 1992 when 16-year-old Yoshihiro Hattori, an exchange student in Baton Rouge, Louisiana, went to the wrong house to attend a Halloween costume party dressed as John Travolta in *Saturday Night Fever* and supposedly mistook the order 'Freeze' for 'Please' (according to the Japanese media) by the paranoid owner of the house, Rodney Peairs, who proceeded to blow Hattori away with his .44 Magnum. English teachers throughout Japan suddenly felt the need to write 'ashes' and 'hashish' on the blackboard and work on pronunciation with emphasis on the position of the tongue. The comedy duo 'Downtown' Hamada and 'Downtown' Matsumoto lampooned Muramatsu in a spoof on the television program *Downtown's Comedy Show*. A week later, Muramatsu would shoot himself dead with his gun, but on August 14th, the second day of Winston's detainment, he was fighting for his professional life, which he felt was the only life he had.

An editorial in the *Asahi Shimbun* raised the question that the Americans were so aggressively raising: If Muramatsu really believed that the American had swallowed an illegal drug, why had he not ordered x-rays to be taken? The big shots at the Drug Enforcement Agency and the National Police Agency were very critical of Muramatsu in private but decided, for the time being anyway, to support him publicly because public criticism of one of their own would have amounted to public self-criticism. So they backed up Muramatsu with his own answer: X-rays aren't 100% reliable, and whatever it was that the American had swallowed, whether it was an illegal drug or not, was going to have to be shat out sooner or later, and there was no harm in waiting an extra day or two in the name of national drug enforcement. They certainly weren't betting on it, but they were hoping that the American was going to shit out some controlled substance. Then they could show magnanimity by sending the drug smuggler back to America with a lifetime ban on re-entry instead of doing what they had every right to do: throw him in jail in Japan. Maybe they would even give Muramatsu a citation for excellence just to rub the Americans' noses in Winston Baldry's prohibited shit.

With American newspapers from coast to coast carrying the story and reporters from ABC, NBC, CBS, and CNN giving live updates from Ōsaka International Airport, President Clinton was forced to speak out, and he made his most vociferous appeal to a foreign country concerning the treatment of an American citizen since appealing to the Singaporean government six months earlier on behalf of Michael Fay after the 18-year-old was sentenced to caning for spray-painting cars. President Clinton spoke with Prime Minister Murayama personally over the phone and expressed his sincere wish that Mr. Baldry's human rights be respected. Clinton's appeal was somewhat effective, as it had been in decreasing the number of strokes with the cane that Michael Fay ended up receiving, and Winston was allowed to get off the toilet every two hours for three minutes to stretch his legs.

After three days with lots of fruit but no success, Winston decided to give written consent to be given an enema. Marshall George, who had been speaking frequently with Winston via mobile phone during Winston's confinement on the portable toilet, was asked to be present as a witness–to Winston's signing of the agreement, that is. The last thing the police wanted to be accused of, at this point, was coercing the American man's consent. George was on his way to America, however, to discuss how things presently stood (and how Winston presently sat) with Larry King on *Larry King Live*. So Ambassador Mondale made the three-hour ride on the bullet train from Tōkyō to Ōsaka to witness the signing.

The enema accomplished what it was supposed to accomplish, and after a very thorough stool test, Winston had a load off his mind as well as off his bowels. The news flashed up on the Motogram on Times Tower in New York's Times Square, and people who had placed bets were checking their tickets. A photo of Ambassador Mondale shaking hands with a haggard Winston Baldry went straight to the Associated Press. Winston was given back the cremation jar with half of its original contents and let go without an apology. Ambassador Mondale led Mr. Baldry out of detainment to freedom and turned him over to Junko Teratani. After making a stop at the airport bank so Winston could change dollars into yen, they were escorted outside through a media swarm buzzing with the clicking of cameras and a barrage of questions that commingled into a clangorous jumble from the pack of bustling press people jockeying around with TV cameras and microphones. Finally making it to a stretch limousine arranged for them by the American Embassy, they sat in the back seat behind darkened windows and breathed simultaneous sighs of relief. Junko looked back out the rear window and watched the swarm become smaller and smaller before saying what she had expected to say to Winston three days before: "Welcome to Japan."

They arrived at Junko's house in Kyōto's Sakyō Ward a little before 5:00. A whirring *TV Tōkyō* helicopter that trailed them all of the way from the airport filmed them getting out of the limousine. The driver helped Winston with his suitcases and said goodbye to him at the genkan* after receiving his autograph. Junko's ten-year-old son, Kōsei, who was leaving the house with a long-handled net to catch cicadas with, said "Hai' (Yes) and dashed off after Junko told him, "Kurakunaru made ni kaette kinasai yo." (Come home before dark.) Following Junko's example, Winston removed his shoes, stepped into house slippers, shuffled through the house, and stepped out of the house slippers to walk in stocking feet on the tatami† of the air-conditioned guest room, where there was a small party going on for several other Americans for whom Junko had arranged housing and was acting as a liaison. The special occasion was the annual spectacle of Daimonji,‡ which they would all go out to see later.

Winston received applause fit for a celebrity. Junko's husband, Nobuhiko, a section chief at the NHK Culture Center in Kyōto, stood up to introduce himself and formally present Winston with his meishi.§ Everyone else stayed seated at the kotatsu** and greeted Winston in turn upon being introduced by Junko. There was a lady who would be

---

* front entrance of a house.

† woven floor mat, also used as a unit of measurement.

‡ event marking the close of Bon, in which a big bonfire in the shape of the kanji for 'big' (大) is built on Mount Daimonji in eastern Kyōto to bid farewell to the ancestors' spirits.

§ name cards, which also include place of emploment. position, address, and phone number. Handwritten name cards were first used in the early 19th century.

** low heater-table with legs about 14 inches high, on which a futon is placed over the frame and under the tabletop.

teaching English at a high school in Kyōto, a man who would be teaching the history of western civilization at a high school in Ōsaka, and five high-school students, three girls and two boys, who were on student-exchange programs in Kōbe, Ōsaka, and Kyōto. They were all very aware of Winston's ordeal and had been looking forward to receiving some entertaining firsthand information. So he became and remained the unwilling center of attention until Junko said that Winston-san probably wanted to take a shower, whereupon Winston gladly followed her to the furo.* He said OK after she explained how to turn the shower on and off and how to use the water-temperature control, and said OK again after she added that the bath water was ready in case he wanted to get in after showering.

He took his clothes off and rolled the cover off the *furo*. Skipping a shower, he stepped straight into hot, bluish-green nyūyokuzai† water for a few minutes before stepping out, lathering himself with soap, and stepping back in. After shampooing his hair and dunking his head into the bluish-green water to rinse it, he pulled the plug and stepped out, leaving a ring around the tub. He came out of the *furo* looking fresh in clean clothes and went back into the guest room, where the guests were talking about this and that while occasionally watching a televised game of the 76th National High School Baseball Championship at Ōsaka's Kōshien Stadium that Nobuhiko was very interested in. Junko was coming and going and coming again to put more food on the *kotatsu* that was already covered with makizushi,‡ potato salad with slices of cucumber in it, edamame,§ de-crusted, quartered ham & egg and egg & cucumber sandwiches, and watermelon, plus various beverages, such as beer, sake, plum brandy, orange juice, and cold barley tea. "This is self-serve. There are some silverwares in case you prefer instead of chopsticks," Junko said to Winston. He sat himself down cross-legged at a corner of the *kotatsu* next to the fellow who was going to be teaching the history of western civilization. Nobuhiko stood up and went over to fill Winston's glass with beer, then went around and refilled everyone's glasses and led them all in raising their glasses and saying "Kanpai!" (Cheers!) After a chorus of deep sighs of refreshing beery satisfaction, Nobuhiko hollered "Oi, biiru!" (Hey, bring some more beer!) to Junko, who had already gone to the kitchen to get more beer.

Focus on the Winston Baldry fiasco gradually faded, mainly because he didn't really want to talk about it, and isolated conversations sprung up. The lady who was going to be teaching English was talking to Nobuhiko about the recent fall of the Liberal Democratic Party and the shaky, new coalition government headed by Tomiichi Murayama of the Social Democratic Party; the two high-school boys were talking about

---

* Japanese bath, which you get into *after* washing and rinsing.

† packaged bath powders.

‡ long roll of sushi, wrapped with seaweed.

§ boiled and salted soybeans in the pod.

the "awesome" and "totally cool" video games on their host families' Famicoms (Family Computers); and the three high-school girls were talking about problems they were having with their host families, including one girl's account of how she caught her host father stealing a pair of her panties. The fellow seated next to Winston was busy looking through the Employment Section of the *Mainichi Daily News,* but he put the newspaper down to talk to Winston.

"Are you going to make some extra money teaching English?"

"No."

"Why not?"

"I'm a *geography* teacher."

"That doesn't make any difference. You're a native speaker. That's the only qualification you need. Me, I'm a history teacher, but I got a job teaching English on evenings and on Saturdays at Nichibei English school in Ōsaka. I can make an extra ¥90,000 a month teaching there over and above my teacher's salary of ¥180,000. Plus, I picked up a couple of private students who are coming to my house for ¥3,000 an hour. Here, let me pour you some more beer. That's the way it's done here in Japan. You never pour your own beer, unless you're alone of course. So after school starts in a couple of weeks, I'll be bringin' in about ¥300,000 a month. That's $3,000! And I've been in Japan less than two weeks."

"Holy moly!"

"Yeah. And I'm tryin' to pick up some more classes. I've been goin' to the Pig & Whistle pub in Ōsaka at night to talk to other foreigners about what's going on. Sometimes people leave and are looking for a replacement. I put an ad in the *Kansai Time Out* monthly magazine offering private classes, and I gave Mr. Teratani my résumé because I'd like to get my foot in the door at NHK. I had some business cards made too. Here's one." Winston looked at the card that read JAMES D. RICHARDS, ENGLISH CONVERSATION INSTRUCTOR and gave his address and phone number. "Keep it. I had 500 made. You can get 'em made at Takashimaya department store here in Kyōto. I'm thinkin' about having some fliers made too. I've got a lot of openings on Sundays, and I can still squeeze in some other classes here and there during the week."

"You mean you're teaching seven days a week?"

"Yeah. Why not? The money's great. That's what I'm here for. What else is there to be here for? It's easy money too, like takin' candy from a baby. I'm gonna rake it in. The dollar's back up to 101 today, but I think it'll go back down below 100 again. I hope so. I hope it goes down to 90. I'll be laughin' all the way to the bank. One year here and I'll save about $20,000. That's a nice nest egg, but I'm not just gonna sit on it. I'm gonna use it to make *more* money, a *lot* more money. Japan is ripe for business opportunities. Did you know that there's no frozen orange juice in this country? They've got little bitty refrigerators, and frozen orange juice would be a good space saver. That's just one of my ideas. I've got a lot of ideas. I'll tell you about more of 'em some time. Give me a call."

"All right. This beer is going straight to my bladder. Where's the bathroom?"

"You came from it just a little while ago. The restroom, which they call the toilet, is where you want to go, unless you're planning to piss in the bathtub. You wouldn't be the first person to do it. I made the mistake the first day I was in this country. Junko brought me here and I asked her where the bathroom was, and she directed me to the *bath* room. But with its square shape and that blue-colored water that looks like Tidy-Bowl Cleaner, how was I to know that the bathtub wasn't a Japanese toilet? It's a good thing I had to go Number One and not Number Two, although I'm sure *that's* been done before too. The toilet is down the hall on the right. There's a urinal in it. That seems to be standard. The toilet is the non-flush Japanese-style, so if you have to go Number Two, be careful not to fall in."

"I don't think I'll be having to go Number Two for a long time."

"I sure as hell wouldn't think so. But don't feel bad. Some poor bastards have to get enemas every day. Don't stay in there too long. I've got to go too."

Upon finishing his business in the toilet, Winston came back into the guest room and walked on the *tatami* without realizing that he was still wearing the red, synthetic-rubber toilet slippers. After his attention was calmly called to the alarming fact, Nobuhiko set up his karaoke set and was soon singing *My Way*. Junko served coffee and homemade cake while waiting her turn so she could sing *Ue o Muite Arukō* (Let's Look Up While Walking), known in America as *Sukiyaki*. Winston ate half his cake and suddenly felt strange. "Were there any nuts in the cake?" he apprehensively asked Junko, who replied, "The frosting was with mince pecans. Do you allergy of nuts?" Straight back to the toilet he went. Down on his knees with his head near the hole, through which a three-week heap of fly-infested shit was perfectly visible, he vomited and vomited until finally falling asleep from exhaustion.

The port city of Kōbe had a large and diverse foreign population scattered among its nine wards. 500 Vietnamese lived in the southern ward of Nagata and constituted the largest ethnic group in the ward after the 9,000 Koreans living there. It was a poor side of town badly in need of urban renewal. A disproportionate number of elderly people lived in old areas crammed with small shops and factories. 6,500 people worked in the ward's 450 synthetic-shoe factories and made synthetic shoes that George Piper would have been very critical of. Junko Teratani could have picked a better ward in Kōbe for Winston Baldry to live in, like the well-to-do Chūō Ward, but Shingo and Kimie Tsujimoto were relatively well-off and had a second house that they put up for reasonable, temporary rent through the Japan Foreign Teachers program that Junko was involved in.

Shingo and Kimie Tsujimoto lived in a better part of Nagata Ward and ran one of Japan's 22,000 bookstores. Their bookstore was attached to their house. Next to their house was another house that was also theirs. Both houses were quite old, built shortly after World War Two in the traditional way with wooden frames and tiled roofs. The second house was for their son, Yōichi, and his wife, Sachiko, to live in, but Yōichi died of karōshi* two years before, shortly after Sachiko gave birth to a baby girl, and Sachiko left with the baby to go back and live with her parents in Yokohama. The Tsujimoto's daughter, Kumi, was married to a salaryman† with whom she had been living at his parents' house in Ōtsu, in Shiga Prefecture, since returning from a four-day honeymoon in Australia that they preserved with Fuji film in two big photo albums. Kumi's husband, Yoshiyuki, didn't want to move into the Tsujimoto's second house, even though it would have been more convenient for him to get there and back from his company's office in Ōsaka, because his mother didn't want him to. So the house was open, and the Tsujimotos, wanting to internationalize themselves for all of their neighbors to see, wanted an American, a white American of course, to live there.

Junko and Winston stepped out of the taxi they had taken from JR (Japan Railways) Shin Nagata Station and got Winston's suitcases out of the trunk that automatically opened and closed. Junko led Winston into the Tsujimoto's air-conditioned bookstore, My Book, where Mr. Tsujimoto was working behind the counter and several teenagers were browsing through manga.‡ She introduced herself to Mr. Tsujimoto and introduced Mr. Tsujimoto to Winston. After agreeing that it was hot ("Atsui desu ne"), Mr. Tsujimoto led them into his house, where Mrs.

---

* death from overwork.

† corporate workers. In their dark suits and ties, Japanese salarymen are modern-day samurai insofar as they devote their lives to the companies that employ them, and do so with the dedication displayed by Lieutenant Hirō Onada, who maintained his post in a cave in the Philippines until 1974 because he didn't know that the war was over.

‡ comic books, often as thick as big-city telephone books.

Tsujimoto greeted them in seiza* and followed the greeting by saying, "Atsui desu ne." Mrs. Tsujimoto served green tea and sweets and talked with Junko in Japanese because her English was very limited. In fact, the only thing she could say of any real length was 'I can speak English only a little'. Junko translated for her and for Winston and enabled Winston to answer her most pressing questions, viz. where in America he was from, what his impressions of Japan were, why his beard was white, and if he could use chopsticks. After those questions were answered, Mrs. Tsujimoto led Junko and Winston to her second house, which had new *tatami* mats in two of its four rooms. One of them was the living room, as it had a *kotatsu* in it. She turned on an electric fan and showed them around the house, which smelled slightly of mildew from not having been aired out much during the hot, humid summer. She made a stop at the *furo* to explain how to run the bath water and how to turn on the gas to heat the bath water, and added that there was a sentō† just down the street if he preferred that. After getting a box of Kyohō grapes out of the refrigerator, Mrs. Tsujimoto invited Junko and Winston to sit down at the *kotatsu,* on which there was a thermos, a tea pot and tea cups, green tea, and rice crackers. As a matter of course, Mrs. Teratani and Winston were seated on the tokonoma‡ side. Mrs. Tsujimoto sat opposite them, poured tea, and said that she hoped that Winston would teach English to her and some of her friends, a group of three or four, maybe five or six, depending upon the time and the day, as her friends were involved in such things as calligraphy, flower arrangement, and tea ceremony, not to mention the full-time job of being mothers to their husbands. Winston grabbed a few of the big, purple grapes and ate them with the skins on. If there had been some apples, he would have *really* shocked the ladies by grabbing one and biting into it after shining it on his shirt. "Suimasen!" (Excuse me!) shouted a sushi-shop man who slid open the *genkan* door and came right in with a platter of assorted sushi that Mr. Tsujimoto had asked to be delivered. After exchanging formalities and saying "Atsui desu ne", he left, leaving the three of them with the sushi. Winston followed the example of the women by taking the tiny, red cap off one of the little plastic-fish containers of soy sauce to squirt the soy sauce onto the sushi but unfortunately squirted Mrs. Tsujimoto in the eye. "Suimasen!" (Excuse me!) shouted a woman who slid open the *genkan* door and came right in with a honeydew melon. After exchanging formalities and saying "Atsui desu ne", she said that she had heard that a gaijin§ would be living there and that she had come to welcome him and give him the honeydew

---

* upright kneeling/sitting position.

† public bath-houses. There were 23,000 at the time of the Tōkyō Olympics in 1964, but they have been rapidly decreasing since and now are used mostly by elderly people, who still use them for socializing as well as for bathing.

‡ alcove for flower arrangements and scrolls.

§ foreigner, specifically a western foreigner, which is why Japanese who travel to western countries refer to the native people as 'gaijin'.

melon and ask him if he would teach English to her three-year-old son, who was presently enrolled in a juku* for preschoolers so that he would hopefully get into prestigious Keiō Yōchisha kindergarten in Tōkyō and then slide all of the way into Keiō University, thereby guaranteeing him a job at an elite company. Mrs. Tsujimoto asked the woman if she would like to join them for sushi, but the woman said that she had to pick her son up from his private mathematics lesson and backed her way out while bowing incessantly and making the customary apologies for having bothered them. Junko said that she also had to be going in order to be back in time to prepare dinner for her husband. She told Winston to call her if he had any problems. Mrs. Tsujimoto left with Junko after telling Winston through Junko that she would come back in a couple of hours to take him to a nearby restaurant for okonomiyaki.†

Winston breathed a deep sigh of relief to finally be all alone. So this house would be his home for half a year. He walked around the house again and made a much closer inspection, then sat down on the floor against a wall in a room between the living room and the kitchen that he decided would be his office. My God it was hot, and My God it was humid! His short-sleeved shirt was sticking to him. Sweat was running down from his armpits. He took his sweaty shirt off and threw it across the room. What a week! What a nerve-racking, culture-shocking week! He sat against the wall with his legs stretched out for almost an hour, exhausted. Finally picking himself up, he trudged to the *furo* to take a refreshing, cold shower. Upon opening the door, he saw a gokiburi‡ scamper into the corner. Outside the house a minute later, which is how long it took him to put his sweaty shirt back on and grab his bags and get the hell out of the house with the intention of going straight to the airport and taking the next plane home, he calmed down enough to go back inside and call Junko Teratani. Junko said that there were many cockroaches, especially in the older houses, and that he should go to a pharmacy and buy a very strong cockroach-killing gas that came in canisters and was much more effective than the little cockroach-killing houses called Gokiburi Hoihoi. She said that three canisters would be enough for a house his size and added that he should set the canisters off the next morning because he would have to stay out of the house for about eight hours. As for this night, she suggested that he go to the public bath down the street that Mrs. Tsujimoto mentioned.

The question he was faced with outside the public bath was which of the two entrances was for men. His question was soon answered when an elderly man wearing a yukata§ and carrying a senmenki** came out of the entrance on the left. Upon entering, Winston came alongside a little

---

* cram school. In 1994, there were 47,500 jukus in Japan.

† pancake-like dish containing cabbage and meat and/or squid. It is especially popular in Ōsaka and Hyōgo Prefecture.

‡ Japanese cockroach, which is black and up to two inches long (and can fly).

§ casual cotton kimono.

** wash basin used for bathing.

counter with a woman seated behind it. He gave her a 'How much is it?/I have just arrived from another planet' expression. The woman wrote down 450 on a piece of paper. Winston pulled out coins from his pocket and was carefully examining each one when the woman finally pulled his hand closer and picked out four 100-yen coins and one 50-yen coin. After receiving a towel and a wrist band with a locker-key attached to it, he apprehensively walked into the locker room, where an elderly man was in long underwear and a haramaki.* Another elderly man came in from the bath area holding his wash towel over his private parts. Winston found his locker. A couple of minutes later, he took his wash towel and entered the bath area with nothing on except his wrist band. There were five baths of different sizes, ranging from very large to fairly small. In three of them, steam was rising in densities that showed hot, hotter, and hottest. Two men were seated up to their necks in the hotter one with their wash towels on their heads. There was a long, shallow pool with a cold waterfall that a man was standing under. There was also a sauna, out of which came a man with irezumi† over his entire torso. Two elderly men lathered with soap were seated on bluish stools at the washing faucets vigorously washing themselves with wash cloths. Winston sat on a stool at one of the faucets and poured water over himself again and again, adjusting the water-temperature control from the shades of red to the shades of yellow to the shades of blue. When he had washed away all of his sweat, he went over to the least steamy of the steamy baths. He sighed a pleasureful sigh and closed his eyes upon sitting deep down in the hot water.

"Dochira kara?"

He opened his eyes and saw the fellow with *irezumi*. The tattooed part of him was submerged and appeared to be floating in front of him. His name was Yasumasa Kanamori. He was the number-two man in the Kuramoto-gumi crime syndicate, which was affiliated with the Kōbe-based Yamaguchi-gumi, the biggest of them all with one-third of Japan's 85,000 yakuza.‡ He had a huge head and a panchipāma.§ He looked like a gorilla, and he repeated himself.

"Dochira kara?"

"Pardon?"

"What is your country?"

"America."

"America big country. Japan little country."

"Have you been to America?

"Please once more."

"Have you been to America."

---

* cotton waist band worn especially by older people to keep their internal organs warm.

† tattoo. Japanese tattooists do their work by hand instead of with machines and stick the needles deep into the skin.

‡ Japanese mafia. The three largest groups are the Yamaguchi-gumi, the Inagawa-kai, and the Sumiyoshi-kai.

§ Japanese English for 'punch-perm', which is a short, tight Afro perm.

"I go America many time. Business. Hawaii very like. What is your job?"

"I'm a geography teacher."

"Jogging teacher. Sportsman. Sports very like. Keirin* number one like. What is your name?"

"Winston."

"Say me more one time."

"Winston."

"Weenstone. I am Kanamori. Please be to enjoy dinner together."

"Well, I—"

"You will my guest."

"Well, all right."

"I am waiting."

The gangster stood up and stepped out of the bath, revealing tattoo work so extensive that he looked like he was wearing a green short-sleeved shirt and matching shorts. Fifteen minutes later, when Winston was ready to leave, there was a big, black Cadillac with darkened windows parked outside. A young man with a *panchipāma* was leaning against the front door, smoking a cigarette. He flicked away the cigarette before opening the door for the 'jogging' teacher. Winston got in reluctantly and sat next to Kanamori. He didn't want to offend the man because he seemed rich enough with a 'chauffeur'-driven Cadillac to be a very important member of the community, perhaps the mayor. "You like Korean food, Mr. Weenstone? Me very like. We go Korean restaurant. Very good," the mobster said and off they went with the younger man behind the wheel.

Wearing a sweatsuit and massage sandals, Kanamori entered the restaurant smoking a Kent cigarette. Winston sat down at a table with the two *yakuza*. A middle-aged woman promptly came over to greet Kanamori and give them oshiboris.† Kanamori put out his cigarette while keeping his eyes fixed on the menu and ordered a couple of kimchi‡ dishes and two large jockeys of draft beer, one for himself and one for Winston. After slowly wiping his face and the back of his neck with the *oshibori,* Kanamori took the last cigarette out of his pack and crinkled the pack.That was the signal for the younger *yakuza* to run out and get his boss another pack of Kents. Kent was a very popular name in Japan. In addition to Kent cigarettes, there were the two foreign TV celebrities named Kent: Kent Gilbert and Kent Derricott. Neither of those squeaky-clean Kents, both of whom were Mormons, would have been caught dead with a guy like Kanamori. "Kanpai!" (Cheers!) Kanamori said upon raising his beer to Winston.

When the younger *yakuza* returned with a new pack of Kents, Winston noticed that the fellow was missing a fingertip on his left little finger, a sure sign of a *yakuza* who at one time had been ordered to take a knife to the finger at the first joint and turn the fingertip in for having

---

* bicycle racing at velodromes, where a lot of gambling goes on.

† rolled-up wet cloths given at restaurants and coffee shops.

‡ Korean cuisine consisting of red-hot, garlicky, fermented vegetables.

done something that displeased his boss. It was almost automatic to look from a man's *panchipāma*, another *yakuza* trademark, and see if he was missing a fingertip on his left pinkie. Prosthetic fingertips were now available to *yakuza* who wanted to get out of the racketeering business and not have the permanent finger-pointing stigma. Many older *yakuza* had been dropping out since the passage of the Anti-Organized Crime Law in 1992, which finally designated *yakuza* as criminal organizations and provided means of making life financially difficult for them. The number of young recruits was in decline because the gangster business was no longer seen as a good business to get into. Older *yakuza* like Kanamori waxed nostalgiac about the *yakuza* heyday in the '60s and '70s, when there were half as many *yakuza* as policemen and there was a long-standing understanding between the *yakuza* and the police that had since become more short-standing. Kanamori was big enough to still be doing pretty well, although there was nothing pretty about it. "From now we go Ōsaka," he said after they finished their beers. Before Winston knew it, he was back in the Cadillac, seeing no compelling reason not to go with the flow. Kanamori was impulsive, aggressive, and arrogant, perhaps even violent. There was no doubt about any of that, but Winston did not feel threatened. Kanamori seemed to like him and was being friendly to him in his own way. Besides, it was a chance to become acquainted with a Japanese person on just his first day in town and get driven around to see some sights. "You like whiskey?" Kanamori said while pouring Chivas Regal into two glasses at a small bar in the large back seat. "Scotch whiskey very good, number one," he continued while adding water. "Kanpai!" (<u>Cheers</u>!) he said and talked to Winston through thick, swirling cigarette smoke about Hawaii and then to someone else on his mobile phone that he shouted at before hanging up in disgust.

"Her no good. Maybe I get new girlfriend. I have three girlfriend. You like beautiful lady?"

"Yes, but—"

"From now we go nōpankissa."*

Tennōji Street was like many streets in Ōsaka with its neon-lit restaurants and bars, but it was the most famous street in the city for *nōpankissas*. "Ah, Kanamori-san! Irasshai!" (<u>Welcome, Mr. Kanamori!</u>) shouted a man in a suit standing outside the entrance that a slightly intoxicated Winston followed Kanamori through while the cigarette-smoking gangster talked to someone else on his mobile phone. "Ah, Kanamori-san! Irasshai! Futari desu ka?" (<u>Welcome Mr. Kanamori! Two people</u>?) said the manager on the inside, who led them across a mirrored floor to a table for two that a waitress in a miniskirt (and no panties) promptly showed up at to bring them *oshiboris* and take their orders. Still talking on the phone, Kanamori leaned over and looked straight down at the mirrored floor beneath her as the smoke from his cigarette went up under her miniskirt and partially clouded his visibility.

"You like, Mr. Weenstone?" he said after finally ordering two iced coffees without looking up.

---

* kissa (tea shop) with waitresses who do not wear panties.

"Well, I um um—"

"I very like."

Winston was dazed. He leaned back in his chair with bloodshot eyes from the smoky ride in the car. The customers were all men, and every single one of them was smoking. His eyes were burning. He would have had a headache if not for the analgesic effects of the alcohol. Their waitress soon came back with their two iced coffees, plus two more iced coffees and two mixed juices for customers at another table. Again Kanamori leaned over to look up by way of looking down. Unfortunately, the waitress lost control of the tray and spilled all six drinks on Winston. Kanamori leapt up and knocked her down with a slap across the face. Shouting like a madman, he dragged her by the hair across the mirrored floor toward the door. The manager and two other men restrained him in a respectful way and tried to calm him down as he continued shouting at the top of his lungs about the ineptness of the no-good waitress that had mistreated his friend. Winston wiped himself with a towel that was brought while saying that no harm had been done. "Very regret," Kanamori said when they were back in the Cadillac and heading to Jūsō Music, the most famous place in Ōsaka for decadent strip shows. Winston wanted to escape, but he certainly didn't want to insult this volatile man. "I would really like to go home," he said but was told, "More another place we go."

"Ah, Kanamori-san! Irasshai!" (Welcome, Mr. Kanamori!) said the manager of Jūsō Music, who led the mobster and Winston to two open seats at the base of the stage, on which a completely naked lady was using a vibrator to bring the second show, the masturbation show, to a climactic conclusion. Kanamori lit a cigarette, ordered two small tonic drinks, and sat with his arms folded at his chest as the third show, the 'open' show, began. A cigarette-smoking naked lady, platinum blond down low as well as up high, came out and sat wide open on the edge of a chair, and proceeded to put the filter end of the cigarette into her vagina and draw on it. "Her my type," Kanamori said and clapped loudly as she inserted a small blowgun and shot off darts, popping balloons that were attached to the wall. Winston Baldry, the conservative from Corvallis, was shocked. He had never even imagined anything like this. He felt ashamed to be in such a place. He wanted out and he wanted out now, but he didn't have the faintest idea how to get back home and he didn't have enough money to spend the night at a hotel. He felt at the mercy of Kanamori, and he hated being at the mercy of such a jerk. "Please take me home," he said to the racketeer as the entertainer turned her back to him and bent over to look at him through her legs. He tried to redeem himself by looking completely uninterested, and she responded to his indifference by kneeling down before him at the edge of the stage and pulling his white beard to her platinum-blond pubic hair, making it impossible to tell where one ended and the other began. It broke everyone up, especially Kanamori. Winston sat pensively as the entertainer danced away and saw her out of the corner of his eye crouch down over a customer's bottle of beer and pick it up (without using her hands). "I don't mean to offend you, but I'm leaving," he said to Kanamori as the racketeer answered his mobile phone. He headed straight for the door but stopped in his tracks upon hearing a terrifying yell from the mobster. Turning around, he saw what had drawn the attention of everyone else, including the entertainer, who now stood motionlessly 'holding' the customer's beer bottle: an alarmed Kanamori screaming on his mobile phone. Then Kanamori was moving fast. "Ikō!" (Let's go!) he said to Winston without breaking stride. The next thing Winston knew, he was back in the Cadillac, speeding back to Kōbe. Tomohiro Takahashi, boss of the Kuramoto-gumi syndicate, also affiliated with the Yamaguchi-gumi, had been shot by two gunmen while coming out of a bar in Kōbe's Sannomiya district. His bodyguard was dead and he was being rushed to the hospital by ambulance. That much was clear, but that's pretty much where the clarity ended, although there seemed to be little doubt that it was a 'hit' carried out by henchmen of the Azumi-gumi or its affiliate, the Seiyuki. Winston was scared of the speed of the car and the insanity of the horn-honking driver. At amusement parks, Winston refused to go on any ride faster than the Ferris wheel. He was holding on tight and watching himself doing high-speed tailgating and passing cars like they were in neutral. Leaning forward, he saw the speedometer registering 160, which he mistakenly thought was miles, not kilometers, per hour. By the time they came to a sudden stop and parked outside Sannomiya Station, he was a basket case. He was as white as a ghost and his nerves were shot. Through the darkened windows of the parked Cadillac, he saw many police cars, many big cars, and some gaisenshas.* Hundreds of bystandsers were bystanding. This was obviously a crisis. Seeing Kanamori chewing out a policeman while other policemen looked on, he wondered if Kanamori was perhaps the chief of police. Adrenaline was still racing through him from the wild ride. He was tingling from head to toe. He took a deep breath, got out of the car, and went over to where the driver was smoking a cigarette and watching his boss hollering at the policeman. "Excuse me, but how can I get back home?" he asked, hoping deep down that the tough-looking man would be kind enough to take him back. "Eigo wa zenzen dame" (I can't speak English) the man snapped and turned away. Winston looked at the gaisenshas. There were three of them. Their owners, like the owners of the hundreds of other gaisenshas throughout Japan, received a great deal of financial support from yakuza and wielded considerable political clout, which was clear by virtue of the fact that they were allowed to parade their vehicles through the busiest of the big-city streets and blast their recordings at deafening levels in an outrageous disturbance of the peace. Winston watched two of the gaisenshas leave in a hurry, then turned his attention back to Kanamori, who was huddled with several guys with panchipāmas. Apparently Takahashi had been shot in the upper arm and would be OK. Twenty yakuzas had already been sent to the hospital to provide protection for him. The two gaisenshas had left to go there too.

Kanamori's driver finally wedged his way in to ask his boss what to do with Winston. Kanamori flicked his backhand with an order for one of

---

* military-looking trucks with barred windows and external speakers. They are owned by ultra-nationalistic right-wingers who want to bring back the emperor system and the glory days of Japanese Empire.

the younger guys to take him home. The nod ended up being given to the driver of the third *gaisensha*. Before Winston knew it, he was in the front seat of the truck with a tough 20-year-old kid who had become an *adult* delinquent on the last Coming of Age Day. He was the son of a bitch and a bastard, which made him a 'bitchard'; but 'Dick wasn't short for 'Bitchard' like it was for 'Richard'–'Dickhead' was. He had orangish-brown dyed hair, actually more orange than brown, which meant that he was more than a little rebellious. He tapped the last Seven Stars cigarette out of its pack and into his mouth and threw the empty pack out the window. Then he lit the cigarette and took off. Grabbing an opened can of Georgia coffee from a can holder, he drank what was left in it and threw the can out the window. He turned on the CD player that had a Public Enemy CD in it, then ate the last of an order of takoyaki* and threw the Styrofoam container out the window. After another big drag on the cigarette, he grabbed a comb from behind the sun visor and combed his hair. Then he threw the comb out the window and said "Shimatta!" (<u>Damn it</u>!) "DO YOU PLAY BASEBALL?" Winston asked upon seeing a metal baseball bat next to the kid. But he wasn't heard above the blaring rap music and didn't say anything else except "TSUJIMOTO'S BOOKSTORE". Given the content of Public Enemy's lyrics, it would have been more appropriate to have said "TSUJIMOTO'S MOTHER-FUCKING BOOKSTORE".

Without an address or even the name of a district, efforts to find Tsujimoto's bookstore were so frustrating that the kid's I-don't-give-a-shit attitude got taken to its limit. He turned on the *gaisensha* recording full power. People at home gnashed their teeth and went to their entrances to see what in the hell was going on. Many of them put their hands over their ears while watching the *gaisensha* pass by. Before long, or rather *after* long, Winston's neighbors saw him step out of the front seat of the *gaisensha* and go into his house.

---

* grilled balls of flour, egg, octopus, and ginger, which are covered with a thick sauce.

'Idobata kaigi' (Meeting around the well) is a Japanese expression referring to women getting together and gossiping, and the gold medal for gossiping has got to go to Japanese women. Winston gave the women in his neighborhood a lot to talk about on the morning after his arrival home by *gaisensha*, but they were still just getting their jaws warmed up when three fire trucks rushed to his house with their sirens wailing. Smoke, coming out of every cranny and crook, had enveloped the house shortly after Winston set off twelve cockroach-killing canisters. Junko Teratani told him the day before that three would be enough, but he wanted absolute certainty. After setting off the twelve canisters, he fled to a nearby coffee shop, My Coffee, where he had a breakfast that took much longer to order than to eat because of a language problem that began when he came in looking completely confused and said to the man behind the counter "Do you serve breakfast here?" and then tried "Do you have breakfast here?" "Can a person have breakfast here?" and "Can you eat breakfast here?" Finally, the man's wife came out from the kitchen. Thinking that perhaps this *gaijin* wanted to have breakfast, she said "Mōningu?"* Winston said "Good morning" back and then said "Do you serve breakfast here?" "Is it possible to have breakfast here?" "Can I order breakfast here?" "I would like to eat breakfast," and "I want breakfast." After performing a pantomime of buttering a slice of toast and eating it, he succeeded in making himself understood. He had just received the *mōningu* when a construction worker came in and ordered the weaker coffee called Amerikan kōhii, almost always called 'Amerika' for short, by saying "Amerika" to the man behind the counter before staring at the *gaijin*. "Yes, I'm from Corvallis, Oregon. Winston Baldry. Nice to meet you," replied Winston. He had just asked for another cup of coffee with the mistaken notion that the endless-cup-of-coffee policy applied in Japan when Mrs. Tsujimoto, who used a spare key to get inside the smoky house, discovered the truth just in the nick of time to stop the firemen from turning on the hoses. The smell of the cockroach-killing gas lasted for days and was still detectable two weeks later on this day, September 1st, the first day back to school for high-school students–and high-school teachers.

Carrying his briefcase, Winston left his house at 8:15. Having already timed it (and re-timed it) from his house to Shin Nagata Station at two different speeds, leisurely (13 minutes) and slightly in a hurry (nine minutes), he was on his way to catch the 8:32 train, meaning that he had decided to walk very leisurely, as walking slightly in a hurry in the humid heat would have been very uncomfortable. People were using the word 'zansho' (lingering summer heat) and still eating cold-noodle dishes like sōmen, reimen, zarusoba, and hiyashi udon. Wearing a necktie with a

---

* Japanese English for 'morning', but means 'breakfast set'–typically a triply thick slice of buttered toast, a scrambled egg, a tiny lettuce salad, and a cup of coffee.

short-sleeved shirt, a rare sight in Japan, Winston wanted to arrive at the station a few minutes early so he could get in line and hopefully get a seat. "Ohayō gozaimasu" (Good morning) he said with a tip of his hat to his neighbor across the street, who was at her second-story window spreading out her *futons* on the first-floor roof so they would get dried and fluffed up by the sun. He didn't know her by name, but he knew her by face, as was the case with several others in the neighborhood. Crossing over to the other side of the street, the east side, he walked in varying shades of the houses that even now, at this early hour, didn't extend past his already damp armpits but did extend over the heads of three little primary-school girls coming toward him on their way to school in their navy blue uniforms, yellow hats, and red knapsacks. "Haro, haro, haro," they said and giggled among themselves and then giggled some more when Winston said "Hello" back.

A dragonfly landed on his shoulder. He nudged it off, but it came right back. He slowed his step and looked at it staying motionless before flying off and circling him. Stopping, he raised his hand above his head with his index finger pointed upward, and it landed on his fingertip and stayed there even after he resumed walking. His armpits were already getting itchy. That was bad enough. What was really bad was when his ass and the insides of his upper legs sweated and itched. The ointment he bought at the local pharmacy, My Drug, wasn't helping because he couldn't stop scratching himself, especially at night. "Oshiri o kaka-naide" (Don't scratch your ass) the pharmacist told him while a woman was waiting next in line. Never in his life had he experienced such muggy weather. He slept with two fans blowing on him because one was not enough. He kept his *furo* filled with cold water so he could take frequent plunges during the day. In order to get out of the heat and into air conditioning, he spent a lot of time in coffee shops, which was the main reason for the popularity of coffee shops in the 1960s. (They were popular in the 1950s because they had television sets.) The coffee shop Winston frequented, My Coffee, was a new coffee shop with a sign over the entrance that said 'Since 1993'. He had the *mōningu* there every morning except this morning. This morning he breakfasted at home on Kellogg's Corn Flakes, the most popular of the very few breakfast cereals available, which he bought along with other groceries at the neighborhood grocery store, My Shop. Walking with as much of himself in the shade of the houses as possible, he came behind an old, bent-over woman pushing a baby carriage—a common sight as baby carriages gave older women support in addition to providing space for groceries and other things. The dragonfly flew off his fingertip and landed on the old woman's baby carriage. Stepping to the side and passing by her, he glanced inside the baby carriage and saw a cabbage doll. Suddenly, there was a shriek and an "Abunai!" (Watch out!) behind him. Turning around, he saw a *futon* slide down off the roof of his neighbor's house and onto the three giggling primary-school girls, knocking them down. After going back and helping the now not-giggling girls get out from under the *futon* and saying "Dō itashimashite" (You're welcome) to their "Arigatō gozaimashita" (Thank you very much), he had to quicken his step from very leisurely to plain leisurely.

In addition to 'Ohayō gozaimasu', 'Dō itashimashite' and 'Arigatō gozaimashita', Winston had learned a few other words and expressions, but not enough to get him very far at all. He felt very lucky to have become acquainted with Naito-san, a friendly woman who ran a nearby vegetable shop and could speak English quite well. She helped him arrange for the English-written *Daily Yomiuri* newspaper to be delivered to his house every morning. Just the day before, she went with him to JR Shin Nagata Station and helped him buy a two-month train pass between there and Hyōgo Station, where he would be getting off to walk to Minami Kōbe High School to teach world geography. After re-passing the old, bent-over woman and her cabbage doll on his way to the station, he saw Naito-san putting up a reed screen in front of her vegetable shop to keep the sun out.

"Ohayo gozaimasu, Naito-san. Genki desu ka?" (Good morning, Mrs. Naito. How you you?)

"Ah. Ohayō gozaimasu, Weenstone-san," she said and exclaimed "Eeeehhhh!" while stroking her jaws in reference to Winston's clean-shaven face.

"I shaved my beard off last night."

"Wakaku mieru." (You look young.) "You look young."

"I've heard that before. Have a nice day."

"Weenstone-san mo. (You too.) You too. Ganbatte ne. (Do your best.) Do your best."

"I will. Sayōnara."

"Sayōnara. Goodbye."

Winston ran a hand over his clean-shaven face. It still felt strange. It looked strange too because the lower half of his face was white, whereas the upper part was dark with a tan. He shaved his beard off because he didn't want to continue standing out and being stared at wherever he went. In the two weeks he had been in Japan, he had not seen a man with so much as a mustache. Nor had he seen anybody with white hair, as everybody with white hair dyed their hair black or, in the case of many older women, a soft violet that often was a hard purple. His white beard made him stand out way over and above the eye-catching fact that he was a *gaijin*, another word he had learned and had already heard too many times. Up ahead, in the middle of the next block, a bakyūmukā* was parked with its big hose out and pumping. Winston didn't know enough about the situation to make a well-advised detour

---

* Japanese English for 'vacuum car', which is a truck with a hose used for sucking refuse from non-sewer toilets. Unlike in the Edo Period (1600-1868), when collectors paid or traded for natural 'human fertilizer' and rich folks' manure fetched a higher price because they ate better food, vacuum cars, still frequently seen in 1994 in rural areas and older urban areas, charged a fee for the service.

but wished that he had when he came alongside the truck and got blasted full force, full on, full hose, full shit. He held his nose and picked up his step, and picked it up some more until he was into a run to get away from the stench of the percolating shit. By the time he got to the station, sweat was pouring down his brow and running down from his armpits. The right side of his boxer shorts had crept up and was sticking to the crack of his now sweaty and itchy ass. His pants were rubbing against the heat rash between his legs. He went up the steps and passed the ticket man with his wallet open to show the man his train pass, then went down the stairs to the platform, scratching his ass and trying to get his boxer shorts back down where they belonged.

Thanks to his mad dash from the shit-sucking truck, he arrived as a train was departing and was therefore able to get first in line for the 8:32 train. Alongside him came a middle-aged woman who happened to be an obatarian.* People came behind them and stood orderly in double-file. He took his *Daily Yomiuri* out of his briefcase and stood the briefcase upright between his legs, unaware that a letter had fallen out. Scratching his ass some more and still trying to get his boxer shorts back down, he glanced at the front page and caught the news about the hoopla surrounding the countdown, now just three days, to the opening of Kansai International Airport, the continuing American problem with Castro and the Cuban boat-people crisis, and more controversy about compensation for the 300 or so survivors among about 200,000 young East and Southeast Asian ladies used as sex slaves (but referred to in the press as 'comfort women') for Japanese front-line troops during World War Two. A woman standing in line behind him, who saw the letter fall but waited for somebody else to point it out because she felt uncomfortable communicating with *gaijins,* finally picked up the fallen letter and gave it to him. "Arigatō" (Thank you) Winston said. "Nihongo ga jōzu desu ne" (You speak Japanese very well) the woman replied.

The letter, forwarded to Winston via the American Embassy in Tōkyō like thousands of other letters he received from supportive Americans who sympathized with what he went through upon arrival in Japan, was from a representative of the laxative company ex-lax offering him "a six-figure sum" to be their pitchman like Mr. Whipple used to be for Sharman toilet paper. Winston hadn't kept the letter because he was interested, although that six-figure sum was certainly tempting; he just hadn't gotten around to reading all of the letters in that particular stack. He put the letter back into his briefcase with about fifty other letters that had come undone when the rubber band holding that stack broke. He gathered the scattered letters and put them into the pouch of his briefcase, where he had been keeping letters from colleagues and friends. One letter was from George and Adele Piper. He took it out and re-read it.

---

* pushy middle-aged woman. The word was coined in the early 1990s from 'obasan' (middle-aged woman) and the monster movie *Battalion.*

Dear Winston,

We're so happy you decided to stick it out instead of coming right back after that horrible ordeal you went through. But it's not everyone who gets their picture in the papers shaking hands with a former vice president of the United States of America. We're trying to get a print of that picture so we can have it enlarged and glossed.

I can't imagine cockroaches as big as you described in your letter. That would be enough to make me come back. But we enjoyed Japan so much when we were there four years ago, even though I had a bad cold and was blowing my nose everywhere we went. It's so rich in culture. And the people are really wonderful and polite, even if they do slurp their noodles. You haven't eaten sushi, have you? We were shocked to learn about some of the things they eat over there. We tried to use chopsticks once but gave up. Fortunately, we could get continental breakfasts and American-style dinners at our hotels. And we were pleasantly surprised at how many McDonald's there are. What a life saver! We went out once with the group to a Japanese-style restaurant. What a disaster! I don't know how they can sit on the floor at those low tables. It cut off the blood circulation in one of my legs, and when I got up to go to the restroom, my leg gave way and I fell down and almost killed myself!

We're leaving for Mexico in a couple of days. Of course, we'll send you a postcard. Well, I'll turn you over to George now. Enjoy your stay in Japan. We're so thrilled that you are expanding your horizons like we have. Experiencing new and different cultures is so deeply rewarding.

Love,
Adele

Hey, Mr. Celebrity!

We're going to have that picture framed! You sure look better in that picture than you did on CNN. Andy Warhol was right, but you were famous for a lot longer than 20 minutes. Too bad you weren't back here to appear on Oprah Winfrey. Some guy in Vermont won $87,000 by predictiing the exact time you would move your bowels.

What Adele failed to mention about her fall at the restaurant in Japan is that she landed right on top of the table just after the waitress brought another round of food, and she lay there for the longest time until she was sure her back wasn't broken. We had to take her to the hospital for x-rays, and she was laid up in the hotel for two days.

Glad to hear from you. It took only four days for your letter to get here. That's faster than it sometimes takes to get a letter from here to Portland. Hope you're not still suffering from culture shock and having so many cultural problems. When we were over there, a guy told me a story, and he swore it was true, about an American man who went to Japan on business and was taken by his Japanese business associates to a traditional Japanese restaurant. After a while, he went to the restroom to take a pee, and when he came out, there was a woman in a kimono standing in front of him and holding out a finger bowl. As he was tall and she was short, she was holding the bowl at the level of his you-know-what. So he figured it was a Japanese custom for guys to wash their peckers after they take a pee and decided that while in Rome one should do as the Romans do. So he unzipped his fly and pulled out his pecker and dipped it into the bowl. Well, you can imagine how shocked the woman was, but she figured that it was a custom for American men to wash their peckers after peeing. The guy who told me the story called it a case of double cultural misunderstanding.

As Adele mentioned, we're heading for Mexico. Looking forward to an excellent two-week tour. Of course, we won't drink the water. I'll conclude by saying that we're proud of you for taking the first step on the road to becoming international like us.

Take care,
George

PS Enclosed with a column Dave Barry wrote about you is a letter from Australia addressed to Wallis. We're wondering if it's from someone who found her chain-message in a bottle. Wouldn't it be something if it makes it to Japan?

The Pipers' wonderment in George's PS was correct. The letter was from a woman in Bundaberg, 130 miles north of Brisbane. It contained a picture postcard of the Gold Coast, a picture so beautiful that Wallis would have laminated it and put it on the bathroom wall with her other favorite postcards. The woman wrote that she had done as requested. Winston knew that strong winds would carry it south along the eastern shore and send it either west through the Bass Strait or east in the Tasman Sea toward New Zealand. The only way it could theoretically make it to Japan would be to get carried south of New Zealand and back across the Pacific Ocean, then up the coast of Chile and Peru and back out. That wasn't likely. Likelihood, of course, could get taken for a ride if another shark were to swallow it. There were many sharks off the coast of Australia.

" . . . Kiken desu kara, go-chūi kudasai" (Be careful because it's dangerous) came a taped woman's announcement that millions of people heard every day. Nobody could have told you exactly what the woman said in entirety because nobody was really listening. Nobody really cared, except Japan Railways, which liked to provide as many announcements as possible, both on and off the trains. The 8:32 train pulled in at 8:32, as a matter of course. Passengers gushed out because they were getting out or getting pushed out. Winston and the *obatarian* split apart by stepping aside, and two long single-file lines formed on either side of the gush. The *obatarian* wedged her way in sideways past the people getting off, and the people behind her followed her lead. A fellow in line behind Winston, who wished that he had gotten in line behind the *obatarian* instead of the *gaijin*, bolted and headed straight through the center of the passengers trying to get off, and he was followed by the people behind him. After everyone got off and everyone stormed on, Winston was able to get himself all of the way onto the jam-packed train with a helpful push from the JR man, who blew his whistle inches from Winston's face before the doors closed. But the doors reopened because the last door closed on Winston's leg. After the JR man helped Winston get his leg all of the way in, he blew his whistle inches from Winston's face and the doors closed. But they opened again because this time the door closed on Winston's briefcase. Winston created enough space to put the briefcase and his newspaper between his legs and managed to raise his right arm up to the curved area just above the inside of the opened door. The JR man blew his whistle again inches from Winston's face and the doors closed. But they opened again because Winston's hat fell off and was lying over the small gap between the train and the platform. With his left arm pinned against him and his right arm providing the leverage that was keeping him all of the way on the train, he took his hat from the JR man the only way possible: with his teeth. The JR man blew his whistle again inches from Winston's face and the doors closed and the train took off. Pressed against the door with his hat in his mouth and his nose turned sideways against the door window, Winston said to himself, "Like a sardine in a can!" And that sardine had a very itchy ass.

At Hyōgo Station, Winston got off and went with the flow until he was out of the station and on his way up the street that led to Minami Kōbe High School. It was an old, concrete, three-story building built during Reconstruction after its precursor, a two-story concrete building, was destroyed by a bomb dropped from an American B-29 in the spring of 1945. A big, iron gate to the school grounds was opened and closed by the gateman and caretaker, Miyajima-san, who sat near the gate in an old, wooden booth that was not much wider than a telephone booth. "Ohayō gozaimasu," Winston said to him for the third time, having come to Minami Kōbe High School twice before, once for a test run and once for orientation. At orientation, he met the principal, Hirota-san, and the vice principal, Mitsuzuka-san, whose teeth were crooked and crookeder, respectively. He also met several teachers and office workers, including Kenji Maekawa, who would be assisting him as a translator in world geography in addition to doing his regular job as an English teacher, and Rika Koga, a pretty office lady who stared at him with stars in her eyes because she was a big Hanshin Tigers baseball fan and, with the beard Winston had then, she thought he looked like Randy Bass, who played for the Tigers from 1983 to 1988 and led them to the championship in 1985.

He walked on concrete with students, who wore school uniforms designed by Hanae Mori. When he got to the two-door entrance, he held the door open for a female student behind him. She was uncomfortably confused by the gesture but went anyway and was followed by a wave of students, one after another, hurrying to get past a door that they didn't have to exert any energy to open. Seeing no letup, Winston stopped holding the door open and cut in. A boy collided into the back of him and started a chain reaction that ended up involving more than twenty students. Inside the entrance, Winston put his shoes into a small locker and took out a pair of slippers. He shuffled in the slippers to the teachers' lounge, where several people were present. One of them was Maekawa-san, who said, "Good morning, Weenstone-san. Eeehhh! You shaved your whiskers!"

Maekawa would have been tall for an American, which meant that he was very tall for a Japanese. He was three inches taller than Winston, who was average in height for an American, which meant that he would have been a little tall for a Japanese. Maekawa's English was pretty good, certainly better than the vast majority of Japanese high-school English teachers. For example, he could say 'This is a book' instead of 'Jizu izu a buku'. He passed the 1.5 Level of the EIKEN examination and scored 610 points on the TOEFL examination. Even so, he had a bad habit of conjugating irregular verbs in mid-sentence and saying things like, "I haven't–take, took, taken–taken the TOEIC examination yet." After greeting Winston, he resumed talking to, or rather listening to, a young, overweight American lady named Shannah Pearl (Pāru-san), who would be the ALT (Assistant Language Teacher) in his English classes.

Shannah would have been attractive if she were thinner and didn't have a toughness about her that suggested that she could bite your head off. She hardly ever smiled because there was so much wrong with the world. Environmentalism, political correctness, and women's rights kept her very busy complaining. At college, she protested against the existence of a reproduction of a Hellenic statue of Athena, the goddess of wisdom, on the basis of sexual harassment insofar as the toplessness perpetuated the notion that women are nothing more than sexual objects, and she succeeded in getting the university to remove the offensive statue that had been there for 45 years, which greatly reinforced her sense of the power she wielded. When Winston came into the teachers' lounge, she was saying to Maekawa-san, "We've got to do something!" in reference to the destruction of the Amazon rain forest.

Terada-san, one of the office ladies, who were first and foremost tea servers and second and secondmost ashtray emptiers, saw Bōrudorii-sensei (Teacher Baldry) go into the teachers' lounge and naturally followed him with a cup of green tea. "Nihongo ga jōzu desu ne" (You speak Japanese very well) she said when he said "Arigatō" (Thank you). Backing her way out of the room while repeatedly bowing, she got whacked in the behind by the door that had been pushed open by Vice Principal Mitsuzuka, who came in and greeted Winston with, "Ah, Bōrudorii-sensei. Dōmo. Eeehhh! Hige o sorimashita ne" (Ah, Teacher Baldry. Thank you. I see that you shaved your beard) before going over to discuss something with Maekawa. While Winston was sipping his tea, Rika Koga, the Hanshin Tigers fan, came in. Named after Rika-chan Ningyō,* she was every bit as pretty as her namesake and was often called a *bijin* (beautiful woman). People said that she looked like the popular actress Masako Natsume, who died of leukemia nine years before. At first, she was disappointed because Bōrudorii-sensei had shaved off his beard, but on second look, she thought he still looked like Randy Bass as the slugger looked after shaving off his beard in a Gillette commercial. After introducing herself in English ("My name is Rika Koga") and giving him her *meishi* with the telephone number highlighted with a yellow marker, she backed her way out bowingly. Winston finished his tea and went over to introduce himself to Shannah Pearl, who he didn't meet at orientation because she wasn't there, being too upset after an encounter on a train with a chikan† who ended up with a bloody nose.

"Hello. My name's Winston Baldry."

---

* Japanese answer to Barbie, which first appeared in the mid-60s.

† dirty, old man; groper. Virtually every young lady in Japan experienced chikans, but the problem was taken so unseriously by the male-dominated government that it fell under the Nuisance Prevention Ordinance.

"So *you're* Winston Baldry. Hey, I'd sue their asses off if I were you. But I thought you had a beard."

"I did. I shaved it off yesterday."

"I'm Shannah Pearl. Are you also a JET person?"

"No. To tell you the truth, I flew in an airplane for the first time in my life just a couple of weeks ago when I came to Japan."

"Wow. No, I mean are you a member of the Japan Exchange and Teaching program?"

"Oh, I'm sorry. No, I'm not. I'm on the MEF–Mombushō English Fellows program."

"Never heard of it. I'm on the JET program. There are about 25 applicants for every one of us who get accepted. I'm really excited about applying the teaching skills I learned at Princeton."

"I'm going to teach world geography here."

"Oh."

"Where are you from?"

"Cincinnati. Actually, I was born in Dayton, but we moved to Cincinnati when my father joined a big law firm there. So I lived there until I went away to Princeton."

"I'm from Oregon."

"Oh. I was in Oregon once, on a school field trip to save the spotted owl. I want to help raise the level of awareness over here. Did you know that 15,000 square kilometers of the Amazon rain forest were deforested last year. Within ten years, half of it will be gone. I think that–" She suddenly stopped talking because the mathematics teacher, Sanada-san, a humorless middle-aged man who only laughed at jokes made by his seniors, had come into the room and started smoking. "Isn't the teachers' lounge non-smoking?" Shannah blurted out and created a hush. Sanada looked up at her, drew on his cigarette, and let out a long stream of smoke before turning his attention to his class list. Shannah stomped out of the room with tears in her eyes. Maekawa was the first to break the silence. "Weenstone-san, you look young. How long had you– grew, grow, grown–grown your whiskers?"

At 9:00, the bell rang and Vice Principal Mitsuzuka led Maekawa-sensei and Bōrudorii-sensei out of the teachers' lounge and up to Room 203, where 43 noisy students gradually quieted down. Mitsuzuka-san gave a speech to the class about the new teacher, 'Weenstone Bōrudorii', with information about what country he was from, what state he was from, what city he was from, what his profession was, what subject he taught, and what university he taught at. After telling the students to do their best in order to become international, he left. Maekawa-sensei proceeded to give a speech about the new teacher, with information about what country he was from, what state he was from, what city he was from, what his profession was, what subject he taught, and what university he taught at. "Hello. How are you?" Winston said habitually without expecting a response and was shocked when everyone in the class said in unison, "I am fine, thanks. And you?" "Not bad. Can't complain," Winston said but was nudged by Maekawa and told that he should say 'I am fine, too'. So he said, "I am fine, too." Then he picked up a stick of white chalk and wrote his name on the blackboard ("My name is Winston Baldry") and drew the borders of the United States ("This is the United States of America") and drew the borders of the state of Oregon ("This is the state of Oregon") and put a dot in western Oregon ("This is the city of Corvallis"). Turning to the students, he said with translation-help from Maekawa-san, "I am from the city of Corvallis, in the state of Oregon, in the United States of America, in the North American continent, in the world. You are from Kōbe, in Hyōgo Prefecture, in Japan, in Asia, in the world. Our countries are far apart, separated by the Pacific Ocean, the largest of Earth's oceans, but we live in the same world." He spun a globe that was on the lectern, then picked up the class list and called roll by reading Roman letters of the students' names that Maekawa had written next to the kanji.* Lots of laughter ensued because of his mispronunciation of the vowels and the western tendency to put an accent on one of the syllables. He did as badly as Ronald Reagan did when the then American president pronounced the name of then Prime Minister Takeshita (correctly pronounced Tä-kay-shee-tä) as Tayk-a-**shit**-a.

It took him ten stressful minutes just to call roll. It would have taken less time (and gotten less laughs) if he had not assumed that their responses 'Hai' (which means 'Yes', but in this situation means 'Here') were hellos and had not said "Hi" back to each and every one of them. Deeply sighing, which brought more laughter, he put the class list down, wiped his brow, and rolled out two large maps of the world—a map commonly used in Japan and a map commonly used in America. With Maekawa's assistance, he put them up on the blackboard with colored blackboard magnets. Making frequent stops for translation by Maekawa, he commented that Japan was in the center of the Japanese map and America was in the center of the American map but neither country was really in the center because the world is a roundish ball, not a flat rectangle. Turning the globe, he said that all of the oceans, continents, countries, mountains, lakes, rivers, and other topographical features of this planet that English speakers call 'Earth' and Japanese call 'Chikyū' are the subject matter of geography. Maps, first made by Babylonians on clay tablets almost 4,500 years ago, are very useful in studying geography, he went on to say, but world maps have misrepresented the actual size of countries and continents because of mapmakers' nationalistic and racial biases and consequently both maps on the blackboard were proportionately inaccurate. With Maekawa's further assistance, he took both of the maps down and put up a Peters Map, which he explained was made by a German historian named Arno Peters and showed countries and continents according to their actual, proportionate size. Then he said, "Look how big Africa really is. Look how small

---

* ancient Chinese ideographs, of which about 2,000 are commonly used.

Europe really is. Are there any questions? None? Any thoughts about what I've said? None at all? Well, let's play a game."

Desks were pushed to either side to make room for three teams of eleven members and one team of ten members to stand single-file facing the front of the classroom. The first person on each team was given a pen and a sheet of paper with the alphabet written on it from top to bottom. On 'Go', they had to dash up to the map and find a country that began with the letter A and print its name correctly next to the A, then hand the pencil and paper to the next person on their team and go to the back of the line while the next person dashed up to the map to find a country that began with the letter B, and so on. The object of the game was to beat the other teams in getting all of the way to Z. After a couple of rounds, the students lost interest and started chattering and playing until the lines were un-linear. By the time the chairs were pushed back and everyone was seated again and finally quiet, class was almost over and it was time to give them their homework—a questionnaire consisting of five questions: (1) How many continents are there in the world? (2) How many oceans are there? (3) How many countries are there? (4) What percent of Earth's surface is covered by water? (5) What country do you want to go to and why?

Three more 50-minute classes and five more hours later, Winston was finished for the day and mentally wasted, but at least he was going home before rush hour. He would have gotten a seat if another *obatarian* hadn't body-checked him in her maniacal pursuit for the seat. He was able to hang on to a strap, though, and even had some elbow room, which enabled him to feel more like a human being and less like a canned sardine. He badly needed a couple of beers. For the past week, he had been going to a neighborhood *okonomiyaki* place named Tanuki for dinner and drinking three large 633-milliliter bottles of Kirin Lager beer, which he liked almost as much as the Henry Weinhard's beer he drank back in Corvallis. The *obatarian* got off at the next station and Winston was able to sit down, next to a guy dozing off with a Cup Sake in hand. Winston loosened his tie, leaned his head back, and took some deep breaths with his eyes closed until he felt the fellow's head, which had been bobbing farther and farther down to the side, come to a rest on his shoulder. He shrugged the guy half awake and back up, but the guy fell right back to sleep and his head started bobbing again until it landed right in Winston's lap. He pushed the guy's head back up just after the train stopped at the next station. The guy woke up, realized that it was his stop, made a mad dash to get off the train before the door closed, and barely made it. Then he ran alongside the train as it pulled away, banging on the window and seeming to be yelling at Winston, who didn't know what to make of it until he looked down at the floor next to him and saw the guy's shoes.

Winston was at Tanuki as soon as it opened at 5:00. As he'd been going there for a week, he was acquainted with the woman who ran the place while her husband played mahjong.* She was Korean. Her father was one of hundreds of thousands of Koreans brought to Japan during World War Two to do slave labor and make up for the loss of Japanese men conscripted for the Japanese Imperial Army. Her husband was a third-generation Korean whose grandfather was forcibly brought to Japan after Japan colonized Korea in 1910. Like most second- and third-generation zainichi,† they had never been to Korea and couldn't have spoken Korean if their lives depended on it; and like the vast majority of the 700,000 *zainichi,* they used Japanese names to avoid discrimination because hatred of Koreans ran deep, so deep that even long-time permanent-residence didn't entitle them to vote, much less attend state-run schools. Winston greeted the woman, Yoshiko Shinohara, and had the usual. On his way home, he bought two big 500-milliliter cans of Asahi Super Dry at a vending machine. Nothing was in his little mailbox except an electric bill that was all Greek to him and a handbill explicitly advertising pornographic videos. He unlocked his door and went in, took off his shoes and stepped up onto the *tatami,* set his briefcase down, turned on both of his fans, stripped down to his boxer shorts, leaned against the wall, took a big swig of beer, and slid down along the wall to the floor. "Holy moly, what a day!" he said and scratched his itchy ass.

The next day was another day, with some differences but with uncanny similarities. One of the differences was that he bought *three* cans of Asahi Super Dry at the vending machine on the way home from Tanuki. He popped one of them open immediately and had almost finished it by the time he completed the one-minute walk from the vending machine to his house. Holy moly, he thought as he slid down along the wall again in his boxer shorts. Finishing his beer, he crushed the can and threw it for the trash can and blankly watched it hit the rim and bounce off. Thank God it was Friday and the next day was one of the two monthly no-school Saturdays. He had two full days to recuperate. Sure as his name was Winston Baldry (or Winston Bōrudorii), he needed recuperation. Wow, he was wound up! Wow, he was beat! Wow wow, his ass was itchy! He shot his arm out and caught a mosquito in mid-air. After clenching his fist tightly to make sure he had killed it, he opened his hand and saw it fly away. He leaned over across the *tatami,* grabbed his box of mosquito coils, and lit one. Then he leaned back against the wall and opened the third can of beer. In addition to recuperating, he had to think of some way to get the students interested so he didn't feel like he was talking to the walls, or at least keep them occupied with something to do besides talk, write letters, read *manga*

---

* board game with 136 tiles, played by four people. Originally from China, the game became popular in Japan in the early 1900s. There are about 25,000 mahjong parlors in Japan.

† Korean residents in Japan. Osaka has the largest population of zainichi: 120,000.

and fashion magazines, and sleep. That wasn't going to be easy. He crawled over to his briefcase and took out the questionnaires they completed for homework. He wanted to see their answers to the question 'What country do you want to go to and why?' One at a time, he went through them: Australia–I want to shopping; Hong Kong–To shopping; Hawaii–I go to shoping; Australia–I want to looking at koara; Canada–I go to ski; America–I go to shopping; French–I wont go shopping; Swiss– I eat cheeze; Hawaii–I want to shopping; Singapore–I like to shopping; Italy–Dericious pasta; Australia–Somehow; Hong Kong–Shoping; Finland–I meet Santa Claus; America–I wont to meet Kebin Kosner; Singapore–I want to shopping; Australia–I go to shopping . . .

"Gojōsha arigatō gozaimasu. Osore irimasu ga jōshaken o haiken itashimasu" (Thanks for taking the train. Sorry, but I have to check your tickets) said the JR man, holding his hat at his chest after bowing to the passengers in the fourth car of the shinkaisoku (new rapid express) heading toward Kyōto. Seated next to the window beside a vacant seat, Winston didn't hear him or even see him. He was plugged in to a Sony Walkman with big over-the-ear Panasonic headphones. With his eyes closed, he was listening to relaxing 'alpha' music that had become part of his regimen in a losing battle against stress. He had been drinking more beer than he had ever drunk before and was having the guy at the local liquor store deliver it to him by the case on the back of his motor scooter. He kept a beer at arm's length while taking his long evening bath, into which he put special therapeutic bath powder said to relieve stiff shoulders. Every night before going to bed, he rubbed the ointment Tiger Balm into his neck and temples. He put strips of the medicated plaster Tokuhon onto his shoulders every morning and peeled them off while drinking his first beer of the evening, which was within two minutes of his arrival home from Minami Kōbe High School. He was receiving a weekly Sunday anma* that helped, but not for long because by mid-week his nerves were on edge again and on their way to being shot. Mrs. Tsujimoto recommended acupuncture, but he didn't like the idea of having needles stuck into him. Mr. Tsujimoto recommended moxsa,† but that became out of the question when he saw the many scars the size of vaccination marks on Mr. Tsujimoto's upper arms. Concerned people extended their greetings to him with the question 'Katakori wa dō?' (How are your stiff shoulders?) and offered various suggestions that included yoga, T'ai Chi, aerobics, jogging, swimming, machine training, and 250 golf swings a day, all of which required some degree of energy, which he didn't have to any degree. He was thinking about dragging himself to a doctor for a check-up to see if something was physically wrong with him. He spent his weekends lying around and recuperating, and preparing for the next week's classes.

It had now been six weeks since he arrived in Japan—one week since his anal itch had cleared up—and he hadn't gone out anywhere to speak of, except to a Minami Kōbe High School faculty party on September 30th, at which Rika Koga was present. Looking especially pretty in a kimono, she offered to take him the following Sunday to see Kazamidori no Yakata and other western-style houses in Kōbe that foreigners lived

---

* Japanese massage taken with one's clothes on. Unlike shiatsu, which involves finger pressure on some of the 657 tsubos (pressure points), anma, often done by blind people, focuses on rolling stiffness out of the muscles.

† heating treatment in which a kind of plant is burned on certain parts of the skin to get one's system back into balance.

in during the Meiji Period (1867-1912) and the Taisho Period (1912-1925). He declined the invitation by saying that he had too much preparation to do for his classes, but the real reason was that he felt it was too soon to go out on a date, as it hadn't even been five months since Wallis died laughing. A part of him, though, really wanted to go out with her, and it shouldn't be necessary to mention which part of him it was. While he was talking to Rika at the party in basic, broken English, the Japanese History teacher, Masaharu Ikenouchi, grabbed Shannah Pearl's breasts and said, "Ōkii mune ya ne." (You've got big tits.) Rika had stopped going to faculty parties because Ikenouchi had done the same thing to her not once but twice, but she wanted to go to this party because Winston was going to be there and she liked Winston because he looked like Randy Bass, the former first baseman for the Hanshin Tigers. Had Winston been there at the party wearing a Hanshin Tigers uniform with Bass's number 44 on the back, she would have creamed her kimono. She adored the back-to-back Triple Crown winner, who arguably had the greatest season in Japanese baseball history with a .350 batting average and 54 home runs in a 130-game schedule. He might have equalled (or even surpassed) Sadaharu Ō's record of 55 home runs* in the final game of the season if he had not been thrown nothing but ridiculously outside pitches in all five of his appearances at the plate by the pitchers of the Yomiuri Giants, who happened to be managed by none other than Sadaharu Ō. Perhaps Ikenouchi would have grabbed Rika's breasts again if Shannah Pearl hadn't been at the party. If he had, Rika was finally prepared to show him a little fighting spirit, but she certainly wasn't prepared to take things as far as Shannah had taken them by going beyond the charge of sexual harassment to the charge of sexual assault, with photos of a bruise on her left breast to present as Exhibit A or, rather, Exhibit Double D. Shannah was a tough woman. Rika was a pretty tough woman herself. Divorced Japanese women had to be.

Aside from that party, the only time he went out to socialize was ten days before on a national holiday (Autumnal Equinox Day), when he went no farther than Ashiya to have dinner at the home of Donovan Wood, an Australian man he met one day on the train platform while waiting for the train back home after another grueling day at Minami Kōbe High School. That dinner, prepared by Donovan's Japanese wife Chie, was the first well-balanced meal he'd had in a very long time, even though he got violently ill eating ground nuts that were in a spinach-sesame dish. His diet was perhaps part of his problem. He breakfasted on Kellogg's Corn Flakes or Kellogg's Genmai Flakes. For lunch at school, he brought a banana or two, as other fruit was so expensive. For dinner, he had Seafood Cup Noodles, which he ate at home, having stopped going out for dinner at Tanuki because he wanted to be alone, all alone. The little pieces of dried octopus in the Cup Noodles were the

---

* Ō hit 55 home runs in 1964, when they played 140-game schedules.

extent of his protein intake. One day, when My Shop had a special sale on Cup Noodles, he bought 35 of them and needed two large plastic bags to carry them home in. If not Cup Noodles, he boiled Bon curry sauce in the bag–he had settled on medium hot–and poured it onto three slices of the thickly-sliced white bread that came four slices in a pack. Hoping to make up for a lack of variety in a diet that would have been completely vegetableless without the little pieces of dried seaweed in his Cup Noodles, he took multi-vitamin pills. To keep himself charged at work, he drank several cups of Nescafe instant coffee, into which he added the non-dairy powdered creamer Creap. He capped off his banana lunch each day with a small 100-milliliter bottle of tonic, either Oronamin C or Fibe Mini, available in one of the many vending machines across the street from the school.

He managed to make it through work OK, but by the time he got home, he was beat, and by the end of the work week, he was wiped out. Aside from stepping out, stepping slowly, to get groceries at My Shop, wash his clothes at the koin randorii,* and get his massage, his steps were few and far between. He sat around the house and watched a lot of TV on his new Hitachi bilingual television. Mostly, he watched sports, usually a Yomiuri Giants baseball game because hardly any other games besides Giants games were televised. Occasionally, he watched a J.League soccer game. Until the fall basho† ended a week before, he watched *Sumo Digest* every night. When there weren't any sports on, he watched quiz shows like *Naruhodo the World* and *Sekai Fushigi Hakken*. If there happened to be a bilingual movie on, he used the bilingual feature of his TV to make Perry Mason, Columbo, John Wayne, Harrison Ford, and others speak English instead of Japanese. Most of the movies were violent American action movies. The best part about watching some of them was watching the introduction by Yodogawa-san, the enthusiastic octogenarian with gray hair and black glasses. The night before, Winston watched the samurai drama *Zenigata Heiji* and then a program in which bikini-clad young ladies were brought into a pigpen one at time, tied up spread-eagle on the ground, and doused with buckets of pig slop before hungry pigs were released into the pen to lick the slop off them while they wiggled and screamed. He had decided to subscribe to the satellite station WOWOW and buy a VCR so he could tape movies as well as rent videos from the local video-rental shop, My Video. On this day, Sunday, October 2nd, the Asian Games, featuring Chinese steroid-filled women, was opening in Hiroshima. That was something Winston considered worth watching. But he'd made up his mind that on this day, no matter how tired he was, no matter how weak

---

* Japanese English for 'coin laudry', meaning 'laundromat'. As Japanese, almost without exception, hang their laundry outside to dry, laundromats are very hard to find.

† sumō-wrestling tournament. Six major tournaments are held in a year, each lasting for 15 days.

he felt, no matter how much preparation he had to do, no matter what, he would make a trip to Kyōto and go to Kinkakuji Temple to finally settle his outstanding IOU.

Five days before, September 27th, was the day of the harvest moon, which people celebrated by eating a sweet dumpling called *dango*. That night, there were many traditional festivals. The rice harvest had actually begun two weeks before and would continue until the middle of October in colder areas. Now, on this second day of October, some harvested fields were black from being burned to put nutrients back into the soil. Some had brown mounds of rice shells that would be used for field-burning or tipi-like stacks of straw that would be used to protect vegetables from frost. Many still-unharvested fields had scarecrows, some that looked like humans, but most of which were just big, yellow-and-black balloons that looked like eyes. Winston didn't see the rice fields. Nor did he see the driving ranges, billboards, neon signboards, shops, stores, apartments, and manshons.* His eyes were closed. The JR man had to tap him on the shoulder to make him aware that he was being asked to show his ticket. After the JR man stamped his ticket and moved on, Winston resumed listening to alpha music with his head-phones on and his eyes closed—until he was tapped on the shoulder again, this time more forcefully. The forceful tapper was *not* a JR man. The fellow repeated himself after Winston took off his headphones.

"Where are you from?"

"Watashi wa America-jin desu." (I'm American.)

"No, no, no. Please be to speak English. I want to practicing my English."

"No, thanks."

Back on went the headphones. He cranked up the volume and closed his eyes, hoping that the man would go away but conscious that he had sat down beside him and was talking to him. Trying to ignore him, he kept his eyes closed until the guy started nudging him. Then he angrily pulled off his headphones with one hand.

"What's the problem?"

"Do you like sushi?"

That did it. Winston got up and moved to another seat, next to a guy using a cordless electric shaver. Across from him were two high-school girls sharing a box of Glico Pocky chocolate-covered sticks while paging through *Jump* magazine. "Gaijin ya. Mite" (Look! There's a foreigner) one of the girls said to the other one. Nobody else was paying much attention to him, but until a few days before, he was unknowingly followed everywhere by a plainclothes policeman because of suspicion that he had *yakuza* connections and was perhaps a Mafioso seeking ties with the Kuramoto-gumi that his 'friend' Yasumasa Kanamori was the number-two man in.

---

* Japanese English for 'manshion'–apartments built by private developers since the 1960s, but called 'manshon' (manshion) for image reasons.

At Kyōto Station, Winston put his knapsack on and got out. Still listening to alpha music with his headphones on, he went with the flow along the platform and down the stairs, past the JR ticket-takers and out where people, people, and more people were coming and going, crisscrossing and crosscrissing this way and that way. Standing in complete confusion between Ogawa Coffee and the subway ticket machines, he looked for any indication about where he needed to go to take a bus to Kinkakuji. "You look lost. May I help you?" said a Canadian lady who lived in Kyōto. She had such large lips that Winston suddenly remembered what 'Spike' Gallagher, a kid in his elementary-school class once said about another kid in the class, Chuck 'Bahama Lips' Talbott: "He's got lips like he's been sucking on doorknobs." "Yes," Winston replied after he lowered his headphones and she repeated herself, "I want to take the bus to doorknobs–I mean Kinkakuji Temple."

"Kinkakuji or Ginkakuji?"

"Kinkakuji."

"Go that way about 200 meters. You'll see a kiosk. Turn left there and go up the stairs. You want bus 205."

"Thank you."

"No problem."

"That's what *you* think."

It was a beautiful, sunshiny day in Kyōto. In front of Kyōto Station at the place for bus 205, Winston stepped forward from under the canopy and looked up at Kyōto Tower. The observatory provided a good view of the city, but he didn't have time for that today. He had an appointment to meet Donovan Wood at the Gosho (Imperial Palace) after finishing his business at Kinkakuji.

Bus 205 soon came with its green seats, except for two gray seats with signs above them in Japanese saying that they were for 'silver citizens', i.e. elderly people. Not knowing any better, Winston sat in one of the silver seats next to a young lady who knew better but didn't care because it wasn't September 15th, Respect for the Aged Day. A couple of borderline elderly people–It was difficult to tell which side of the border they were one because all silver citizens dyed their 'silver' hair– had to stand among the swaying straphangers. Cramped in the small double-seat with his knees pressed against the back of the seat in front of him, Winston had his knapsack on his lap. On the knapsack, he had a Kyōto city bus map that Donovan had given him along with the book *Kinkakuji* by Yukio Mishima. He focused on the purple line on the map showing the route of bus 205, which ran up Karasuma Street, over Shichijo Street, and up Nishiōji Street. He turned off his Walkman and lowered his headphones, and tried to listen to the tape-recorded announcements in Japanese that were muffled by the bus's motor. A sign at the front of the bus showed him that the fare was ¥200. Leaning with difficulty just far enough to the left to reach into his right pants pocket and take out his coin purse, he saw that he didn't have ¥200 in coins. Leaning again to the left, he put the coin purse back, then leaned with even more difficulty to his right to reach into his left pants pocket and take out his wallet. He took out a ¥1,000 bill and leaned again to the right to put the wallet back. He saw a woman seated up front get up from her seat, put a bill into a machine next to the driver, and receive change back in coins, and understood that he would have to do the same. Then he slipped his hand into his knapsack and took out a letter from the Pipers that he had received the day before. He read it again while keeping one eye on where he was in relation to where he was going on that purple line.

Dear Winston,

Your letter was waiting for us when we got back from Mexico. Sorry to hear that your classes aren't going as well as you had hoped. It sounds like you're drinking an awful lot of beer. Please don't drink too much or you'll damage your liver. I hope that you're gradually getting adjusted to the food. I could never get used to raw fish! We didn't think the food in Mexico was nearly as good as it is at the Taco Bell here in town. Do they have Taco Bells in Japan? I know they have Kentucky Fried Chickens because we ate at one. The only problem we had in Mexico, aside from Montezuma's Revenge, which I mentioned in the postcard we sent to you, was when we got separated from our tour group in Mexico City and had to go right back to our hotel and spend the rest of the day there. But we thoroughly enjoyed our trip. The Mayan ruins were absolutely breathtaking. I don't think George put down his video camera during the whole trip. Are you going to buy a video camera? They're really great for traveling. Well, I'll turn you over to George now. Enjoy your stay in Japan. We're so thrilled that you are expanding your horizons like we have. Becoming international is its own reward. We're enclosing another letter from Australia addressed to Wallis. It's interesting that her bottle made it down there. She would have been so excited.
Love,
Adele

Hi Winston!

It's great that you're learning to speak a little Japanese. One of the best things about group tours is that you don't have any language problems. When we were over there, I was really impressed with how well-dressed and well-groomed everyone was. I wasn't very impressed, however, with the quality of their shoes. If you need another pair, let me know. It must be difficult to find shoes big enough for you over there. Are you coming home for Christmas? We'd love to hear about your impressions of Japan and show you our videos of our trip to Mexico. Kenya is next on our list.
Take care,
George

PS I almost forgot to tell you about what happened to George when we were in Mexico. He handed a little shoe-shine boy a $10 bill for a shoe shine that cost about a dime in pesos because that's all he had at the time, and the boy ran away with the money without even shining his shoes. Anyway, George chased him and slipped on donkey poop and then slid like a baseball player in freshly laid cement, ruining both his suit and his shoes. You should have been there.
Adele

PPS Well, I'm not going to let Adele have the last word, not when she broke two more high heels and lost a gold earring. But from now on, I'll have my shoes shined at the hotel. I see I'm running out of space. All the best.
George

The enclosed letter from Australia addressed to Wallis was sent by a boy who lived near the southern coastal city of Adelaide. In his mappy mind, Winston opened up a map of Australia. The bottle had evidently gotten carried south along the eastern shore and then had been swept west through the Bass Strait. Now, its logical course would be westerly, clear across the southern shore and then up the western coast, unless easterly winds (farther out) prevailed and sent it back. Strong easterlies could still send it all of the way back to South America and conceivably past Cape Horn, through the Strait of Magellan, and up the coast of Argentina. It would be interesting to see where the next letter would come from. Wallis would have indeed been very excited.

After forty minutes on the bus, Winston knew he was getting close but didn't know exactly where he was on the purple line until there was a helpful announcement in English: "Next stop is Kinkakuji Temple." Several people got off in front of him, putting in ¥200 tickets or ¥200 in coins. He put the ¥1,000 bill into the slot with the head of Natsume Sōseki facing up, and the bill went in and came back out. He turned it over and put it back in with the head of Sōseki facing *down,* and it went in and came back out. The driver grabbed the bill, flattened out a crease in it, and put it in, and it went in and came back out. Grabbing it again, the driver flattened out a couple of small wrinkles and put it in, and it went in and came back out. After finally being given change for the ¥1,000 bill by another passenger, Winston was able to pay the fare and get off. On the corner, there was a sign with KINKAKU-JI written in blue, under which was a red arrow pointing the way.

He walked through the main gate and paid ¥400 for an admission ticket given to him along with an information-leaflet with Japanese on one side and English on the other. Having read Mishima's book *Kinkakuji,* he knew some things not mentioned in the leaflet, such as the matter of the psychologically disturbed monk-in-training who sent the temple up in smoke in 1950. He walked on a gravel path that winded around to an opening and said, "Holy moly!" There it was, Kinkakuji, the Temple of the Golden Pavilion, and there *he* was, the only person without a camera. Everybody was either taking pictures or posing for pictures. The younger posers were flashing the V-sign without any idea what it meant aside from being a posing necessity. It was picture-taking madness there at that best picture-taking place, with the largest of the little islands on Kyōko-chi (Mirror Pond) in the foreground of the glistening golden temple. Winston walked on a path leading behind the temple. At the back of it, he leaned against a low bamboo fence and wondered where in the hell and how in the hell he was going to empty Wallis's ashes without being seen, as there was no letup in the horde of people passing by. Fighting against the flow, he walked back to the front and went to a dead end where a little wooden gate was locked with a padlock. He took off his knapsack and squatted down with his back against a tall bamboo fence in the shade of a couple of momiji.* People were continuously posing near him and in front of him, but it was nevertheless the most private part of the best part. The only feasible way to do it, he figured, was to take some ashes in his fist, a little at a time, and nonchalantly drop them over the low bamboo fence onto the moss that surrounded Mirror Pond. He opened the knapsack and took the top off the urn. *Well, here I am, Wallis. Right here at Kinkakuji. It really is beautiful. I wish you could see it. I know you wanted to come here. There were so many places you wanted to go. I'm sorry. I was a jerk. I always made excuses. I always talked about someday, but someday never came for you. I got in the way between you and your dreams. I should have taken you on some nice trips so you had more to look forward to than where your bottle was going. It made it to Australia, by the way. That's its third continent. Right now, it's probably heading west in the Great Australian Bight. There's a chance it could make it to Africa if it gets swept up the west coast of Australia. If I sell the house, I'll make some arrangment with the post office so I can keep getting letters from people who find the chain-message. I really don't know what I'm going to do with the house. It's not home anymore without you there. I sure took a big step by coming to Japan. You must really be shocked if you can see me. I remember, on the day you died, you said that you'd like to have your ashes thrown at Kinkakuji. Well, that's what I'm here to do. Sorry I can't put all of your ashes here. The police took some for lab tests because they thought your ashes were hashish. Pardon?*

Winston's 'Pardon?' was directed at a man who was a member of a group of American Psychiatric Association psychiatrists in Japan on an APA trip. They were staying at the posh Miyako Hotel while in Kyōto.

"Would you like to talk about it?"

"Talk about what?"

"I'm a psychiatrist. I can help you."

"Who said I needed help?"

"You've lost someone, haven't you?"

"I don't want to talk about it."

"Talking about it is an important part of the healing process."

"I don't want to talk about it to *you*. I don't even know you."

"My name is Theodore Herbelsheimer. I have a Ph.D. from Stanford and 25 years of clinical experience. Why don't you open up to me and tell me what you're feeling?"

"Please leave me alone."

"I've had six books published and more than 40—"

"I DON'T CARE."

"OK. Fine. I tried to help you, but you don't want any help. I charge $175 an hour in my private practice, but I was willing to give you a few minutes of my clinical skills free of charge. But OK, no problem. It's your loss, not mine."

---

* Japanese maple tree.

"Is there some problem over here, Ted?" asked a concerned member of the group who had become aware of the altercation. "No," Herbelsheimer replied to his colleague. "This guy's just being a pain in the ass. But that's *his* problem. Let's go." And away they went, to pose with other members of their group.

Winston stayed there for a few more minutes until he was ready. Then he reached into his knapsack and into the urn. With a fistful of ashes, he walked over to the low bamboo fence and leaned forward against it. Pretending to be admiring the beautiful temple, he dropped the ashes onto the moss. Three more times he did this at three different places as he made his way to the back of the temple. Mission accomplished, he went up some steps, past a second pond, an old tea house, and a souvenir shop, and then back out.

On Nishiōji Street with his headphones back on, he got his directional bearings and flagged down one of the country's 250,000 taxis. After jumping back when the automatic door sprung open, he got in and pulled the door closed as it closed automatically and told the driver to take him to Karasuma-Marutamachi by saying, "Karasuma-Marutamachi kudasai." (Please give me Karasuma-Marutamachi.) This was only the second time he had taken a taxi in Japan, and what impressed him the first time impressed him again. Over and above the whiteness, the spotlessness, and the cleanliness of the car itself, the well-dressed, well-groomed driver was wearing white gloves.

Winston listened to his alpha music while the taxi driver listened to a baseball game between the Seibu Lions and the Kintetsu Buffaloes. The Lions had already clinched first place in the Pacific League, which was nothing new, and would be playing in the Japan Series against either the Yomiuri Giants or the Chunichi Dragons, who were going down to the wire in their battle for the Central League championship. As the driver turned and went east on Marutamachi Street, the Lions' first baseman, Kazuhiro Kiyohara, hit a home run off the Buffaloes' pitching ace, Hideo Nomo.

TAXI DRIVER: *(upon stopping on Marutamachi Street near its intersection with Karasuma Street)* Hai. Karasuma-Marutamachi desu. (OK. Here we are at Karasuma-Marutamachi.)

WINSTON: *(forgetting that he had his headphones on)* Karasuma-Marutamachi?

TAXI DRIVER: Hai. Karasuma-Marutamachi desu.

WINSTON: *(after taking off his headphones)* Karasuma-Marutamachi?

TAXI DRIVER: Sō desu. (That's right.)

WINSTON: *(wanting to be completely sure)* Karasuma-Marutamachi?

TAXI DRIVER: Koko ga Karasuma-Marutamachi desu yo. (Hey, this place here is Karasuma-Marutamachi.)

WINSTON: Arigatō. (Thank you.)

Winston paid the taxi fare and got out. Forgetting that the door was automatic, he slammed it shut. After putting his headphones back on, he did as Donovan told him to do. He walked east along Marutamachi Street to the Gosho's southern entrance and went through the big, wooden gate, then headed north on the gravel of the wide pedestrian road. Donovan said he would be sitting under a tree somewhere on the right. As it was a beautiful Sunday, many people were at the Gosho. Most of them were walking on the gravel or sitting on a bench; some were sitting on the grass. Donovan was sitting under a spruce tree that had three wooden poles supporting heavy branches that extended way out.

Donovan Wood was 46 years old. He had been living in Japan for 15 years, but sometimes it seemed to him like only yesterday, or not so long ago anyway, that he was knocking around with a backpack on his back. With money he saved working on the family sheep farm in Queensland, Australia, he headed straight for Kathmandu. This was in 1971, still in the hippie heyday that gave Freak Street its name, and this was before there were any *Lonely Planet* guidebooks to carry around like *Bibles*. In fact, Donovan gave Tony Wheeler the idea for the name of his guidebooks. He happened to bump into Tony and his wife, Maureen, in Pokhara two weeks after having met them at a pie shop in 'Pig Alley' in Kathmandu. Maureen said, "Hey, it's a small world," and Donovan replied, "Yes, but it's a very lonely planet." In those days, Donovan had a beard and long hair that he pulled back into a ponytail. Now he had a goatee and shorter hair that made him look more respectable. He had put on several pounds with time, and time had faded not only his once dark-brown hair, but also, and more surprisingly, his once green eyes. Now, one eye was grayish green and the other bluish gray. The bluish-gray one, his right eye, was his good eye. He 'lost', as they say, his left eye when he was 12 years old. Since then, he had a glass eye, and for quite some time, it needed to be replaced with a new one, a bluish-gray one.

Doing the lowest of low-budget traveling, Donovan bummed around for eight years, the first four in Nepal and India. On the day after King Birenda's ostentatious coronation in Kathmandu on February 4th, 1975, he set off for Europe and spent two years on the cheap in an old Volkswagen van. Sometimes he stopped to make money doing farm-work, which was much more laborious than selling magic mushrooms to beach bums like himself in Goa, India, where he earned the nickname 'the Mushroom Man'. After Europe, he went to Egypt, with his top priority being to see the Grateful Dead perform at the Pyramids on September 16th of 1978. Next was Iran, where the Shah had been keeping things peaceful in the oil interests of Uncle Sam for 36 years. Little did he know how unpeaceful things were about to become. He was teaching English in Tehran when the Islamic Revolution broke out and ended up fleeing with the Shah. He didn't actually flee *with* the Shah but two weeks after the Shah left on January 16th of 1979. He would have left *before* the Shah if he had an American passport to show instead of an Australian one, for America, not Australia, was the Great Satan. A few passport-stamps later, he was in Pakistan, making money by smuggling guns into Afghanistan. This time he got out long before the shit hit the fan. The Russians rolled in on December 31st of 1979, but Donovan was long gone a full three months before that impending 'rollation'. He showed up in Japan on a rainy October 7th of 1979. It was the day of the 35th general election, which had a low voter turnout because of the rain but didn't make any difference because Japan was (and would remain for another 14 years) essentially a one-party system, with the one party being the Liberal Democratic Party. Kakuei Tanaka, forced to resign as prime minister in 1974 for taking bribes from Lockheed to get him to influence All Nippon Airways (ANA) to buy Lockheed aircraft, was still *de facto* running the show. Ōhira Masayoshi was the prime minister. Emperor Hirohito was still alive and kicking and publishing articles about jellyfish. Japan had still not come to terms with its militaristic past, and straightforward apologies for its wartime aggression were still a long way off. Market-deregulation had not yet begun, but the continuation of the economic miracle inspired books like Ezra Vogel's *Japan as Number One,* published that very year. Japanese knew that America still had a hold on number one, but the country was oozing with optimism and banks started a lending binge that would come back to haunt them in ten or twelve years. It was the year that three-time Triple Crown winner Hiromitsu Ochiai began his pro baseball career with the Lotte Orions. Kitaonoumi, the greatest sumō wrestler since Taihō, was still going strong, with the next great sumō wrestler, Chiyonofuji, just up and coming. Pink Lady (Mie and Kei) was (or were) still the pop-music rage, with Seiko Matsuda's debut one year away. Karaoke was a thing of the future. The TV music program *The Best Ten,* hosted by Hiroshi Kume and Tetsuko Kuroyanagi, was popular with young people. Many teen idols had double-eyelid operations to give them the western-look that was fashionable because good-looking *gaijins* appeared in one soft-sell television commercial after another. None of them looked like Donovan Wood, but that didn't matter because of the huge demand for English teachers. His main reason for coming to Japan was because he was told that Japanese girls were crazy about western guys and were ready for action. He showed up with an old backpack, 35 American dollars, and 200 grams of condom-sealed Afghanistanian hashish up his ass, in his stomach, and in the hollow of his left eye, over which he was wearing a patch. (His glass eye was in a jar with some marbles.)

In those days, and for several years afterward, the demand for English teachers far exceeded the supply, and native English speakers didn't need any other requirement, not even having made it through kindergarten. Now it was very different, not with respect to a kindergarten requirement, but with respect to the supply that had been driven by the surging yen. Now there were so many young people, mostly Americans, competing for teaching jobs at language schools like NOVA, ECC, Berlitz, and Tōza, or working as ALTs (Assistant Language Teachers) at middle schools and high schools on the rapidly expanding

JET program, that *gaijins* in the larger cities were getting stared at much less frequently as if they were aliens from outer space. Consequently, there was a sharp decrease in the number of children crashing their bicycles. Foreigners had been coming to Japan in ever increasing numbers since the mid 1980s, when the yen started packing a punch. Bangladeshi, Pakistani, Iranian, Brazilian, Peruvian, and Chinese men were welcomed by bigwigs of construction companies and factories that could use them as cheap labor. Thai and Philippino ladies were welcomed by *yakuza* that could use them as strippers and prostitutes. Westerners were welcomed because they were white. Americans were especially welcomed because they were Americans. Japan still had an American complex that developed after Japan surrendered to America and Emperor Hirohito said over the radio that he wasn't really a god. America became the new god or, at least, a sort of heaven that they could catch glimpses of through Hollywood movies. America was good, America was great, Americans were more than welcome, and Americans came. The 'invasion' of young Americans started really snowballing in the late 1980s on the downward slope of the U.S. dollar, but even before then, *gaijins* were commonly assumed to be Americans. Donovan was rejected as an English teacher at a couple of places because he was not American. He was even told at one place that he was not qualified to teach English because he was not a native English speaker. Perceptions had changed since then. People teaching English in Japan were no longer assumed to be Americans, thanks mainly to the JET program that started in 1986. Half of the 4,500 'JETs' were from Britain, Canada, Australia, and New Zealand. America was no longer heaven. In fact, America was scary with its gun-culture in which 20,000 people were murdered a year. Australia had replaced America as the number-one travel-choice for Japanese. Now the Gold Coast was like a Japanese enclave. Now they all knew that Australians spoke English. Now Donovan had a job teaching English at a university.

Donovan was a seasoned veteran. The veterans were mostly men because ladies couldn't put up with the sexism and the sexual harassment for long. Most of the veterans started off in the language schools, but they'd long ago said sayōnara and jumped off that one-for-you/five-for-me merry-go-round. They'd gone through the phase of going over to South Korea so they could come back with a new three-month tourist visa or working things out for a renewable six-month cultural visa studying something that required having to do as little as possible. Many of them were now married to Japanese ladies. Most of those with master's degrees were teaching part-time at one or more universities. Donovan was one of the elite, with a full-time professorship at Kōbe Gakugei University. They couldn't very well refuse a candidate who had graduated with an M.A. in Applied Linguistics from Harvard and a Ph.D. in Language and Literacy Education from Oxford. "Bugger 'em if they can't take a joke," Donovan said to himself while putting together his résumé.

Donovan's big secret was nerve-racking at first. No one doubted it, though, so no one checked it out. He certainly looked like a scholar with the pipe he smoked to play the part. Eight years had now passed, and his academic history was part of the pride of Kōbe Gakugei University. The president of the university, Tetsuaki Kurokado, respected Wood Kyōju (Professor Wood) for his scholastic achievements and proudly introduced him as having advanced degrees from both Oxford and Harvard. The introductions made Donovan uneasy because Crown Prince Hironomiya wasn't the only Japanese to have gone to Oxford, and Crown Princess Masako wasn't the only Japanese to have gone to Harvard. There were some Britons and Americans coming to Japan, even on the JET program, who had gone to Oxford or Harvard, and Donovan dreaded being introduced to a fellow Oxonian or Harvardian eager to talk about their alma maters. Six months before, President Kurokado introduced him to a new part-time English instructor at Kōbe Gakugei University, Gregory Martin, who really had graduated from Oxford. "Wood Kyōju also graduated from Oxford," Kurokado told Gregory, who was eager to talk about Bodleian Library, Divinity School, Sheldonian Theatre, etc. with a fellow Oxonian. "Which college did you go to?" Gregory asked Donovan, who didn't even know that Oxford was an umbrella name for thirty colleges in the city of Oxford. Chewing on half a mochi* that one of the office ladies brought him with a cup of green tea, Donovan saw no other way of answering Gregory than by pretending to choke on the mochi. Shrieks, shouts, and cries for help filled the room. Donovan's performance would have been considered overacting if it had been considered acting. As it was, it was considered nothing less than an emergency. Several people choked to death on mochi every year, especially during the New Year's holidays, and Donovan seemed to be well on his way to becoming a statistic. Nothing helped until Gregory applied the Heimlich maneuver. Donovan ejected the mochi and slumped to the floor, unable to say anything at all except "Iranai" (It's not necessary) when the ambulance arrived. After that, Donovan avoided Gregory like the plague and was antisocial to the point of arrogant, which passed him off in Gregory's eyes as an Oxonian through and through.

To cast a mold of his fictional tracks, Donovan went on his 1994 summer vacation to both Oxford and Harvard to get a feel for his 'alma maters'. As for Oxford, he decided that he had graduated from Balliol because it was considered the most radical, and therefore the most fitting for his personality. He was prepared to talk about a wide range of things Oxonian, from the river Cherwell to Blackwell's book shop to the Pelican Sundial at Corpus Christi college to pubs like the King's Arms, the White Horse, and Eagle and Child (which he knew he should call the Bird and Babe like the locals do). After school recommenced in

* rice cake made from pounding steamed rice.

September, he was much less standoffish to Gregory and even told him which college he went to. "Really! I went to Balliol too! Who was your personal tutor?" Gregory said. Fortunately, Donovan was eating another *mochi,* and he almost choked to death again.

He was high on hashish when he put his bogus résumé together. It was in the fall of 1985. At the time, Donovan was teaching company classes and private classes, but barely making ends meet. He and Chie and their five-year-old identical triplets were living in a 2LDK (two little rooms plus a little living room, a little dining room, and a little kitchen) in a shabby apartment building pretentiously named Villa Yamamoto, from where Donovan could see no light at the end of the tunnel. The only people aware of Donovan's big lie were Chie, her parents (Tsutomu and Mitoko Natsuki), her brother Junichirō, and Donovan's two closest friends, Jarod 'Kiwi' Bailey, a New Zealander, and Tony Sheppard, a Canadian. Chie's family wasn't going to spill the azuki* for reasons of status, not to mention money. The Woods became rich. They were now living in a big, beautiful house in affluent Ashiya. Tsutomu and Mitoko boasted of the eminence of their son-in-law as a way to impress people.

In addition to teaching at Kōbe Gakugei University, Donovan used his fluency in Japanese to do translation-work for several companies. He made about ¥850,000 (then A$11,000/US$8,500) a month. When he came to Japan in October of 1979 with 35 American dollars, he figured he'd stay for a year at most and then hit the road again. That was before he met Chie Natsuki, a 23-year-old fairly pretty and very orgasmic receptionist at the Berlitz language school in Ōsaka, where he was teaching conversational English. The rest is history. He and Chie had been married just over 13 years, and the 'trippers', as Donovan called their triplet daughters (Mari, Misa, and Megumi), were 13 years old and in their second year of middle school.

Donovan was dying to get out of Japan the way many Liberal Democratic Party members were dying to form or join other political parties when they saw the LDP boat start sinking in 1993. The difference was that Donovan's boat wasn't sinking; it was sailing along just fine. It was hard for him to walk away from such big and easy money, with four months of paid vacation thrown in. In addition to that, and this was a big addition, he was respected. He was Professor Wood, a great scholar with advanced degrees from both Oxford and Harvard, the two most prestigious universities in the world, and he was living in a country with a university-fixation equaled by none. Even graduates of Tōkyō University, the most prestigious university in Japan, couldn't help bowing their heads in awe of Donovan's scholastic achievements. He was forever being asked to co-chair forums, be a panelist at symposiums, and speak at international conferences, seminars, and workshops. One week before, he was invited to be the main speaker at an international

* red beans. As red is an auspicious color, azuki boiled with rice (sekihan) is often eaten on festive occasions.

JALT (Japan Association of Language Teaching) conference. The week before that, he was invited to be the moderator at the Tōkyō Colloquium international roundtable. (All invitations were politely declined with the explanation that he couldn't spare the time because he was very hard at work completing a trilogy.) Things had turned around for this farm boy from Queensland who never went to college and bummed around for years to the beat of Bob Marley, whose greatest distinction before becoming Professor Wood was being the Mushroom Man. So ego gratification entered the equation, but fraud was also there as a constant. The A$750,000/US$550,000 or so in wages he'd earned under false pretenses over the past eight years from Kōbe Gakugei University constituted major fraud that could have put him in prison for years. To protect his savings in the event of his bank account at Sanwa Ginkō in Kōbe being frozen, Chie withdrew money from the bank account every three months and wire-transferred it from a different bank under a fictitious name to a bank account they had at the National Australian Bank in Melbourne.

He would have also been looking at some time in the slammer if he were to get nailed for possession of hashish, which he always had on hand because he bought fifty grams at a time from a French fellow living in India who smuggled hashish into Japan twice a year for a big, fat profit. He considered the hashish a necessity, though, because he still enjoyed getting high. Besides, it helped him blow his mind away from the triplets, who drove him crazy with their immature adolescence and whiny yakkity yakking. They had the run of the house, and it was either retreat or surrender. So he retreated—to a room he made soundproof, which the triplets called the Forbidden Room because they were not allowed to go into it under any circumstances whatsoever. That's where Donovan holed himself up, read books, watched videos, listened to music, drank beer, and smoked hashish.

Sitting there now at the Gosho with his back against the big spruce tree, Donovan was rolling a cigarette with Drum tobacco, which he preferred to the pipe he still smoked purely for show. He saw Winston stepping over the low fence while licking the cigarette paper. He wasn't in a particularly good mood on this day because he discovered that the triplets were selling their panties to a thriving business establishment that sold middle- and high-school girls' unwashed panties to older guys who got off on sniffing them. When Donovan wasn't in a good mood, he could be confrontational. There were many Donovan Wood stories. On one occasion, at a jazz bar, he broke a painting over the head of a guy who referred to his triplet-daughters as hāfu.* On another occasion, he stormed out of his house at 7:45 a.m. with a full carton of eggs and threw all ten eggs at a campaign truck. On both occasions, he was given sincere apologies. In the bar incident, he was apologized to

---

* Japanese English for 'half', but used to refer to a person who is half Japanese and half something else.

simply for being made angry; in the campaign-truck incident, he was apologized to for a violation of the Public Offices Election Law, which allows campaign trucks to disturb the peace only between 8:00 a.m. and 7:00 p.m. Donovan Wood was like a daruma,* always returning to an upright position when pushed over. He was, after all, the distinguished Professor Wood. He lit the cigarette and began smoking.

"Hi, Donovan."

"I thought for a minute you were wearing giant earmuffs, mate."

"I couldn't get those blasted Walkman headphones to fit in my ears right. They kept coming out, especially when I was walking. These stay on."

"Are you sure you don't need a special license to walk around with those friggin' things on? How long is the cord?"

"Five meters. I have it wrapped up in my bag."

"So what you're saying is that you could put the Walkman down and walk around it like a dog tied to a long leash."

"I didn't think I was saying that. But I am saying that I can turn the world off by turning my Walkman on."

"That's one way of keeping the stress down, mate. Me, I've got my soundproof room."

"You sure picked a nice tree to sit under."

"I'm very particular about the trees I sit under, and I don't care to associate with people who aren't. Here's part of my newspaper. Have a seat."

"I've got my own seat, thank you—also a *Daily Yomiuri.*"

"Not a bad paper on Sunday because it's got the world report of the British paper the *Independent* as a supplement. Their cartoons sure leave a lot to be desired. *RamenHead* is the worst form of humor to appear in the English papers here since *Gaijin* was in the *Mainichi Daily News* several years ago. I wouldn't read the *Mainichi* if it were free. I used to buy the *Asahi Evening News* once a week for Alan Booth's column, but I stopped buying that rag when he died last year. How about a beer? I've got a couple wrapped up that are still a little cold."

"I sure could use one."

"Here you go. Cheers! So how'd your business go at Kinkakuji?"

"Fine. I'll empty the last few bits right here. There. That's the last of it."

"You could have found worse places. These are the grounds of the Kyōto Imperial Palace. The nobility used to live in this area during the Heian Period. Nobunaga, Hideyoshi, and Tokugawa Ieyasu all spent some time here. I wouldn't be surprised if all three of them pissed under this tree, not at the same time of course. So what did you think of Kinkakuji?"

"Impressive."

---

* legless and armless dolls representing the founder of Zen Buddhism, Bohhidharma, whose legs and arms atrophied after nine years of meditation in a cave. When pushed over, darumas always come back to an upright position.

"Also overrated, which is why it's over-touristy. I can think of many other temples where I'd prefer to have my ashes scattered. That reminds me–I've got to write my will one of these days."

"A guy on the flight coming to Japan told me his uncle wrote in his will that he wanted his ashes packed into a fireworks and shot off. He's the guy who had me greeting the airport authorities with 'Watashi wa kichigai desu'."

"Forgive me for laughing. Hey, did you feel the earthquake last night?"

"Yeah. I forgot all about it. It woke me up. That's the third one I've felt since I've been here."

"They say another big one is going to hit Tōkyō one of these days."

"It's not just Tōkyō that's at risk. There are about 2,000 active faults in Japan. A big one could hit here too."

"It would take something like that to get me out of here."

"Sounds like you're pretty settled."

"Four of us are. One of us is pretty *un*settled. I've got to get out of here before the bull shit takes me down like quicksand. I feel like the guys on the trains standing near the doors with cigarettes in their mouths and their lighters perfectly in place to light them the very second the doors open at their stops."

"Why don't you get out?"

"I've got four roots, all female, and uprooting three of them would be a major uprooting. I missed a chance a year ago, before they started middle school. I'm definitely not going to let them go to high school here."

"Why not?"

"Because it makes them too submissive. Right now they've still got some spunk. For example, they were on the train the other day, coming back from a friggin' karaoke box, and some guy was masturbating in front of them."

"Holy moly!"

"99.99% of Japanese girls and ladies in that situation are going to passively move away without reporting the matter or raising any hell at all, which is why there are so many perverts and gropers on the trains."

"So what did the triplets do?"

"Mari grabbed him by one arm, Misa grabbed him by the other arm, and Megumi grabbed him by his pecker. They may not look like much, but they're tough little shits. Mari and Misa kept his arms locked and Megumi pulled that poor bastard from one end of the car to the other while he screamed bloody murder. Megumi told me she was twisting while she was pulling. I was biting my lip to keep myself from laughing. When the train stopped and the doors opened, she pulled him out onto the train platform. I wish I would have been one of the hundreds of people watching. She pulled that sorry bastard along the train platform and was pulling him up the stairs when the JR guys intervened."

"What did the JR guys do?"

"Nothing, of course. The guy apologized, so they let him go, even though he'd been caught red-handed, or I guess I should say red-peckered."

"Probably black-and-blue-peckered. They seemed like such nice, sweet girls when I met them last week."

"You don't have to live with them, and you can thank Buddha for that. Any one of them would be enough to drive you crazy. Then there's the sibling rivalry that's three times as bad because they're identical triplets. Last week, there was hostility in the house because Misa received a higher prize than Megumi and Mari at a kingyo-sukui contest, which involves scooping up little goldfish from a low water tank with paper nets. It was held by the National Kingyo-sukui Game Association. You can't imagine. Now they're bugging me about buying them all horses, and they probably want a descendent of the great Japanese racehorse, Shizan. One of our neighbors has got a horse, you see. It's a good thing they're not old enough to drive, or they'd be wanting their own cars, probably Mercedes Benzes because one of our neighbors has got one. They think I shit money."

"Sounds like you live in a rich neighborhood."

"'Rich' isn't the word. 'Status' is the word. I used to have a used Mazda Familia, but Chie said I was shaming her, so I got pressured into spending the equivalent of about 40,000 US for a Toyota Celsior."

"Holy moly!"

"Now she wants me to buy another one—his and hers. Got to keep up with the Katōs, you see. It isn't enough that I am paying ¥250,000 a month in rent for a house I had to pay ¥750,000 in gift money for the privilege of renting."

"*I'm* beginning to think you shit money."

"If I'm shitting money, it's chump change compared to what my neighbors are shitting. A neighbor lady bought a sweater a couple of months ago at the gift shop in the luxurious Nikko Hotel in Guam where she was staying and paid ¥90,000 for it. Her husband is the main man for the import of beef for the McDonald's in Japan, so it's just a drop in the McBucket for them. The guy across the street sent his son to medical school at Teikyō University, which costs about 80,000 US a year—after about a 60,000 US entrance fee. The son of one of our other neighbors got married in August. Chie gave a present of ¥50,000 so we wouldn't seem cheap. Anyway, the bride was from Fukui, which meant that the bridegroom was obligated to give the bride's parents about 100,000 US and the bridegroom's parents were obligated in turn to spend twice that much for furniture for the couple."

"I've heard that weddings are unbelievably expensive over here."

"Hotel weddings are the biggest rip-off in this country. A simple hotel wedding and party would run you about 30,000 US for two hours. When all is said and done, you'd spend about 70,000. If you were fairly well off, it would be about 100,000. My neighbors probably spent 200,000. They had the affair at the posh Hotel Ōkura in Kōbe and had a couple of famous comedians as MCs. But the biggest joke was that the couple got divorced right after they got back from their honeymoon in Australia. That's called a Narita Divorce."

"Why do you suppose they got divorced?"

"I *know* why they got divorced. The kid's mother told Chie. The girl had gone on some trips before and had some experience traveling abroad and dealing with people, whereas the guy was a basket case. She had to be the one in charge of dealing with hotel staff, waiters and waitresses, and everybody else. He was like a helpless little child, and she got disgusted with him. The kid's mother blamed the girl for not opting for a Honeymoon-Pac, in which the guide goes everywhere with you, even to the restaurants, so you don't have to deal with anybody. The guides do everything for you except wipe your arse and tuck you in bed. You might as well be wearing a diaper and be sucking on a pacifier. But he was just a typical guy. One reason that western guys are popular with Japanese ladies is that Japanese guys don't measure up to their expectations. They've seen too many guys in Hollywood movies and too many otokoyaku* in the Takarazuka Revue."

"What kind of a wedding did you and Chie have?"

"Low budget. It had to be. I didn't even have enough money to buy her a decent ring, which is supposed to be three times your monthly salary. I gave her a cheap moonstone ring I bought a few years before in Sri Lanka. Her father took one look at it and said I'd insulted her and him and his whole family and all of his ancestors. At the time, I was making only ¥200,000 a month. That meant that I was supposed to spend ¥600,000 on a friggin' ring. I had ¥6,000 to my name."

"So what did you do?"

"I borrowed the money from her father, which didn't leave me much leverage. He might as well have been standing over me with a samurai sword. We got married on one of the inauspicious days called butsumetsu† because it's cheaper. We had both a Shintō-style wedding ceremony and the party at a hotel, and it was a rip-off from the commemorative group photos to the cream of corn soup. But things have changed since then. Now Chie's got a big diamond ring and her father recently came to *me* for a loan. What's this coming up the road?"

"It looks like a camera crew."

"Followed by two limousines? More like some celebrity's entourage, I'd say."

Behind the two limousines was a van that had 'Sun Music' written on it. Behind the van was a crane-like machine on big rollers. Three men got

---

* women of the 370-strong all-female Takarazuka Review, who play romantic, debonair men.

† bad days in a month for holding certain events. Weddings on butsumetsu are naturally much cheaper than on taian (good days), for which reservations need to be made as much as six months ahead. Butsumetsu and taian are determined by astrologers.

out of the first limousine and one man got out of the second limousine. The four of them looked at Donovan and Winston. Donovan put out his cigarette and began rolling another one. "It looks like we're going to have to contend with some bull shit," he said.

After some consultation among the four men to decide who was the best at speaking English, one of them came over. Donovan lit his cigarette.

"Excuse me. We are wanting—"

"Tabun sonna ni kantan ja nai to omou kedo, Nihongo de hanashite kuremasen ka." (Not that it would make you feel any more at ease, but you can talk to me in Japanese.)

"Ah, Nihongo ga shabereru no desu ka." (Ah, can you speak Japanese?)

"Mite no tōri." (Evidently.)

"Suimasen ga, ko no ki no shita de bideo o toritain desu. Dō ka koko o noite kuremansen ka?" (I'm very sorry, but we're going to shoot a video under this tree. So would you be so kind to leave?)

"Dame desu yo. Koko ni wa nanzen mono ki ga aru deshō. Hoka no ki o sagashite kudasai." (No. There are thousands of trees here at the Gosho, so please find another one.)

"Mōshiwakenai kedo, koko ga ichiban ii basho nan desu." (I'm really sorry, but this is where we want to shoot the video.)

"Rimujin ni aidoru ga notte iru no?" (Is there a teen idol in one of those limousines?)

"Hai." (Yes.)

"Onna no ko, otoko no ko?" (A boy or a girl?)

"Suimasen ga, koko o akete kudasai." (Please do us a favor and move.)

"Ryōhōtomo to iu wake dewanai deshō." (It has to be one or the other.)

"Onna no ko desu." (It's a girl.)

"Miyazawa Rie nante yuwanaide. Boku mukatsuite shimau." (Don't tell me it's Rie Miyazawa, or I'm going to throw up.)

"Chigaun desu ga—" (No, but please—)

"Dare desu ka?" (Who is it?)

"Chotto ne." (Please.)

"Bājin ka dōka nante kiite inai yo." (I didn't ask you whether she's a virgin or not.)

"Iya!" (What a thing to say!)

"Namae o kiiteiru dake ja nai ka." (I only asked you what her name is.)

"Asami Kaori desu." (Her name is Kaori Asami.)

"Kiita koto ga nai. Kashu desu ka?" (Never heard of her. Is she a singer?)

"Sō desu yo." (Yes.)

"Ikutsu na no?" (How old is she?)

"Jūhassai desu." (Eighteen.)

"Kaori-chan ga kono ki no shita de utatte iru tokoro o toru tsumori desu ka?" (Is the plan to shoot a video of Kaori-chan singing a song under this tree?)

"Sō desu." (Yes.)

"Hōnto ni utau no, soretomo kuchipaku na no?" (Sing or lip sync?)

"Kuchipaku desu yo." (Lip sync.)

"Ano kikai wa kōsetsuki na no?" (And is that machine over there an artificial-snow dropper?)

"Sō desu." (Yes.)

"Shinjirarenai! Jā, dōzo yatte. Watashi-tachi kamawanai kara, demo kasa o ni hon kashite kurenai ka na. Jinkō-yuki ga kakaranai yō ni." (Incredible! Well, carry on. Don't mind us, but we'd appreciate it if you'd give us a couple of umbrellas so we don't get covered with artificial snow.)

"Suimasen. Yappari doite kuremasen ka?" (I'm sorry, but you'll have to leave.)

"Warui desu kedo, watashi-tachi ga saki ni kitan desu." (Well, I'm sorry, but we were here first.)

"Komatta nā." (This is difficult.)

The man went back to report to his boss, who knew that Kaori-chan wanted to have the video shot under that particular tree because it was under that tree that her boyfriend had given her a stuffed Doraemon* when they came to the Gosho in the spring on their high-school class trip. The boss came over.

"Dōshitan desu ka?" (What's the problem?)

"Sore wa watashi no serifu da yo." (That's my line.)

"Nihongo ga hanaseru no ka?" (Can you speak Japanese?)

"Swahirigo de wa hanashite inai yo." (I'm not speaking Swahili to you.)

"Watashi-tachi wa tokubetsu kyoka o morattan desu yo. Anata-gata wa koko ni iru kenri wa nai." (We have special permission. You can't stay here.)

"Anata wa reigi o wakimaeneba naranai. Moshi Beat Takeshi ga baiku no jiko de ima mo nyūin shite iru koto o shiranakattara, kokora atari ni kakushi kamera ga atte kare ga yarase o shitan ja nai ka to omou. Hoka no ki o mitsukenasai." (You should take a course in human relations. If I didn't know that Beat Takeshi was still hospitalized from his motor-scooter accident, I'd think that there was a hidden camera somewhere around here and this was one of his spoofs. Go find another tree.)

---

* popular cartoon character. A cat-like robot that travels in a time-machine, Doraemon helps Nobita, a weak primary-school boy.

The boss signaled for the three men to come over and said, "Kono ki ga iin desu." (We want this tree.) Donovan waited until the four of them were standing in front of him and blew out a smoke ring. Then he threw a *meishi* at the feet of the boss.

"Watashi wa ju-go nen Nihon ni sunde imasu. Kenri mo wakatte imasu. Sore ga watashi no bengoshi no meishi desu. Iyagarase o yamete hoka no ki o sagashinasai." (I've been living in Japan for 15 years. I know my rights. That's the name card of my lawyer. Stop harassing us and go find yourselves another tree.)

"Kaori-chan wa *kono* ki ga iin desu." (Kaori-chan wants *this* tree.)

"Jā, naze anata-tachi ojisan janakute, Kaori-chan jishin ga watashi-tachi ni tanomanai no?" (So why isn't Kaori-chan over here talking to us instead of you guys?)

"Watashi-tachi wa kanojo no manējā nan desu." (We're her managers.)

"Sonna tsumaranai shigoto yoku yatte irareru ne. Mazu Yūseisho ga kijun o mōkete, sonna tsumaranai aidoru o dasu hōsōkyoku kara hōsōken o toriagete shimaeba ii no ni." (I'm surprised you've got the nerve to admit having such a job. The first thing the Posts and Telecommunications Ministry should do to start setting some standards is revoke the broadcasting license of any broadcaster that shows ridiculous teen idols.)

"Iikagen ni shiro!" (That's enough!)

The boss stomped back to the limousine to call the Gosho police on his mobile phone. Donovan explained the sitiuation to Winston, who suggested that they move to another tree but agreed to stay because Donovan was adamant about playing this out. Before long, a black police car came slowly on the gravel and stopped. Two policemen got out and spoke with the boss for a couple of minutes before walking over to Donovan and Winston. Wanting to go on the offensive of the ensuing exchange, Donovan greeted them with a smile.

"Omawari-san, watashi wa ju-go nen Nihon ni sunde irun desu. Eijūken mo motte imasu. Watashi no tomodachi to watashi wa koko ni suwatte imashita. Dare ni mo meiwaku o kakezuni tanoshinde ita no ni ano hito-tachi ga totsuzen yatte kite watashi-tachi ni koko o sare to iun desu. Koko ni tatte iru yonin wa yakuza mitai nan desu. Boss wa tokuni iatsuteki nan desu. Watashi wa mōsukoshi de shiko o fumitaku natte shimattan desu. Kono atari wa nanzen mo hoka no ki ga aru no ni, naze ka Kaori-chan wa kono ki ga ii rashii desu. Dakara manējā janakute kanojo jishin ga koko ni kite tanomu beki desu. Marude yūmei na Monzaemon no kabuki no naka de shisha ga Shunkan ni saigo-tsūkoku o watashita toki mitai ni. Moshi kanojo ga jibun de kite, kono ki ga dōshitemo iru to iu no nara hanaretemo ii yo." (Officers, I've been living in Japan for 15 years. I have permanent residency. My friend and I were sitting here minding our own business and having a nice time, but these people suddenly came up and had the nerve to tell us to leave. There were four of them standing here like *yakuza*. The boss was especially confrontational. I almost expected him to do the traditional sumō-wrestling leg-lifting foot stomp. There are thousands of other trees around here but, for some reason, Kaori-chan wants this one. So she should be talking to us instead of her managers, who have been coming over here like the imperial envoy giving Shunkan the ultimatum in Monzaemon's famous Kabuki play. If she tells us herself why it has to be this particular tree, we'll leave.)

"Hōnto?" (You will?)

"Sō shimasu yo." (Yes.)

They looked at each other, shrugged their shoulders, and went back to tell the boss. The boss had a talk with Kaori-chan, who cried and demanded that the *gaijins* be made to go away. After a few minutes, one of the managers came back and told Donovan that Kaori-chan couldn't come over but wanted them both to have an autographed photo of her. Donovan thanked him for the photos and said that they'd wait for her to become able to come over.

"Suimasen ga dame nan desu." (I'm sorry, but it's a bit of a problem.)

"Dōshite?" (Why?)

"Kanojo wa hazukashigari desu." (She's shy.)

"Manējā to ittara uba mitai na mono deshō. Dōshite shitsukete inai no?" (Being her manager is like being her babysitter, isn't it? Why don't you help her grow up?)

"Komatta nā." (This is really difficult.)

The fellow headed back for another conference, then came back.

"Otsuki to issho nara iin desu kedo." (She'll come over if she can have the group behind her. Please allow this.)

"Mō san mai buromaido o kuretara ii yo. Watashi wa musume ga san nin iru. Minna baiorin no shindō to iwarete imasu. Jiman ja nai keredo, yoku Ōsaka Shinfonii Hōru de enso surun desu yo. Dakara Kaori-chan no buromaido hodo ii mono wa nai to omoun desu." (OK, but I'd like three more autographed photos. I have three daughters, all of whom are violin-playing prodigies. I don't like to brag, but they often play at Symphony Hall in Ōsaka. So I'm sure they'd like nothing more than an autographed photo of Kaori-chan.)

"Wakarimashita." (All right.)

"Ima no wa jōdan da kedo." (That was a joke, by the way.)

"Wakarimashita." (I understand.)

Right after he returned with three more autographed photos, there should have been a drum roll. Kaori-chan, wearing a big, red bow in her hair that matched her mini-skirt and bobby-socks, stepped out of the second limousine. With the group behind her for moral support, she came over like she was going to her own execution. She stopped a safe

distance away with her head bowed, unable to say anything. Donovan
let her suffer for a minute before breaking the silence.
"Anata ga kuchipaku suru no wa nan no uta?" (What's the title of the
song you're going to lip sync?)
"Watashi no Kokusai-teki na Kurisumasu no Yume." (My International
Christmas Dream.)
Donovan put his hand to his left eye. "Yume mite iru ga ii yo. Buromaido arigatō. Dātsu ni demo tsukau yo. Hora! Uketotte!" (Dream on,
miss. Thanks for the autographed photos. I'll use them for dartboards.
Here's something for you. Catch!) She caught what Donovan tossed to
her and looked at it curiously. "Watashi no gigan desu. Biidama asobi ni
tsukatte" (It's my glass eye. You can play marbles with it) Donovan
said. Kaori-chan dropped the glass eye and ran back to the limousine in
full-fledged hysteria. "I'll say it again," Donovan began after picking up
his glass eye and leading Winston to the Marutamachi subway station,
"I've got to get out of this country before the bull shit takes me down like
quicksand."
They took the subway and got off at Kyōto Station. Winston followed
Donovan through the underground to Avanti department store to get
foreign beers at a little liquor store on the first floor. "I like my women
thin and my Guinness Stout," Donovan said and took three Guinnesses
out of the cooler. "They have Guinness Extra Stout too, but I don't drink
that because I can't say that I like my women extremely thin. What are
you going to get for yourself?" Winston grabbed three Budweisers, not
the American 'King of Beers', but the Czechoslovakian-made Budweiser
that was made in the kingdom of Bohemia long before there was an
empire named Anheuser-Busch. They had their first beers while waiting
for the train to come in on the Nara Line and were on their second beers
when they got off at JR Fushimi Inari Station after just a four-minute
train ride. Outside the station, they waited for a chance to get across a
one-way street.
"Would you care to eat barbecued sparrow on a stick, Winston?"
"No, thanks."
"Can't say that I blame you. There are five or six shops down that way
that sell it. Another specialty of Inari, although you can get it at many
other places, is Inarizushi, which is fried tōfu wrapped around rice."
"So if I had one, I'd be able to stand up at a function and say, 'I had
Inarizushi at Inari!'?"
"Yeah, but why would you want to? Besides, I've got a couple of
bentos* that Chie made for us."
"No sushi, I hope."

---

* Japanese boxed lunches, which are put together with attention to appearance, as
Japanese dishes are said to be for the eyes. (French dishes are said to be for the nose
and American dishes for the stomach.)

"None. No nuts either. Sorry again about the ground nuts in the spinach dish the other night. I didn't think you were going to stop throwing up."

"Neither did I. Sorry I wasn't better company."

"What are you talking about? You were very entertaining. The trippers have been imitating you throwing up ever since. I threatened to take away the pagers they use to keep in constant touch with their goofy friends if they do it one more time during dinner."

They walked under a huge, orange torii* and up the road toward Fushimi Inari Taisha. Finishing their second beers, they put the empties in a waste can near the guards' station. They walked up stone stairs and through the Main Gate, on either side of which were enormous statues of seated foxes. Foxes were believed to be messengers to Fushimi Inari Taisha from the gods. A few people were throwing money into the money slot in front of the Hall of Worship. Donovan and Winston walked around the Hall of Worship and headed up to the Main Shrine.

"This is a different kind of Buddhism, isn't it?"

"It's not Buddhism, mate, it's Shintōism. Whenever you see a *torii* gate, it's Shintō. In case you didn't receive today's itinerary, the plan is to climb Mount Inari and walk down it on the north side to Tōfukuji, which is a Buddhist temple. This particular Shintō shrine is *the* place to pray for good business. Paying naturally goes with the praying. About two million people come here during the New Year's period."

"Sounds like good business for the Shintō priests."

"At a few thousand yen a crack, it's not bad. Chie is more generous than most givers. She's going to be the death of me if the trippers aren't. And to think her name means 'wisdom'! The first place she talked me into driving after talking me into buying the Toyota Celsior was to a Shintō shrine, where I paid a Shintō priest ¥5,000 to spend a couple of minutes waving his paper pompon back and forth across the car with its doors and hood open. She later took the license-plate number to Tanukidani Jinja here in Kyōto, which is the shrine that specializes in providing protection for cars, and paid ¥5,000 for a one-year good-luck charm to put in the car. I was surprised she didn't pay ¥10,000 for a five-year good-luck charm. She must have figured we'd trade in the Celsior after one year and get a brand-new car, probably a Porsche. Other jinjas† specialize in this or that. Kitano Jinja here in Kyōto is the one to go to for luck in passing entrance examinations, so there's a herd of students going there in January and February. A young lady in my neighborhood recently made a pilgrimage to Izumo Taisha in Shimane Prefecture to pray for luck in romance. She's got a mug on her that looks like the old pro wrestler Giant Baba would look like if he were wearing a wig, so she's going to need all of the luck she can get.

---

* gateway at a Shintō shrine.

† Shintō shrines.

Another lady in my neighborhood dragged her impotent husband to Kurama Jinja to increase his virility. A week later, he had a heart attack during sex and died right on top of her."

At the Main Shrine, several people were in various stages of throwing money into the long money slot, swinging the long strips of red and white cloths to ring the bells overhead, clapping their hands together, and bowing in prayer. Inside the Inner Worship Hall, a good-luck-in-business ceremony was going on with a Shintō priest performing the rituals on an elevated platform before fifteen or twenty kneeling people. Donovan and Winston walked around to the side of the Main Shrine, from which direction came a fellow in a high-tech, electric wheelchair. They stepped off the stone path to let the fellow pass by.

"Did you see the control panel on that wheelchair, mate?"

"Pretty high-tech."

"It had more buttons than a high-tech toilet, and I wouldn't be surprised if it can function as one and even meet the high standards of the esteemed members of the Japan Toilet Association."

They stood and watched the fellow heading to the front of the Main Shrine.

"That's something you don't see very often in Japan."

"A high-tech wheelchair?"

"No. A disabled person in public."

"Come to think of it, he's the first disabled person I've seen in the six weeks I've been in this country. Why is that?"

"It's considered shameful, so it's hidden. This society sweeps things under the rug for the sake of appearances."

The man in the wheelchair stopped in front of the Main Shrine and threw a 100-yen coin into the coin slot. Upon leaning forward to grab the long bell-ringing cloth, he accidentally touched a bad control-panel button to touch at that time. The 90kg wheelchair shot out from under him and went in reverse down the stairs. The feeble man held onto the bell-ringing cloth and swayed, trying not to fall. Donovan ran over and steadied the man as the wheelchair crashed into the low, orange fence surrounding the Hall of Worship and put a dent in it. Two guards and two other men carried the heavy wheelchair back up to the Main Shrine. Donovan helped put the man back into it as a ceremonial dance began at a nearby platform. "Yoisho," the man sighed upon sitting back down safe and sound.

"Dōmo arigatō gozaimashita." (Thank you very much.)

"Iie." (Not at all.)

"Nihongo ga jōzu desu ne." (You speak Japanese very well.)

"Tarzan no yō ni rōpu ni burasagaru no ga jōzu desu ne." (You swing like Tarzan very well.)

Donovan and Winston walked back to the side of the Main Shrine and out along a little stone path to a big stone path and up some stairs where pigeons were standing around. One was walking fast to stay away from a little boy in a Miki House sweatshirt and squeaky, novelty shoes. They turned right at an ancient shrine dedicated to the protection of the emperor and went up more stairs, past a big general-worship shrine. Two palm readers were seated to the right near the start of a tunnel of big, orange *toriis* so close together that they were almost touching.

"Fortunetelling is big business in Japan," Donovan said. "I wouldn't be surprised if its number three—behind the car industry."

"What's number one?"

"*Pachinko.* Fortunately, Chie isn't a *pachinko* maniac. She throws a fair bit of money away on fortunetellers concerning the trippers, though. You'd think she'd go to an astrologer because she could get a three-for-one deal but, no, she goes to the ones who examine the strokes of the *kanji* of their names. She ought to write a book called *How To Waste Money.*"

One big *torii* after another stood for one big company after another, with the names of the companies on the opposite sides of the *toriis* in black *kanji*. There were names of steel companies, private universities, heavy industries, hotels, kimono stores, car companies, restaurants, golf clubs, tour companies, driving schools, construction companies, and on and on. Tall trees on either side of the *toriis* shaded the rest of the stone-block path unshaded by the *toriis*. Omikuji* were tied to the ends of some of the lower branches.

"Is Chie shopping today?"

"No. She got stuck today because it's Seisō no Hi, Cleaning Day, in our neighborhood. Every neighborhood has got these cleaning days, one in the spring and one in the fall. The thought of her cutting weeds and cleaning the drainage ditches brings a smile to my face."

"Why aren't you doing it too?"

"Are you kidding? I'd rather pay the ¥10,000 non-participation charge to the block leader. Unfortunately, I'm going to be the block leader next year. I was elected because they say it's my turn. That means that Chie's going to get stuck doing all of my block-leader duties, just like all of the block leaders' wives get stuck doing, because I'm not going to be an exception."

"That's male chauvinism."

"Call it whatever you want. On the plus side, it will give her an excuse to spend more time gossiping with the wife of the sub-block leader. Anyway, she's more cut out for being a block leader than I am. She's a born blockhead."

"How can you say that about your wife?"

"Be thankful she isn't *your* wife."

"She seems like a nice lady."

"'Seems' is the operative word there, just as it was when you said that the trippers seemed nice. If ever there was a culture where appearance

---

* fortunes written on pieces of paper that are received at Shintō shrines after drawing lots.

doesn't square with reality, it's this one. If I can give you any advice at all, it's not to take these people at face value."

"Are you saying they're hypocrites?"

"No. They don't pretend to be what they're not; they pretend *not* to be what they are."

"What's the difference?"

"They *sup*press instead of *ex*press, and it makes them neurotic."

They came to two tunnels of smaller and tighter *toriis* that were side by side.

"Do we take the left one or the right one?"

"It doesn't matter, mate. We're not driving a car. But don't walk too fast or they might get us for speeding."

"With that last beer, we might be over the legal limit for drinking while walking: DWW."

"Cheers. They both lead to the same place, so take your pick."

Winston chose to stay on the right. They walked past *toriis* that stood for pharmacies, snack bars, hotels, confectioneries, beauty salons, *okonomiyaki* shops, car dealerships, hotels, restaurants, printing companies, and on and on. They came out from the tunnel to a wishing shrine that had hundreds of ema* hanging at the front of it and thousands more hanging on the side of it on wooden racks. Nearby was a chōzubachi.† They used a ladle to wash their hands, then headed through another tunnel of big *toriis* that led them into a forest with big, old trees towering high above them. An old woman using a walking stick and a man who helped support her came toward them and passed by. Then they were all alone on the path. Some *toriis* were bright orange with fresh paint; others were various shades of orange, some almost pinkish. Fresh paint jobs were part of the upkeep costs the companies were expected to pay the Shintō priests. The recession was showing. A few *toriis* were dilapidated; a couple were broken off. Crows were cawing. There was the sound of running water. They came to a T and turned right through more *torii*-tunneling that had a creek on one side and stone lanterns on the other. They had been walking slightly downhill but now needed to go up some steep steps to get to Echo Pond. A young couple was playing janken‡ to see who could win in getting down the steps first. A shop at the top of the steps sold candles and incense for many stone altars on either side of a narrow path off on the right. Small bottles of sake to offer to the gods were also for sale there, as were miniature *toriis* to stack on the altars. A man was praying at the altar of his kelp

---

* wishes written on small sheets of wood that are sold at shrines by Shintō priests .

† old-style wash basin, now mostly seen at temples, shrines, and ryokans (Japanese-style inns).

‡ finger-flashing game of paper/scissors/stone. (Paper covers stone, scissors cuts paper, and stone breaks scissors.) As it can be used to avoid decision-making, Japanese use it *much* more extensively than westerners use a coin toss.

shop on which there were two stone foxes and one live cat. Many of the altars had stone foxes with red or white aprons tied around them; some had candles burning. At the end of the path was a popular, little, wooden shrine at which people prayed for protection against business problems. It had fresh flowers on it. Just past that little shrine was a clearing with a nice view of Echo Pond. Donovan spread out his newspaper on a low concrete wall. They sat down with their legs hanging over the side. A woman came to the little shrine and lit candles and sticks of incense before bowing in prayer.

"Holy moly, those are big goldfish, Donovan!"

"They're not goldfish, they're carp. Here's a *bento* for you."

They opened their *bentos* and their last beers. Donovan threw some rice out to the carp, stirring them up. The ensuing waves made it difficult for a turtle that came over. Three mallards came over also.

"Big, colorful carp were brought over from China a few hundred years ago for the rich folks to have in their ponds as a status symbol, as if the average guy could–"

"Don't move! There's a centipede on your back."

"UWAAAH!"

"I'll get it off you with a chopstick."

"Get the friggin' thing off me!"

"I will."

"Is it big?"

"It's huge."

Winston got his chopstick under the black centipede and flung it off Donovan's shirt. It went up about fifteen feet in the air and came down on the folded hands of the woman praying at the little, wooden shrine. She shrieked and backhanded it off her, and it went sailing between Winston's and Donovan's heads and into the pond, where it was swallowed by a big carp that would become traumatized. Donovan took a couple of deep breaths before getting up and putting things back into his knapsack. He finished his beer and put it into the knapsack instead of putting it into a nearby garbage can. Off they went, back past the altars, past the shop, and uphill through more *torii* tunneling and denser forest.

"I hate friggin' centipedes."

"I saw one wriggling wildly on my kitchen floor when I went back to my house after gassing the cockroaches. It was definitely affected by the gas."

"That's the way they behave when you pick them up with chopsticks."

"Don't tell me that Japanese eat live centipedes!"

"No, and they don't eat dead ones either. But they're really hard to beat to death with a newspaper or even a book."

"I know. I whacked the one on my kitchen floor with a kitchen knife and cut it in half, and both halves kept right on wriggling. There's a big nick on the floor to show for it. The guy who's assisting me in my classes, Maekawa-san, told me that his wife got stung by one above her eye while she was sleeping and ended up in the hospital."

"Listen, I was having sex with Chie once before we were married in the shitty, old rooming house I used to live in, and I wasn't using a condom because they make them so damn small over here that they break even if you *can* get one on. I was just about to pull out when I felt a centipede crawling on my arse. I was too busy screaming and trying to get the friggin' thing off me to think about withdrawing. Nine months later, Chie defied astronomical odds by giving birth to identical triplets without having used fertility drugs."

"That's pretty auspicious."

"And the trippers have been a pain in the arse to me ever since."

"So what do you do with centipedes after you pick them up with chopsticks?"

"I killed them by dropping them into a jar of vegetable oil. Some older Japanese use centipede oil as an ointment. If you go to the Tōji market here in Kyōto on the 21st of every month, you might see guys selling some. You'll definitely see guys selling snake oil with the dead snakes in the jars. It's used as an aphrodisiac, which is another big business in Japan. Several years ago, I was toying with the idea of going into the aphrodisiac business. Maybe I would have turned out as enthusiastic as this joker I met the other day. I threw his *meishi* into the nearest trash can after getting away from him, but I remember his name: James D. Richards."

"That name sounds familiar. Yeah, now I remember. I met him at a party about a month ago. In fact, it was my first night in Japan after coming out of detention. He was going on about getting rich over here."

"Well, he's still going on about that. In addition to teaching English, he's involved with Nu-Skin. Have you heard about it?"

"No."

"Well, it's just a matter of time before you'll be getting a call from somebody you haven't talked to since kindergarten, and they'll give you the Nu-Skin pitch with such reverence that you'll think it's a friggin' religion. This James D. Richards character cornered me while I was taking the train home from work and gave me his rigamarole while showing me graphs about the tremendous growth of this sanctified company that outdid McDonald's in its first year in Japan, and so on. I don't give a flying shit about getting involved in sales and making calls to every Tomatsu, Daisuke, and Haruki. Why are you stopping?"

"I need to take a breather for a second."

"What! You're out of breath already?"

"I'm not used to climbing mountains."

"This is just a hill! Besides, we've hardly started. You're out of shape."

"I haven't been getting much exercise."

"You ought to do a little more than just elbow-lifting. Why don't you get one of those stationary bicycles so you can at least do some pedaling while you're knocking back your beers?"

"I haven't got the energy."

"You're still a young man."

"I feel like an *old* man."

"Listen, what you need to do, and I mean as soon as possible, is get laid. How about that lady at school who's been giving you the eye? What's her name again?"

"Rika. Two nights ago, at a faculty party, she asked me to go with her today to see the old, foreign houses in Kōbe."

"So why didn't you go? She could have shown you an old house and you could have shown her a new love hotel."

"Well, I don't know."

"What's to know? I'm talking biology, not epistemology. You ought to devote a whole weekend to screwing her. You'd feel like a new man."

"I'd probably die on top of her like your neighbor did."

"I can think of worse ways of dying, mate."

"I can too, but I'm still too young to die."

"Now you're talking. So let's get out from under this funeral company's *torii* and keep moving. There's a little udon* restaurant a couple of minutes farther up. We can take a beer break there and get ready for a fair bit of climbing to get us to the top."

"All right. So did you buy anything from James D. Richards?"

"You obviously haven't got me figured out yet. What I finally did was hold out my finger and ask him to kindly pull it, and when he did, I let loose with a loud fart and left. Screw him for wasting my time, as if I've got nothing better to do than listen to him go on about how he's going to make a million dollars and how I can too. I've seen so many of these jokers come and go with their big ideas and their diarrhea of the mouth."

"There's a young American lady teaching English at Minami Kōbe High School. Her name's Shannah Pearl. She can talk your ears off. She goes on about environmentalism, sexism—you name it."

"I'm so tired of these self-righteous Americans coming over here with their more-enlightened-than-thou attitudes. They come at you like a tidal wave."

"She sure went wild at the faculty party. One of the teachers grabbed her breasts. It will be interesting to see what happens. About a week ago, she was trying to get a petition going to boycott an accessories company that's using the brand name BITCH. I heard she sued a guy in college for calling her a 'bitch' on the grounds of verbal assault and won."

"I'm not surprised. How do you tolerate all of that political-correctness bull shit going on in that litigation culture you come from? Here's the *udon* restaurant." They took off their shoes, stepped up onto *tatami*, and ducked under a shop curtain on their way to a low table near a window that looked out onto the forest. "I don't care about being *politically* correct, I just care about being correct. 'Bitch' doesn't have

---

* wheat noodles.

any meaning in the Japanese language. They would pronounce it bichu. It's not offensive to Japanese women, and it won't be until people like this Shannah convince them that it should be because it is to them. She and people like her are as good for Japan as the black bass, which also came from America, are for the indigenous carp in Lake Biwa. The problem is that their influence is growing and spreading like golden rod, which also came from America." An elderly woman came over to them to take their orders. Donovan ordered two bottles of beer and set his Drum tobacco on the table. "People like this Shannah gauge what's OK and not OK according to their own sensitivities and the sensitivities of where *they* come from. Too many Americans seem to think that what's OK and not OK in America should be OK and not OK everywhere. One of the good things about Japanese people is that they listen. They may not agree with you, but they listen. Not some of these Americans. They're just waiting for *you* to shut up so *they* can start talking. And I hate it when they try to impress you as being intellectuals. I don't like genuine intellectuals, much less pseudo ones."

"But you're one yourself. I mean, Harvard and Oxford!"

"Who told you that?"

"One of the triplets—when you made a trip to the toilet the other night. I thought that she was putting me on, but Chie said it was true."

"Well, I don't like to make a big deal about my academic background. But I'm not an intellectual any more than the Japanese so-called talents are talented. If I were an intellectual, I would say something like, 'At the risk of seeming pugnaciously argumentative, I prefer to conceive of myself as a savant', and maybe I'd throw in a little Latin. Please do me a favor, mate, and forget about where I went to school. And I'll remind Chie to button her lip about it."

The woman brought over two large bottles of Kirin Lager and two glasses. Donovan and Winston poured glassfuls for each other, emptied them in single swigs, and poured two more. Donovan stared at the strange creature running wildly on the Kirin Lager label. The kirin* didn't look any more like a giraffe than Chie looked like Cindy Crawford, whose picture was in the ad for the beauty salon she went to before joining the more expensive beauty salon she was presently going to, which had a picture of Claudia Schiffer in the ad. The more expensive one must be better, Chie figured. Besides, if she could look like either Cindy Crawford or Claudia Schiffer, she preferred to look like Claudia Schiffer. She was envious of Cindy Crawford, though, for having been married to Richard Gere, who she was almost as crazy about as Kevin Costner.

Back in the days when Chie was a receptionist at Berlitz, she was so different. Being unmarried, she lived with her parents as a matter of course. She was expected to get married before she turned 26 because

---

* giraffe. 'Kirin' is also used to refer to a winged unicorn of ancient Chinese mythology, and it is this animal that appears on the Kirin Lager label.

then she would be, as the saying went, like a Christmas cake still in a cake shop after Christmas Day (the 25th)–unsalable, unwanted. Now there were many single ladies over 25, but not back then. Back when Chie was 23, she had a couple of years before the 'deadline', so she wasn't yet feeling heavy pressure. She was focused on the newness of her new job and making money for becoming an economic animal. She could overlook the drawbacks of the job, such as the advances of her boss, Imajiku-san, a middle-aged married man who asked her a fairly common interview-question during her job interview: How many boyfriends and sexual experiences have you had? The new teacher came along in the nick of time. He was hardly a knight in shining armor, but he made her laugh. That's why she liked him. She routinely laughed at the jokes of Imajiku and other men above her at work because that was as much a part of the duties of a Japanese working lady as rubbing the guys' backs while they barfed from overdrinking with co-workers and cheering for them at company sports events, but Donovan *really* made her laugh. He was different, and she liked the difference. In a country where rigidity made things so banal, he was refreshingly unpredictable. At the time, Donovan was living in a six-*tatami* room in a boarding house with five other people: three male university students, one would-be university student in his third year at a yobikō,* and a struggling elderly geisha. It was on the floor of that small room that the triplets were conceived with the help of a centipede. Then there he was, pacing back and forth in front of H.I.S. travel agency in Ōsaka, and there *she* was, talking to a famous fortuneteller at Kyōto's Yasaka Jinja. The fortuneteller took into account their birthdates and said that they were compatible. That was what she wanted to hear. She wouldn't hear of an abortion because her cousin had one that left her unable to get pregnant again. So she married the funny man who finally walked away from H.I.S. with his mind made up to stand by her, mainly because he loved to lie by her. Sex with orgasmic Chie was the best sex he'd ever had, and she loved every bit of it, every inch of it, as much as he did. Richard Gere couldn't have driven her more wild. He knew it and she knew it. Richard Gere didn't know it, but that didn't matter. Her parents threatened to disown her if she went ahead and married the *gaijin* but withdrew the threat when they saw its futility and even warmed up after the triplets, their three granddaughters, were born. (Five years later, when Donovan became the distinguished Professor Wood, they became too warm for the professor's comfort.) Donovan was making ¥200,000 a month in the bad old days, paltry for a man with three babies and a wife who had to quit her job. From their little apartment at Villa Yamamoto, there wasn't any more hope in sight than there was a tree. Chie felt confined, as babysitting was non-existent and day-care centers affordable only for the well-to-do. She was envious of her friends who

---

* cram school that prepares high-school graduates for university entrance examinations.

were still working and relatively free. Donovan felt trapped. He stayed out late drinking and looked for any excuse to get out of the house. He stopped making Chie laugh–until an evening in the winter of 1985 when he came home from his job interview at Kōbe Gakugei University with great news, a bottle of champagne, and 100 cream puffs to be the weapons in a cream-puff fight. The first thing Chie wanted after they moved to a house in Sannomiya was a cleaning lady to come once a week because she had more important things to do than cleaning, such as shopping. She became one of the ladies who carry their handbags on their forearms, and her handbag was a Louis Vuitton. She read Japanese fashion magazines like *MORE, With,* and *Elle Japon,* and wrapped herself in ceremony as well as in Chanel, Givenchy, and Valentino. Nothing was too good for the wife of the eminent Professor Wood. Status became supreme, especially after they moved to affluent Ashiya. She pushed for a ¥10,000,000 golf-club membership at Besty Golf golf course, even though neither one of them golfed. She pushed for a health-club membership too, which at least she used for a while before opting for the passive approach offered at the beauty salons and in the many slimming lotions and slimming soaps that had become popular. Sometimes Donovan sat in his sound-proof room wondering what ever happened to sweet, little Chie, who used to ride her bicycle to the station to catch the train to work and did her shopping at bargain sales. She used to like the simplicity of tea ceremony and the atmosphere of izakayas.* Now she had her own top-of-the-line computerized espresso/cappucino maker and preferred fancy French restaurants. The one thing they had in common that bound them together like cement lost its adhesiveness as Chie placed greater and greater importance on Tiffany's diamond rings than on Donovan's gōruden bōrus.† The only thing they seemed to agree on these days was their majority opposition to a five-day school week, because Chie didn't want the triplets at home on shopping Saturday any more than Donovan did. Now sitting there looking at the Kirin Lager label, that *kirin* seemed to be looking back over its shoulder and running scared. Donovan emptied his glass and re-filled it.

"Winston, let me ask you a personal question, which I ask only because you were suspected of smuggling hashish into the country. Do you get high?"

"Not anymore. I smoked a little pot when I was in college."

"And, unlike Bill Clinton, you inhaled?"

"Yes."

"Suppose I had something to smoke–would you want to indulge?"

"Do you have something?"

---

* Japanese-style pub. Originally for poor working people in the Edo Period (1600-1868), they are now popular with even the well-to-do.

† Japanese English for 'golden balls', used to refer to testicles.

"I'm not saying whether I do or I don't. I'm only throwing out a hypothetical."

"Yeah, I guess so."

"Well, it just so happens that I've got a little hashish on me."

"Did you say hashish or ashes?"

"Hashish. And it's not freeze-dried. I'd never heard anything so stupid in my whole life. That Muramatsu must have had a freeze-dried brain. Let's put a buzz on when we get up to the top of this mountain. We'd better get moving if we're going to make it up there in time for the sunset."

Mount Inari was only 232 meters high. Compared to Mount Fuji (3,776 meters), it was like a mole hill. Walking up it was no big deal. Rugby players at nearby Ryukoku University sometimes trained by *running* up it. A little higher up, there were a couple more little *udon* restaurants. Outside one of them was a Pocari Sweat vending machine and a green, phone-card public phone, the kind that had made the old, pink, coin-slot phones almost as obsolete as flip-downs on cans made flip-offs a couple of years before when environmentalism finally got a rare win, that time over concern for cleanliness. The pervasiveness of vending machines was one of the things that amazed Winston initially about Japan, but the whereabouts of some of them, in remote places that seemed to defy strategic marketing logic, was something that continued to amaze him, as did the variety of things available in them, which went far beyond the usual things like beer, soft drinks, cigarettes, and pornographic magazines to include batteries, CDs, even fresh flowers. There were zillions of them in Japan, and it seemed that you could go from the sand of Iwo Jima to the summit of Mount Fuji and not find a single machine that gypped you, testament to the quality of Japanese-made machines.

A man on his way down the mountain, coming from where the refreshments in the very few vending machines were more expensive, came toward Winston and Donovan with a video camera set on his shoulder. Winston froze.

"I thought for a second the guy had a grenade launcher."

"This isn't Bosnia, mate. You couldn't be in a country with less likelihood of somebody blowing your brains out."

"I've read about a few shootings recently."

"They're increasing, but murders here are still relatively very few and far between. Konnichiwa." The greeting was made to four people coming down who said "Konnichiwa" (Good afternoon) back. "There were more murders in New York City last year than there were all over Japan. More people are killed in America in one day than in Japan in one year. I feel completely safe in this country walking anywhere, any time, night or day, and it's nice to be able to say that. People in America are living in fear. Everybody and their mother has got a friggin' gun. Have you got one?"

"No. I live in a relatively safe area. But I thought about getting one after my house was burglarized last year."

"Because you can be pretty sure that a burglar has got a gun, right?"

"Right. But I decided not to get a gun and instead add an electronic curtain-opening/closing device to our home-security system."

"What's next–a moat and a drawbridge? No, thanks. I don't want to live that way. You get paranoid."

"But you've got to have protection."

"What are you doing with your house while you're over here?"

"I rented it out to three college girls who seemed very nice."

"Why do you say 'seemed'?"

"Because they *did* seem nice."

"So you're willing to leave open the possibility that they have turned your house into a whorehouse?"

"No. Well, I mean, if you're talking about a very remote possibility, OK."

"Or maybe a crack house?"

"Yeah, or maybe a gambling house."

"Or maybe a child-pornography photo studio? Hey, are you all right?"

"Yeah. Just a little tuckered out."

"There's not much farther to go. Keep pushing."

"OK. I suppose that crime in America is big news over here."

"They paint America more dangerous than it actually is because that's the way they want to paint it. I sometimes get the feeling that the Japan National Press Club engages in news-fixing the way the construction companies engage in bid-rigging. They showed themselves to all be soybeans in the same pod two years ago when they declared a moratorium on running stories about Crown Prince Hironomiya's efforts to find a bride because they didn't want to put too much pressure on him or perhaps make him feel that he should take down his Brooke Shields posters. The *Washington Post* broke the story about his engagement to Masako Owada. The media over here are run by a bunch of nationalistic old farts, just like the government is, and objectivity goes into their ashtrays with their cigarette butts. So does variation of opinion. You read one newspaper, you've read them all; you see one news program, you've seen them all. I don't mind getting information from the right, but I'd like some information from the left too. Then I'll form my own opinion. The way it is over here, it's a form of mind control. I try to get my students to think a little bit for themselves, but it's like trying to get the politicians to make some genuine reforms instead of just talking about it."

"I don't think the American media is any better. Look at this O.J. Simpson circus. Before that, it was John Wayne Bobbitt, and before that, it was Michael Jackson. They get on one thing and beat it to death, and then they move on to something else. You called the Japanese media bosses a bunch of nationalistic old farts. The American media bosses may not be as old, but they're probably just as nationalistic."

"Probably just as farty too."

"Look at the way the American media covered the Gulf War."

"Ted Turner probably wears stars-'n'-stripes underwear."

"If he does, he could catch a lot of flack from people who want to make desecration of the flag a felony."

"What is it about Americans and their flag? I won't even bother watching the '96 Olympics in Atlanta because it's just going to be a showcase for American flag-waving. I hate watching international sports events anywhere because of all of the friggin' nationalism. The Japanese have got this big thing about becoming international, but they don't understand that you can't start becoming international until you start shedding your nationalism. A good first step is to stop waving the friggin' flag."

"But how can you shed it when it's being force-fed to you?"

"You can't. You've got to get away from the force-feeding. The best way to do that is to get out of your country for a while and stay out—until you can stop thinking about it as being 'your' country and see it objectively."

"That sounds like a long trip. How many people have the time and the money to do that?"

"I didn't say it was easy; I only said I thought it was necessary. If you blow up your TV and throw away your paper, as the John Prine song goes, you can stop being fed nationalism like a goose with a funnel stuck down its throat, but that's not going to help you get a genuine international perspective. I don't see how you can look from the outside until you *get* outside, and you don't need a whole lot of money—unless you're a tourist. There's a big difference between a traveler and a tourist."

"Such as?"

"Travelers don't use credit cards, suitcases with rollers, or video cameras. They don't buy souvenirs, and they don't pose for pictures giving the peace sign. If they see two restaurants side by side, one a dive frequented by locals and the other a fancy place for tourists, they go to the dive, first of all because they might touch down, and secondly because they can't stand being with the friggin' tourists. Tourists are removed; group tourists are twice removed."

"A couple of my best friends are group tourists."

"Well, I don't mean to offend you, and I'm sorry to say this about your friends, but they ruin it for those of us who really want to touch down. Americans used to be the worst, and they're still bad, terrible in fact, but Japanese take the cake and could never be outdone. They give Japan a bad name. I wouldn't be surprised if the flag-carrying guides for the Japan Travel Bureau and other tourist outfits need to be licensed baby-sitters."

"Haven't you ever gone on a group tour?"

"If the day ever comes when I'm traveling on a group tour, I hope somebody shoots me and puts me out of my misery, even if I seem to be thoroughly enjoying it. In fact, if I seem to be thoroughly enjoying it, I hope they bomb me."

Winston picked up his step for the final few steps to the top like a mountaineer ready to plant a flag, which would have caught the attention of the several people standing around nonchalantly and enjoying the view of the southern part of Kyōto with the mountains in the west. Kyōto Tower was imposing but wouldn't be for long because the 31-meter height-restriction for buildings had recently been loosened to allow buildings to go up to sixty meters. Kyōto Hotel led the way; Kyōto Station would soon be following. Winston might have yodeled if he weren't out of breath. He breathed in fresh air on the tree-covered mountain and looked out at the auto-emission smog enveloping the city. With the back of both forearms, he wiped the sweat from his brow and smiled at Donovan, who wiped the smile off his face by pointing at a steep set of steps leading up to the highest point on the mountain.

At the top of the stairs was another complex of stone altars. Donovan and Winston winded their way through it and came out to a clearing with a superb view that extended from northwest Kyōto all of the way south to Momoyama Castle. Nobody was there. Somebody may have been nearby, though, because a Honda Super Cub scooter was lying on its side. "Let's step back into the woods for a few minutes," Donovan said. "Our seats will still be here when we get back. They're reserved."

"They're good seats."

"Front row. I didn't want to take the chance of having a couple of people sitting in front of us with Mickey Mouse hats on."

The forest was mostly pine. It stretched all the way to Yamashina, a couple of hours away on an almost indiscernible footpath. They went about fifty yards into the forest and sat down on the trunk of a fallen pine. A few mosquitoes came around. "Friggin' mosquitoes," Donovan said. He took the empty Guinness can out of his knapsack and pressed down on it near the bottom to make a small dent. Then he took out his Swiss Army knife and used the corkscrew to make a little hole in the dent and another hole in the side of the can. "So that's why you kept the can," Winston said. Donovan took a small piece of hashish out of his coin purse and used his lighter to burn part of the hashish to soften it. He peeled a little piece off and put it over the little hole in the dent of the can. Handing the 'pipe' to Winston, he said, "Here you go, mate. There's a shotgun on the side."

Even before he stepped out of the forest, Winston felt that he had stepped into a new dimension. He was stoned. They both were. They were in the forest for less than ten minutes. It was light then, but getting dark now. Lights were coming on in the city. It was only 5:30, but Japan didn't have Daylight-Saving Time, having given up on that idea after having it for three years during American occupation. There didn't seem to be much sense to it since the guys were coming home late from work anyway. The sun was going down behind the mountains in the west and throwing up some pink into the sky. They stood and watched the sunset as more and more lights came on . . . until it was dark and the city was lit up. Lights were everywhere. The greatest concentration was on the Meishin Expressway. Just beyond the tree line of Mount Inari, a Keihan train was heading north to where it would soon go underground. Way way out, with faint blue lights flickering above it, was a bullet train heading south to Ōsaka. They sat down and looked out. Winston was the first to speak.

"I feel good."

"James Brown. 1965. King Records. The title was actually *I Got You (I Feel Good)*."

"It was a hit when I was in seventh grade. This is the best I've felt in a long time. I've been going through the wringer."

"Well, at least you ought to come out well wrung."

"How do you conjugate that—wring, wrang, wrung?"

"Yeah, like bring, brang, brung, and ding, dang, dung, and meringue, merangue, merungue."

"I'd like to sit in on one of your English classes."

"Sank you. If you go to there, please shit any sheet you want shit. The other day, I was teaching how to go from the adjective 'good' to the adverb 'well': she's a good singer, she sings well; he's a good dancer, he dances well; they're good teachers, they teach well—like that. I told the class to make that sort of sentence, and one kid said, 'He's a good monk, he monks well'."

"So what's wrong with that? He's monking, he has been monking, he will have been monking."

"You should be teaching English instead of geography, mate."

"It probably wouldn't be any less frustrating. A few days ago, I handed out some questions for homework. One of the questions was, 'What would you pack in your suitcase if you were going on a trip to New Zealand in August?' A good answer would have been 'a heavy sweater', 'winter gloves', 'a stocking hat'—something like that. But um—I forgot what I was talking about."

"About what they'd bring to New Zealand."

"Who?"

"Your students. In August. The questions you gave them."

"Oh yeah. The number one answer was 'Cup Noodles'. Number two was 'rice balls'. Another question was 'Where did the Native Americans come from?' The number one answer was 'Native America'."

"If you had asked them to name a famous river, they probably would have said 'River Phoenix'. I know the kind of people you're dealing with. I deal with them all the time myself. I *live* with three of them—make that four of them. But you can't convince me that learning geography is harder than learning a foreign language. I mean, if you say that the Amazon River is in Africa, at least you're in the right hemisphere. In my second year in Japan, I was at a social function in the presence of some sophisticated Japanese ladies, and I was tired because I'd been up late the night before writing letters. One of the ladies commented that I looked tired, and I tried to say that it was because I'd been writing too much, but what I actually said was that I'd been masturbating too much. You should have seen their faces."

"Excited?"

"Hardly."

"A Hong Kong Chinese lady came to Corvallis on a student-exchange program a couple of years ago. I don't know what she wanted to say to her host mother, but what she said was, 'It's nice to meet you. You look like a cow.'"

"That must have made the host mother stop chewing her cud."

"Maybe her ears wiggled and she mooed."

"You're not feeling any pain, are you, mate?"

"None at all, I'm happy to say, except my udder—I mean my bladder—is about ready to burst. I'm going to step back into the forest and take a piss. I'm a good pisser, I piss well."

"I'm so happy to hear that. It would be such a shame if you pissed poorly, which would make you a piss-poor pisser. Shake it easy, mate."

Winston went back among the pines to a place not far from where they had gotten high. That seemed like much longer than just twenty minutes before. It was light then and dark now for one thing, but for another thing, which was the main thing, his perception of time had been altered by the hashish. Like a marathon pisser, he pissed for so long that flying squirrels started squawking to try to make him get out of their territory, unless they were trying to sing along with him as he sang *I Got You (I Feel Good)* while looking up at the stars above the pines. By the time he finally finished pissing, his sense of direction was gone and he didn't have the faintest idea which way to go to get back to where Donovan was. "Holy moly, I'm wrecked," he said to himself and walked into a big spider web. He wiped it off his face, took a few steps in the light of the waning harvest moon, and saw a man standing in front of him. The man was standing under a Japanese larch among the pines. He was motionless, and his head was bowed. "Konbanwa" (Good evening) a startled Winston said, but the man made no response. He stayed right where he was, not moving a muscle. He seemed to be standing slightly above the ground. Around his neck was one end of a rope. He was hanging from a bough of the larch. "DONOVAN!"

Donovan and Winston stood before the dead man. He was dressed in casual wear and wearing a jacket. Behind him was a turned-over bath stool that he had kicked away from underneath him.

"He even brought a bath stool with him. Definitely premeditated, mate. That's probably his scooter back there."

"I wonder how long he's been dead."

"Probably not long. He still looks in pretty good condition."

"Yeah, he hasn't started decomposing yet."

"That's one good thing, I guess."

Donovan stepped forward and felt the pockets of the man's jacket. There was a mobile phone in one of them and a folded sheet of paper in the other. He took out the sheet of paper and read what was written on it by the light of his lighter. "It's a suicide note. He says he's sorry for what he did. I wonder what he did."

"Who knows? Let's get out of here and notify the police."

"What's the rush? This guy is dead meat."

Donovan put the paper back and felt the man's pants pockets. There was an address book in the front left pocket, some keys in the right front pocket, and a wallet in the left back pocket. He pulled out the wallet.

"Donovan, this is a police matter. You can't be going through the guy's wallet!"

"I just want to check his driver's license and see what his name is. His name is Tomoki Itō. He was born on July 18th of Shōwa 41. That's 1966. So he's 28."

"OK. So let's go."

Donovan put the wallet back into Itō's pocket and gave him a push, sending him swinging forth and back. Winston dashed over to stop the hanged man from swinging, but the rope came undone and Itō fell to the ground on top of Winston. Winston pushed him off and stumbled up to his feet. "Let's get the hell out of here," he said. Just then, something started ringing. It was Itō's mobile phone. Winston and Donovan looked at each other. Donovan said, "I'd better answer it, just in case it's a call from God–or Satan."

DONOVAN: Moshi moshi. (Hello.)

CALLER: Donai shitan ya? Gogo kara zutto denwa shite tan ya de. (What in the hell is going on? I've been trying to call you all afternoon.)

DONOVAN: Chotto na. Dō shitan? (It's a long story. What's up?)

CALLER: Aitsu no oyaji ga kane o atsumeru no ni kayōbi made kakarutte yūterun ya. (Her father says he'll need until Tuesday to get the money together.)

DONOVAN: (Looking at Winston with wide-opened eyes, he made a Shhhh gesture with his finger over his mouth.) Wakatta. Doko ni iru no? (All right. Where are you?)

CALLER: Oren chi ya. Mada oshiire no naka ni shibatte iru. Mō shokuryō ga nain de dekaketain ya. Mukai no kōji mo urusai nen. Hayokoi ya. (My place. She's still tied up in the closet. But I've got to get out for a while. I don't have any more food here. And the construction going on across the street is getting on my nerves. Hurry up and get here.)

DONOVAN: Wakatta. (OK.)

CALLER: Ima doko ni irun ya? (Where are you now?)

DONOVAN: Fushimi Inari no chikaku ya. (Near Fushimi Inari.)

CALLER: Eh! Mada Kyōto ni on no? Ichiji kan mo kakaru ya nai ka. Hayokite kure. (What! In Kyōto still! It will take you an hour to get here. Hurry up.)

DONOVAN: Wakatta. (OK.)

CALLER: Matten de. (<u>I'll be waiting</u>.)

The caller hung up. Donovan kept the moblie phone and took Itō's wallet, the suicide note, and his address book. "The caller and Itō here kidnapped a girl or a lady," Donovan said and started walking out of the forest. "I'll explain it all to you on the way back down. We've got to hurry. There's a public phone at the first lookout place. I've got to call the police."

The kidnapped girl's name was Kanako Tatezaki. Her father, Osamu Tatezaki, was the president of Lotte's large chewing-gum division. But Kanako was abducted for money, not for chewing gum. She was on her way home from the private Shōin High School in Ōsaka on Friday with her friend Hitomi Muragishi when two men came by in a stolen Toyota Mark II. The driver was the dead man, Tomoki Itō. The other man, Ryōta Sano, got out and forced Kanako into the car. Kanako was bound, gagged, and blindfolded. She was told that if she caused any problems, they'd cut her ears off like Japanese soldiers did to Koreans under orders from Toyotomi Hideyoshi. Hitomi went to the police, and the police went into action immediately—after some forms were filled out. Itō and Sano laid low and killed time until midnight, then went to Sano's apartment in Ōsaka's Hirano Ward and put Kanako into the *futon* closet. Kanako's parents received a phone call on Saturday morning. They were told that ¥40 million was the price for their 15-year-old daughter's release and that she would be killed if they worked with the police. Itō left in the late afternoon to make it in time for a dental appointment at a clinic near his home in Kyōto's Fushimi Ward. After that, he went to his brother's home to attend a birthday party for his 5-year-old niece. While there, he used his mobile phone to call Sano and tell him that he'd be back there about 11:00 the next morning, Sunday morning. But after going home and drinking, he had a guilt-induced change of mind. He packed his bath stool and a rope on the back of his Honda Super Cub and drove it up the north side of Mount Inari. Naturally, Sano became worried when Itō didn't show up on Sunday morning, but he stepped out to make another quick call to Kanako's parents from a public phone to reiterate the demand and set a deadline for that evening. Kanako's father, who had complied by asking the police to let him handle it, told Sano that he needed until Monday to get the money together.

It took Donovan and Winston twenty minutes to get back down the mountain and back to JR Inari Station. (Donovan told the police when he called them that he had information about a kidnapping and that they should meet him at JR Inari Station.) Four policemen, one of whom was wearing a masuku,* were waiting near two little Suzuki Culture police cars to arrest the two 'kidnappers' coming to turn themselves in like Japanese criminals often do when their sense of shame puts their

---

* Japanese English for 'mask'–a surgical mask worn to protect the wearer from allergens like cedar pollen or protect others from catching one's cold.

sense to shame by prodding them to make a full confession if not commit suicide. After that major misunderstanding was cleared up, the handcuffs were put away. Brushing aside comments about his fluency in Japanese and completely ignoring questions about where he lived, what his name was, and where he worked, Donovan gave the lowdown to a sergeant among the four, Sergeant Tōru Iwakiri. Even though he was higher than a kite, he had his feet firmly enough on the ground to be careful not to run any risk of receiving publicity that could jeopardize the fraudulent foundation that supported his professorship. "Don't give them our names, mate," he said to a ripped, red-eyed Winston midway through his report to Sergeant Iwakiri.

"I already gave them mine."

"Well, don't give them *mine.*"

Several people waiting at the station for the next train listened to Donovan say what he had to say to Sergeant Iwakiri. One of them happened to be a 25-year-old former student of Donovan's, Kentarō Nakatsu, who respected Professor Wood as a teacher because the professor let him sleep during class. As soon as Donovan finished telling the short story that seemed like a tall tale, the police got right down to business, which meant filling out some forms.

"Mazu, saisho ni anata no namae wa?" (First of all, what is your name?)

"Kankei nai." (That's irrelevant.)

"Keishiki desu kara." (It's a formality.)

"Jikan no muda desu yo. Aite wa nakama ni sanjuppun inai ni aitagatte irun desu yo. Mō jikan ga nai. Manyuaru o wasurete kōdō shite kudasai. Kono adoresuchō o shirabete ichiji kan inai no tokoro o sagashite kudasai. Sorekara mukae no dōro de kōji shite iru tokoro o sagashite kudasai." (It's a waste of time. The kidnapper is expecting his accomplice in less than thirty minutes. There's no time to lose. Forget about following your manual and get going. Go through this address book and circle every address that's about an hour away from here. Then check to see which of those places has construction going on across the street.)

"Wareware no shigoto ni kuchi o dasanaide kudasai." (Don't tell us how to do our job.)

"Hito ga shini kakatte iru toki ni, dareka ga yuwana wakaranai desho. Zutto kudaran shitsumon suru tsumori?" (Somebody sure should. Do you really plan to keep standing around here asking insignificant questions while a person's life is at stake?)

Had this conversation been behind closed doors, Sergeant Iwakiri would have had the upper hand, but Iwakiri's awareness of the bylistening bystanders, who had heard more than enough to point fingers at the police if any further delay were to result in a loss of life, changed things. The policeman wearing the *masuku* said that he had gotten the one man's name, nationality, and address in Japan. That was considered good enough. Wasting no more time, they did exactly as Donovan had suggested. Orders were given to check seven places listed in Tomoki Itō's address book. One of them was found to have construction going on across the street: an apartment in Ōsaka's Hirano Ward rented by 29-year-old Ryōta Sano, who had a criminal history of petty theft. Very soon thereafter, a policeman posing as an NHK door-to-door collection person rang Sano's doorbell, but the pretense wasn't necessary. Sano casually opened the door expecting to see Itō. The policeman charged in and was followed by seven more policemen nearby. Sano was held while his apartment was searched. Kanako was found in the *futon* closet and freed. Within the hour, by reason of who her father was, the story was making national television news.

Rice fields were straw-brown empty, except here and there where sparrows, crows, and egrets were still poking around. The change of leaves on ginkgo trees provided a yellow to look at besides the much less appreciated yellow of the golden rod. Pampas grass was swaying. Ginkgo nuts were being roasted or cooked in chawanmushi.* Turnips were being sliced paper thin for senmaizuke.† Non-astringent persimmons were being dried. It was still a little too early for red leaves to be at their best, but the weather was definitely changing for the colder. It was time to start getting out the *kotatsus,* room heaters, winter *futons,* and warm clothes. Many people with western-style toilets were putting terrycloth covers on their toilet seats if they hadn't yet gotten around to having the now standard toilet-seat heating function. It was November 8th. Celebrations were going on in Kyōto to mark the 1,200-year anniversary of when Emperor Kanmu moved the capital of Japan from Nara to Heian Kyō (Kyōto), where it stayed for 1,200 years until Emperor Meiji moved it to Edo (Tōkyō) in 1868. Winston Baldry was at home sitting in his high-tech massage chair, drinking Asahi Super Dry beer and eating Calbee potato chips while watching *Sumo Digest,* which began at 11:15 p.m. Ōzeki‡ Takanohana finished the previous *basho* with a perfect 15-0 record and was guaranteed promotion to *yokozuna* if he could win the present *basho* that began three days before. Takanohana and his older brother, Wakanohana, also an *ōzeki,* were immensely popular, definitely the most popular 'duo' in Japan, with the crown prince and crown princess, Hironomiya-san and Masako-san, in second place. Number three was probably the 102-year-old celebrity women twins, Kin-san and Gin-san. Number four was perhaps Hitoshi Matsumoto and Masatoshi Hamada, of the comedy team "Downtown", or maybe the singing/songwriting team "Chage and Aska". But just one month before, for a couple of days, and a couple of days only, Winston and Donovan were right up there at the top. Winston lifted his bag of low-salt potato chips and poured the last remaining little pieces into his mouth. Then he took a drink of beer and watched *maegashira* Mitoizumi excite the crowd by throwing his fistful of salt high into the air before going out to do battle with *maegashira* Kirishima, an old man for a sumō wrestler at age 35. For Winston, who felt very old for a human being at age 41, the massage chair had essentially become his rocking chair. The next step would have been for him to have the beer going to him via an i.v. machine. He pushed a button on the control panel to make the

---

* steamed soup stock and egg with eel, chicken, or gingko nuts.

† very thin slices of pickled turnips.

‡ second highest sumō rank, after yokuzuna. The ranks in the top division are in the following order: yokuzuna, ōzeki, sekiwake, komusubi, maegashira.

massage rollers concentrate on his upper back and watched Kirishima beat Mitoizumi off the charge and throw him down to the dirt with a hip-toss. Two days before, 45-year-old George Foreman won the IBF and WBA heavyweight titles by knocking out 27-year-old Michael Moorer with a three-punch combination. With nothing more than a huff and a puff, George Foreman could have put lethargic Winston Baldry down for the count. A week before, Mrs. Tsujimoto took Winston to Zhu-sensei, an ethnic Chinese pharmacist, who looked at Winston's tongue, asked him a couple of questions, and gave him some packs of kanpōyaku* to wash down with water before meals. The *kanpōyaku* seemed to be making him feel a little less like ninety years old and a little more like eighty years old.

The headline-making story of the freeing of 15-year-old Kanako Tatezaki at first read the way the National Police Agency wanted it to read, with the anonymous tip seeming almost inconsequential, but a leak to the *Yomiuri Shimbun* on Monday night sent Winston Baldry's name into pronunciation as Weenstone Bōrudorii and into print as ウインストン・ボールドリー : a 41-year-old American bachelor living in Nagata Ward in Kōbe and teaching world geography at Minami Kōbe High School. Donovan and Chie were making love with the 11:00 news program *News 23* on because Chie had gotten hot watching Kevin Costner, in Japan on a promotional tour, being interviewed by *News 23* host Tetsuya Chikushi. Donovan was performing cunnilingus when he heard Winston Baldry's name coming from their bedroom television. He called Winston right away and asked him not to give his name to the newspeople that were already coming with the fury of *maegashira* Terao's tsuppari† attacks, which Winston was now watching *maegashira* Tochinowaka getting hammered with. Although he never rose above the rank of *sekiwake* because he lacked the size to effectively use offensive techniques besides *tsuppari,* Terao could briefly slap anybody silly. Winston watched Tochinowaka get driven back to the edge of the ring with a blitzkrieg of straight-from-the-shoulder slaps to the head before breaking through the onslaught and getting a grip on Terao's mawashi‡ and then bulldozing him back across the ring and lifting him out. A month before, Winston was just trying to get a grip on the situation, and the situation was winding him up tighter than the rush in *tatami.*

On the morning of October 5th, a Wednesday, there was a swarm of newspeople outside Winston's house wanting to know why he had come to Japan, what his biggest impression of Japan was, whether or not he liked sushi, and so on, in addition to the number-one question they wanted to know, which was who his friend was—because it was his friend

---

* ancient Chinese herbal/plant medicines.

† open-handed thrust-attack.

‡ sumō wrestler's belt.

who tricked the kidnapper Ryōta Sano and informed the police. Winston disconnected the phone after calling Junko Teratani and took the day off from work so he could stay behind locked doors and closed fusuma.* Reporters for the *Yomiuri Shimbun*, the *Asahi Shimbun*, the *Mainichi Shimbun*, and the *Sankei Shimbun* were there. Cameramen for Fuji Network, NTV, NHK, and TV Asahi were also there. Junko arrived at one o'clock and, after talking with Winston for half an hour, stepped outside with him to translate while he issued a statement: "I was on Mount Inari with a friend. We were watching the sunset. We'd had a couple of beers. I went into the forest to take a leak. I saw a man hanging there. All of a sudden, his mobile phone rang and my friend answered it. The rest you know, but my friend wishes to remain anonymous because he does not want his privacy to be invaded. I would appreciate it if you would respect his, and my, right to privacy. I just want to do my job. I'm here to teach world geography on a Ministry of Education program to promote internationalization. Thank you. Arigatō gozaimasu."

That evening, the expression 'take a leak' (oshikko o suru) was explained on news programs, and many people improved their English by adding 'take a leak' to their vocabulary and saying, "Chotto tekuriku itte kimasu" (I'm going to go take a leak). As for Winston Baldry, he was well on his way to becoming the most famous urinator in Japanese recorded history, which dates back to the Yayoi Period (300 B.C.-300 A.D.) and the days of Queen Himiko. The Marco Polo Bridge Incident, which triggered the Sino-Japanese War of 1937-1945, started when a Japanese soldier walked off to take a piss and was thought to have been captured by the Chinese. That soldier, whoever he was, played a part in history, but his name is not known. Winston Baldry's name, on the other hand, became very well known. That is not to say that there were plans to erect a statue in his honor like the famous *Mannekin Pis* in Brussels, Belgium, but it *is* to say that it was widely reported, and therefore widely known, that Winston Baldry's going into the forest on top of Mount Inari to 'take a leak' started the chain of events that led to the freeing of Kanako Tatezaki, who became something of a celebrity herself because she had the qualifications for a teen idol: she was cute and had crooked teeth. Not even three months after having been a famous shitter, Winston Baldry had become a famous pisser. Many people voiced their opinions that he should have held it in and gone back down the mountain to use the public toilet—One elderly man said on Mainichi Television that it was disgraceful that the sacred mountain of Mount Inari was being urinated on, especially by foreigners—but an *Asahi Shimbun* survey showed that 77% (99% of the men) saw nothing wrong with him urinating then and there if he really had to go badly. Sitting there now in his massage chair, Winston felt the need to make a trip to the TOTO urinal in his restroom but decided to put it off until the

---

* sliding wooden door.

bow-twirling ceremony signaled the end of *Sumo Digest*. He pushed the button to reverse the rollers on the foot-massage roller that he bought with the massage chair and took another swig of beer from the bottle he held in place on the blanket that was on his lap. No longer drinking from a glass, he was now drinking straight from the 633-milliliter bottle. Five or six bottles a night he was drinking, and an equal amount of urine he was pissing. Four days before, Ronald Reagan publicly announced that he had Alzheimer's disease. Winston couldn't help wondering how many brain cells he himself had destroyed with all of the beer he had been drinking. He would have had a long way to go, though, to catch up to the beer-drinking done by the sumō wrestlers, who didn't seem to have very many brain cells left. He slunk down in the massage chair so that the roller could go all of the way up to his lower neck on the upward roll and watched Akinoshima and Daizen slam heads at the tachi-ai.* Perhaps it was too many head collisions that made the sumō wrestlers appear brain-damaged at interviews, seeming unable to say anything more than 'Sō desu ne' (That's right) and 'Ganbarimasu' (I'll do my best). Or perhaps appearing mentally retarded was their idea of exhibiting the humility that was expected of them by the ultra-conservative, authoritarian members of the Japan Sumō Association. Because of that expectation, there was no emotional display of either the thrill of victory or the agony of defeat in sumō. The victor and the vanquished solemnly bowed to each other before leaving the ring. Even when scoring a major upset, or even when clinching a tournament on the 15th and final day of a tournament, they didn't pump their fists in the air and carry on like Winston had been so accustomed to seeing the hot-dogging American sports players do in a typical American display of emotions controlling the mind instead of vice versa. Japanese, on the other hand (the one not clapping), with their hide-your-honne† mentality, were colorlessly off the other end of the spectrum, where expressionlessness was the prism that dispersed dark, darker, and darkest. Humility, firmly planted by the samurais with their interest in Zen Buddhism in the 12th century and deeply rooted three centuries later with the introduction to the commoners of tea ceremony, was still considered a great virtue, almost as great a virtue for a man as obedience was for a woman.

The media hailed Winston Baldry, the man from Corvallis, who put that city on the map with almost as much exposure as Rie Miyazawa did a couple of years before with a book of nude photos of herself taken in Santa Fe titled *Santa Fe*. He and his mystery foreign friend were lauded for possessing the great virtue of humility in a day and age when most people would have gone for the glory, but they certainly didn't respect Winston's right to privacy or the wish of the mystery hero to remain anonymous. Reporters, photographers, and camera crews stayed

* initial charge in sumō wrestling.

† one's true self, without the mask worn in public.

outside his house until midnight on that night of October 5th and badgered him the next morning as he went to Minami Kōbe High School with the intention of resigning. That day, Thursday, October 6th, newspapers were carrying headlines like 外国人誘拐された少女を助ける (Foreigners Save Kidnapped Girl), ほんとのヒーローは控えめな地理の先生 (Humble American Geography Teacher True Hero), 国際化の星ウインストン・ボールドリー (Winston Baldry: Symbol of Internationalization), 国際人ダマシイを示してくれたウインストンとその友 (Winston and Foreign Friend Show International Spirit), and ほんとのヒーローは誰だ (Who is the Mystery Hero?). At school, Winston's intention of resigning was put on hold by Junko Teratani, who called to tell him about a lucrative offer made through her by TV Asahi for an exclusive, live interview with him and the mystery hero. On his way home from school, he slipped into a public telephone booth and, being careful not to let the reporters standing outside see the number he was dialing, called Donovan.

"Donovan, we're being offered—"

"Where are you calling from?"

"A public phone."

"All right. Go ahead."

"We're being offered ten million yen to go on television together."

"And do what—appear in a Kanebō commercial to promote 'beautiful human life'?"

"No. To be interviewed."

"By whom? Please don't tell me Tetsuko Kuroyanagi on *Tetsuko no Heya* (Tetsuko's Room)."

"The name of the program is *News Station.*"

"With Hiroshi Kume and Etsuko Komiya—I should have known."

"Aren't you interested?"

"No."

"It's one hundred thousand U.S. dollars, Donovan! Holy moly, that's fifty thousand dollars each!"

"Money isn't everything."

"Of course not, but—"

"You go on yourself, mate. You'll probably only be able to collect if you identify me, so go ahead and do it. Just do me a big favor, will you, and give me three steps—I mean three days. Better yet, can you give me four days? I've got a lot to do, and *News Station* isn't broadcasted on the weekend anyway."

"Are you leaving the country?"

"Yeah, and this gives me a good reason to finally get out of here."

"You're not in any kind of trouble, are you?"

"No. No worries about that, mate. But you'll give me four days—until Monday the 10th?"

"Sure."

"Thanks, mate. Cheers." Within thirty seconds of hanging up, Donovan was on the phone with a travel agent for No.1 Travel. After getting everything straightened out, he went into the kitchen. Chie was making brandy balls with extra-old Hennessey Cognac.

"We're outa here!"

"Dō iu imi?" (<u>What do you mean</u>?)

"It's time to pack your clothes after having them dry-cleaned at Be Cleanly and contact the moving company Carry the Tomorrow. Winston is being offered five million yen for an exclusive TV interview in which he'll give my name. He's got every right to do it and he should do it, so don't even suggest that I pay him six million yen not to do it."

"Why are you suddenly talking to me in English?"

"What difference does it make?"

"I can't win a argument to you in English."

"Pigu Raten wa dō? (How about Pig Latin?) Interviewyay isyay onyay ondaymay. Iyay ustjay ademay eservationsray orfay ayay ightflay otay ydneysay onyay undaysay."

"Sore wa Eigo no Pig Latin datta." (<u>That was English Pig Latin.</u>)

Chie didn't want to leave, at least not so soon. There was too much to do. Besides, her yearly elementary-school class reunion was coming up. Besides, the girls were in the middle of their second term at school. Besides, she had already paid for six more months of treatments at Kōbe Aesthetic Salon. Besides, the new Kintetsu department store was having its grand opening soon. Donovan brushed all of those besides aside by saying that they were besides the points and the points were the same points that had kept him clinging to anonymity since the story broke: Becoming a celebrity would involve background checks with the delvers assuredly going into his impressive academic background, and the risk that they would find out the truth simply wasn't worth taking, not at this stage when they had a substantial nest egg that was better broken over some property in Australia than having the yolk sucked out of it in Japan by a district-court judge. Chie knew that disputing the points was pointless and didn't need any metaphors about eggs. She understood the predicament of having her Persian carpet pulled right out from under her and didn't need any metaphors about carpets either. In her heart, she wished that Donovan really had graduated from Harvard and Oxford because then they would have nothing to fear and he would be a celebrity hero and she would be the wife of a celebrity hero. In her mind, she was just as scared as Donovan was about losing their savings, which was enough to buy a nice condominium near the harbor in high-priced Sydney. As the wife of the eminent Professor Wood, Chie had learned both the hard way and the easy way about the difference between barely good, fairly good, pretty good, and very good, and although good was no longer good enough, she understood that they had to get out while the getting was good. So October 9th, 1994 went down in the annals of the Woods' history as Departure Day.

Winston watched Daizen spin Akinoshima off balance and back him out with a choke hold. He groaned as the massage-chair rollers worked circularly beneath his shoulder blades. He had been using the massage chair for two hours every night after taking a long, hot bath into which he put garlic bath powder because garlic was said to be good for stiff shoulders. Two weeks before, he started using big strips of Salonpas medicated plaster instead of the smaller strips of Tokuhon medicated plaster. Tension in his neck made his eyes tired and sore, for which he was drinking garlic-filled tonics and using medicated eyedrops containing vitamin E. The garlic tonics and garlic baths kept away people who wanted to practice their English with him, as well as those who didn't want to. All of that garlic might have repelled Dracula, but it would not have repelled the monstrous media that, a month before, seemed to Winston like gargantuan Konishiki must have seemed like to tiny Mainoumi. Taking a swig of beer, he watched the two sumō wrestlers square off in a weight-differential that was a laughable anomaly.

Once a great, ferocious ōzeki who was almost promoted to yokozuna two years before, Hawaiian-born Konishiki (real name: Salevaa Atisanoe) was now rolling downhill fast and gathering way too much moss. For this tournament, he was down to No. 5 maegashira and up to 269kg (593lb). In his prime, he weighed 30 or 40kg less, but even then was easily the heaviest sumō wrestler in the 1,800-year-old history of the sport. Mainoumi was on the other end of the seesaw plank–the one that needed 170kg (374lb) to balance it. Only 171cm (five feet seven and one-quarter inches) tall, the lightweight Mainoumi had silicone implanted into the top of his head for the day of the official height measurement so he could meet the minimum height-requirement of 173cm, and his ploy was accepted by the Sumō Association in the same sort of way that the police accepted the loophole in anti-gambling laws through which pachinko players received cash by taking their token prizes to the conveniently near, supposedly independent prize-exchange office. The police would have been less likely, though–in fact, they couldn't have been more less likely–to look the other way if a big-name gaijin like Professor Wood could be made to throw gaijins in general into a little more shadow in this Land of the Rising Sun.

Right after making the call from the phone booth on the afternoon of October 6th to inform Donovan about the ¥10,000,000 offer made by TV Asahi for an interview, Winston got back to Junko Teratani. Then she got back to TV Asahi. The new TV Asahi offer was this: They would pay Winston ¥5,000,000 to go on News Station alone on Monday night, October 10th, if he would give them the name of mystery hero in confidentiality on Monday morning so they would have sufficient time to put together a personal profile of the man for the program. After Junko got back to Winston by calling the Tsujimotos, Winston stepped outside and went past the media swarm to call Donovan from the green public phone down the street with a Lotte Chewing Gum telephone card he had been sent with "heartfelt thanks" from Osamu Tatezaki (Kanako's father) along with a smoked ham, Kirin beer gift coupons, a Lotte Orions baseball cap, Lotte chocolates, and a box of assorted Lotte chewing gum, to name just a few of the many things. Donovan told Winston to feel free to give them his name any time after 12:45 p.m. on Sunday, which was the time and day of the Wood family's departure on Qantas airlines. Donovan and Chie's plan was to go about their business as if everything was normal. Donovan requested fixed, round-trip tickets to cover their bases. The next day, Friday, Chie would wire-transfer all but ¥1,000 of their savings at Sanwa Ginkō in Kōbe to their bank account at the National Australian Bank in Melbourne, then give the Sanwa Ginkō bank card to her mother, Mitoko, so she could get Donovan's final paycheck that would be sent to his account on the 25th. On Saturday morning, Chie would pick up the tickets for the flight to Sydney and come back as soon as possible because Saturday, October 8th, 1994 was Packing Day. They would take only one small suitcase each so not to give the impression that they were taking a long trip. Mitoko would send them the rest of their important things later. All of their furniture and appliances would stay. On Saturday, Donovan would call Kurokado-san, president of Kōbe Gakugei University, and their landlord, Morita-san, and tell them that they had to go to Australia for a few days because there had been a death in his family. When they didn't return on Thursday, Mitoko would explain that there had been some problem settling the estate and they would be back as soon as that problem was resolved. Their car would stay in their carport to give the appearance that they really were coming back. Their newspaper would continue to be delivered for the same reason. At the end of the month, Mitoko would explain that there had been an emergency that necessitated staying in Australia indefinitely. Then she would sell the car, the furniture, and the appliances, and keep 50% for her help. That was the plan, but first they were going to have to persuade the triplets to go along with the plan, and that wasn't going to be easy because the triplets weren't going to want to leave their friends and their comfortable lives in Japan. So Donovan decided that the best course of action was to tell them the truth, the whole truth, and nothing but the truth, i.e. they had received a crisis call from the Australian Embassy, based upon intelligence obtained from the American CIA, that a five-man hit squad of Japanese Red Army terrorists would be leaving their base in Lebanon in a few days to come to Japan and kill Donovan for unknown reasons that seemed to have something to do with published comments he had made at an interna-tional symposium pertaining to the Japan-U.S. Security Treaty. At an emergency family meeting on Friday night, that 'truth' failed to persuade the triplets. So Donovan added that the word was that the terrorists were going to torture him first. When that still didn't succeed in per-suading them, he told them what he said he had really hoped he wouldn't have to tell them: his entire family had been targeted. That worked, but not before the triplets gained the concession to have another cream-puff fight on Saturday night like the one they had before they left the old 2LDK apartment in Villa Yamamoto, which they all claimed to remember, even though they were only five years old then–and this time they wanted not 100 cream puffs but 200.

Konishiki wasn't going to throw cream puffs at Mainoumi. With hands as big as meat hooks, he delivered brutal slaps and was, in his prime, a punishing sumō wrestler who hurt a lot of fellow sumō wrestlers. In some ways, Konishiki was a representation of America–so big and so strong and so ready to throw its weight around at the drop of a cowboy hat.

Mainoumi wasn't wearing a cowboy hat and would have looked quite comical in nothing but his *mawashi* if he were wearing one, but he had the proverbial hatful of tricks, not just outside of the ring, as his silicone-implant demonstrated, but especially *in* the ring. He had, in more than a few matches, jumped over a charging opponent and then pushed him out from the big behind. In some ways, Mainoumi was a representation of Japan, the Japan that had been given a psychological boost five years before by Shintarō Ishihara's book *A Japan That Can Say No:* a stubborn competitor not afraid to stand up to an America that had grown too big for its own breeches, and a formidable competitor that frustrated America by not playing according to the rules that America wanted to play by.

Back in the mid/late 1950s, when defeated, humiliated Japan was a poor David with an inferior made-in-Japan slingshot, Japanese well-off enough to have a television set, or lucky enough to have a friend who had one, could derive some vindictive pleasure on Friday nights watching Japanese pro wrestlers like the all-time favorite Rikidōzan, a former sumō wrestler, beat big, bad Americans like Fred Blassie or one of the Sharp Brothers in Rocky Balboa fashion with a dramatic finale of karate chops. It wasn't real, but it was as close to reality as Japan could get to giving America a shellacking until made-in-Japan came to denote such excellence that even Goliath wanted a made-in-Japan slingshot, as well as a made-in-Japan mousetrap, and especially a made-in-Japan car, and the economic miracle had created an economic monster that appeared to Americans sort of like a Godzilla that really showed its teeth in the late 1980s and alarmed Americans by gobbling up such succulent morsels as MCA Movie Studios, Columbia Pictures, the Arco Plaza, the Rockefeller Center, and Pebble Peach golf course.

Sumō was real. There was nothing fake about it. A powerful slap to the head by Konishiki could have killed an ordinary man. Mainoumi was fast and very unorthodox. Their lifetime record going into this match was about even. Winston took another swig of beer and watched Konishiki kick back his legs like a bull does before charging and then get down in his stance to face Mainoumi, who got down in *his* stance so far away from the center that one more step back and he would have been out of the 455-cm-diameter (14'10") ring. Sitting in his massage chair, Winston didn't have to worry about flying sumō wrestlers landing on him like people sitting in the expensive ringside seats had to worry about. Hearing the soft beeps that indicated the end of another 12-minute cycle, he pushed the button to start another 12-minute cycle, pushed another button for the full-back mode, and watched Konishiki charge and Mainoumi do a side-step and Konishiki go belly-down on the dirt.

On Friday, October 7th, three days before the ballyhooed *News Station* interview with Winston Baldry, Donovan felt as if a flying Konishiki had crash-landed on *him*, because that was when he was identified as the mystery hero. He owed that unwanted distinction (and that unwanted weight) to Kentarō Nakatsu, the former student of his who happened to be at JR Inari Station on the evening he was giving Sergeant Iwakiri the lowdown about the kidnapping. Although he respected Professor Wood for having let him sleep during class, Kentarō didn't respect his right to remain anonymous, not when there was money to be gotten for information that the media craved–money for Nintendo and Sega computer games, for instance. After contacting the major newspapers and news stations on October 6th and getting them involved in a bidding war, he ended up selling the information to the *Sankei Shimbun*, which was affiliated with Fuji Television Network, a rival of TV Asahi, on which *News Station* was broadcasted. The story broke the next morning. By the end of the day, Professor Wood's photo, taken from the Kōbe Gakugei University yearbook, was all over the place.

Calls were coming from all over Japan from marketing people hoping to sign Donovan to commercial contracts endorsing such things as Suntory beer, Hitachi washing machines, NEC computers, Aiwa stereos, Toshiba TVs, Daihatsu trucks, Nissan cars, Canon printers, Yamaha scooters, Takeda vitamins, Zōjirushi rice cookers, Pentax cameras, Kao soap, and Glico Kiss Mint. With his great heroism, remarkable academic achievements, and admirable humility, he was considered, in the commercial sense, hot. Being married to a Japanese lady and having the extraordinary rarity of identical triplets fueled the fire. Agents were coming out of the woodwork, jamming the lines, and beating down the door of the brilliant, altruistic, humble Professor Wood. None of the calls were getting through, however, because the first thing Donovan did after getting awakened at 6:10 a.m. by an agent reacting to the front-page headline of the *Sankei Shimbun*, 謎のヒーロー　偉大なるオーストラリア人学者(Eminent Australian Scholar the Mystery Hero), was to disconnect the phone. Reporters and photographers for the *Sankei Shimbun* were already stationed outside his house. A Fuji TV camera crew was there also. By 8:00 a.m., there was a huge buzzing swarm, and there was a sign on the Woods' 'hive' that read 邪魔しないで！(Do Not Disturb!). Television vans were lined up on the street. Fuji TV, TV Asahi, NHK, NTV, TBS, TV Tōkyō, Mainichi Television–they were all there. More than two hundred bystanders had also gathered around with the hope of getting a glimpse of the great man, who was inside thinking that it was too bad it wasn't pouring down rain or, better yet, that there wasn't a great typhoon like the one that thwarted Kublai Khan's invading Mongol armada in 1281. He knew that he had to act like he had nothing at all to hide while at the same time stalling the media until departure time at 12:45 p.m. on Sunday. At 9:00, he saw Kōbe Gakugei University president Kurokado saying live on Fuji Television that Professor Wood had an excellent reputation as a teacher and that he was, in his opinion, a truly international man and, yes, a great man, and that everyone was looking forward to the completion and publication of his trilogy. Donovan turned off the TV, re-connected the phone, and called his sister, Wendy, in Melbourne. So that there would be a KDD record of a telephone call from Australia, he asked Wendy to call him back immediately. Shortly after receiving the call, in which he asked Wendy to call him again the following morning at exactly 9:30 his time, the King Bee stepped outside. Smoking his pipe, he held his hands up to quiet down the hullabaloo in which there were questions like, 'What exactly did the kidnapper Ryōta Sano say to you on the phone?', 'How long have you been living in Japan?', 'Do you have a glass eye?', 'Why did you come to Japan?', and 'Do you sleep in a bed or a *futon?*' He cleared his throat and said that he would have liked very much to stay out there with them on such a nice day and answer all of their questions one by one but wasn't feeling quite up to it at the moment because he had just received a call from his sister in Australia informing him that his 74-year-old father had slipped on a bar of soap while taking a shower and had hit his head and was presently in critical condition with a blood clot on his brain. He added that he was waiting for an update on his father's condition and would accommodate them with a news conference as soon as his mind was more at ease.

The problem with packing was where to begin. "Ippai mono ga aru" (There are so many things) Chie said many times before beginning with her jewelry. There was no way they were going to get everything packed. That became clearer and clearer until it was as clear as the crystal that Chie packed with as much bubble-paper as the china. They needed more boxes, many more, as well as lots more bubble paper and paper tape, but they couldn't get an adequate supply without creating the appearance that they were doing some very serious packing. The cream-puff fight was called off because delivery of 200 cream puffs would have been a little too attention-getting. The loss of that condition made the triplets pout like 13-year-old Japanese girls and come on strong like 13-year-old Australian girls. Donovan relinquished and agreed not to call off the cream-puff fight but merely postpone it, for two nights only, until Monday the 11th, and he let himself get talked into making two more concessions: (1) that the cream-puff fight be held in the suite at the trendy Double Bay hotel, and (2) that there be not 200 cream puffs but 300.

Without enough boxes, the best they could do was put things in neat stacks to be boxed later by Mitoko. Organization was important. Mitoko was the manager. Misa's and Megumi's rooms were designated Gomi no Heya (Garbage Rooms). Mari's room was for the triplets' essential things. Donovan and Chie's room was for Chie's essentials. Donovan's soundproof room was for his essentials. The living room, dining room, and kitchen were to be kept completely unchanged so not to give the impression to anybody let in as far as the *genkan* that the Woods were 'blowing town'.

Winston had thought about 'blowing town' so many times that the thought became a permanent fixture in his mind. "This is killing me," he often said to himself and sometimes thought about the Tsujimoto's son, Yōichi, who died from overwork two years before. On Wednesday, October 5th, shortly after giving his statement to the press with Junko Teratani at his side, he dragged himself behind Mrs. Tsujimoto to her doctor, Yoshihara-sensei, who had not uncommonly gotten into a private medical university by paying a bribe. After first diagnosing Winston as being pregnant and then realizing that he had mixed up the urine samples, he said that Winston seemed to be fundamentally OK and was probably just suffering from stress, which can kill you. The next day, Winston went to school with the intention of telling Principal Hirota that he had to quit for health reasons, but Hirota and Vice Principal Mitsuzuka were behind closed doors all day long trying to quell charges made by Shannah Pearl against the Japanese History teacher, Masaharu Ikenouchi, for squeezing her breasts and saying, "Ōkii mune ya ne" (You've got big tits) at the faculty party a week before. Although Ikenouchi at first denied the accusation, he finally owned up to it because there were witnesses, and he ended up giving Pāru-sensei the ambiguous kind of apology that Japanese politicians routinely gave Asian countries for the behavior of the Japanese Imperial Army from 1931-1945: what happened was unfortunate. That didn't stop Shannah from metaphorically wanting Ikenouchi's dick on a platter, and she was livid when the Kōbe District Public Prosecutors Office reduced the charge from sexual assault to sexual harassment because Ikenouchi did not take her clothes off. Hirota-san and Mitsuzuka-san were doing their best to try to persuade the raging Pāru-san to let the sexual-harassment charge slide, as well as a ¥10,000,000 lawsuit she filed for humiliation and mental suffering. Their argument was that Ikenouchi had the excuse that made almost any kind of bad behavior excusable for Japanese men: he was drunk. As for Winston, he got so drunk that night that he could have gotten himself excused for rape, so long as it was what Japanese called 'soft rape'. (He couldn't have gotten himself excused for murder because, insofar as murder victims were male as well as female (in fact, much more so), there was no such Japanese term as 'soft murder'.) Having decided to stay a few more days and perhaps longer, he needed to find some way, some passive way, to keep the stress from killing him. He seemed to find a way on Saturday, October 8th (Packing Day for the Woods) in a Seibu department store mini-catalog that showed a high-tech massage chair made by National, called Urban Relax, that was on sale for ¥268,000, down from ¥298,000. Because of his celebrity status, he didn't have to put any money down to get it. In fact, the manager offered to *give* it to him if he would agree to be the Seibu November poster-boy. Although he refused that offer, figuring that he would receive ¥5,000,000 on the following Monday (Cream Puff Day for the Woods), they took a photo of him trying out the massage chair, and the photo ended up in every major paper via Kyodo News and created a big demand for the Urban Relax massage chair. Several Seibu staff and many customers wanted Winston's autograph, which had become almost as much in demand as the autograph of the clean-cut, 21-year-old superstar right-fielder for the Orix Blue Wave, Ichiro Suzuki. The owners of Tanuki, the *okonomiyaki* restaurant Winston used to frequent, wanted a large, autographed photo of Winston so they could frame it and hang it above the counter with autographed photos of two other famous people that had been their customers in the past: actor Toshiyuki Nishida, who was appearing in more commercials than child star Yumi Adachi was appearing in TV dramas, and Yutaka Fukumoto, the now-retired base-stealing star of Kōbe's only professional baseball team, the Hankyū Braves, which became the Orix Braves in 1989 and the Orix Blue Wave in 1991.

The Urban Relax massage chair had become more than Winston's crutch; it had become his walker. To take it further, it was to him what Ōsaka Castle was to the Toyotomis during their battles with the Tokugawas in the summer of 1615. Without it, he couldn't have continued. In addition to giving him a new lease on life, it gave him something to look forward to at the end of each working day. He could take a nice, long, hot bath with a cold beer within reach and then sit back in that wonderful massage chair and get massaged while drinking more beer and watching television or a video. That was a whole lot more than Chechen resistance fighters in Grozny or civilians in Sarajevo could have said. He may have been barely surviving, but at least he was barely surviving in relative comfort, and he could derive a little more pleasure from that relative thought. Because of that massage chair, and only because of that massage chair, he never blew town. Donovan never blew town either, and he had only himself to blame—himself and Imajiku-san.

Tadashi Imajiku was the director of the Berlitz language school in Ōsaka, where Donovan taught English conversation in the bad old days during his first two years in Japan. Three and a half months earlier, on June 29th, two days after the U.S. dollar broke the psychological barrier of ¥100, Imajiku, still the director at Berlitz, was at Chico & Charlies Mexican restaurant in the JR ACTI building in Ōsaka with a new receptionist he was in the process of 'job evaluating' (like every other receptionist he tried to 'job evaluate') all of the way to the Peach Pie love hotel, which was his favorite love hotel because it had a couple of rooms with African safari motifs. Donovan happened to be there that evening with his friend Jarod 'Kiwi' Bailey, an unmarried, bald fellow who had suffered more heartbreaks than Tora-san in the 46 *Otoko wa Tsurai yo* (It's Tough Being a Man) movies made until then. They were drinking pitchers of margaritas to celebrate the strength of the yen and help

'Kiwi' get over another heartbreak. It was during their third pitcher that Donovan spotted Imajiku.

Donovan didn't like Imajiku. He hated his infrequent, phony, friendly moods even more than his usual arrogance that was based upon having graduated from prestigious Kyōto University, which he got into by paying a surrogate examination-taker to take the entrance examination for him. What Donovan hated most of all about Imajiku was the way he came on to the receptionists, one of whom, 14 years before, was Chie. Of course, back then, and until just a couple of years before, sexual harassment (sekuhara) did not even have a name. Donovan emptied his salted glass and went over to Imajiku's table.

"Imajiku-san?"

Imajiku washed down part of a cheese enchilada with water. "Hai." (Yes.)

"Oboete inai deshō ga, nan nen mo mae ni Berlitz de oshiete imashita." (You probably don't remember me, but I taught at Berlitz many years ago.)

"Kao wa oboete imasu yo." (I remember your face.)

"Nihon de hajimete shigoto o itadaita koto wa kansha shite imasu. Itsumo otsutae shitai to omotte ita koto ga arimasu." (You gave me my first job in Japan, and I was grateful for that, and there's something I've always wanted to say to you.)

Imajiku cut into his beef burrito with his fork. "Sonna ni kinishinakute ii desu yo." (You don't have to thank me.)

"Iitakatta koto wa anata wa hontō ni busaiku desu ne. Hikigaeru ni nite iru shi, bākōdo no yōna kami wa hazukashii yo." (What I've wanted to say is that you are really ugly. You look like a toad, and you've got the nerve to wear a pull-over hair-style that looks like a bar-code.)

Imajiku was just recovering from his shock when Donovan turned to the new receptionist and said, "Mā, namekuji yori sukoshi wa mashi da ne." (The next step down from this jerk is a slug.) Imajiku pounded his fist down and stood up. Pointing a finger with refried beans on it at Donovan, he shouted, "Dō iu shinkei da!" (You've got some nerve!) People stepped in between them to stop a fight. 'Kiwi' Bailey pulled Imajiku's chair out from behind him while Donovan was politely explaining to the manager that he had merely advised the customer that he should use a fork instead of his fingers to eat his refried beans. Donovan and 'Kiwi' then left, and Imajiku fell to the floor trying to sit back down and hurt his tailbone so badly that going to the Peach Pie was out of the question. That was that, until a little over four months later, when Imajiku saw the picture of the mystery hero in the paper and on television and it all came back to him. With his doubts about the credentials of 'Professor Wood' being as great as his desire to get even, he went back to his old files and found the file of Donovan Wood. There was no mention about him having graduated from either Harvard or Oxford. Thirteen years had passed, so it was possible, but Imajiku didn't think it was likely. He called the Records Department at both universities late that night when it was still morning in New York and afternoon in London. After finding out what he hoped he'd find out, he felt so good that he went to bed and soft-raped his wife.

On Saturday morning, newspapers were running headlines like かなこちゃんを助けたのは、控えめなハーバードとオックスフォード大出の教授 (Low-key Harvard- and Oxford-educated Professor Saved Kanako-chan), 誘拐犯 優秀なるウッド教授には勝てず (Kidnapper No Match for Brilliant Professor Wood), and 村山首相ドナバン・ウッド氏を絶賛 (Donovan Wood Praised by Prime Minister Murayama). At 9:25 a.m., Donovan reconnected his phone in preparation for the requested 9:30-call from Wendy and, at exactly 9:30, received a call from a representative of Kōdansha Ltd. publishing company offering him a big advance to help them write his biography. The next call was from Wendy. After that call, he called Kurokado and Morita and told them that he had just received word that his father had died, so they would be leaving the following day to go to Australia for the funeral but would be returning on Thursday the 13th. After re-disconnecting the phone, he pulled out a few nose hairs to make his eyes water and stepped outside to tell the media the same story. He added that he would give a news conference at 6:00 p.m. on Thursday and apologized for the unfortunate but necessary delay. While he was addressing the media, Chie slipped out and got into her father's car, and her father, Tsutomu, gave her a ride to No.1 Travel so she could pick up their airline tickets.

Meanwhile, Imajiku was making one phone call after another. He was frustrated, however, with the media's unwillingness to take the word of a person who might be trying to defame a celebrity and a national hero who had been praised by Prime Minister Murayama. The police were more receptive but wanted to check out the allegation themselves. In order to check it out, they had to wait until late that night because of the time difference. To put things in a clearer perspective, here's a chronology:

6/29 (evening): Donovan insults Imajiku at Chico & Charlies.

10/2 (Sunday evening): Winston and Donovan find the hanged kidnapper, Tomoki Itō, and report it to the police.

10/4 (Tuesday morning): Winston becomes famous and the media wants to know who his friend is.

10/5 (Wednesday afternoon): Winston issues a statement saying that his friend wishes to remain anonymous.

10/6 (Thursday afternoon): The Woods begin making plans to leave on the 9th.

10/6 (Thursday evening): Winston agrees to go on *News Station* on the 10th.

10/6 (Thursday evening): Kentarō Nakatsu sells his information to the *Sankei Shimbun*.

10/7 (Friday morning): Donovan becomes famous; Winston and Donovan become a famous duo.

10/7 (Friday morning): Donovan announces that his father is in critical condition.

10/7 (Friday afternoon): Imajiku gets suspicious and checks his old records.

10/7 (Friday night): Imajiku calls Oxford and Harvard.

10/8 (Saturday morning): Donovan announces that his father has died and they would be leaving the next day to attend the funeral.

10/8 (Saturday morning): Imajiku starts making whistle-blowing phone calls.

At noon on Saturday, October 8th, Chie returned with the air tickets and a bag of groceries and fought her way through the madness outside to get back to the madness inside. "Ē? Ah, chotto yōji de" (What? Oh, I had some errands to run) she said on her way into the house.

The drawn blinds and closed curtains accentuated the mournful mood at the Woods' residence, and the media joined Professor Wood in mourning the death of his father. Flowers, sent with condolences from all over Japan, were placed near the great man's front door, where presents, like the huge box sent by Osamu Tatezaki, containing everything that Winston Baldry had received from him and much more, were stacked high. The disconnected phone was, of course, understandable, as were the lights that stayed on all night long.

There was no time for the Woods to sleep that night. There was too much packing to do. In his soundproof room, Donovan drank 24-year-old Glenlivet on the rocks and smoked hashish. Unlike Winston Baldry, who was a basket case, Donovan felt relieved. A big load was finally off his mind. He was raring to go. By daylight, he had drunk half the bottle of whiskey and had smoked half a gram of hashish.

Having stayed away all day and all night because housework was not a man's job, Tsutomu arrived at 7:00 and brought in the morning paper that was delivered at 4:30 every day except on 'press holidays'. During the 'Last Breakfast', Donovan picked up the newspaper. ドナバンとウインストンの人気急上昇 (Popularity of Donovan and Winston Skyrocketing) was a front-page headline. He turned to the sports section and read about the final game of the regular season the night before between the two teams tied for first place in the Central League, the Yomiuri Giants and the Chunichi Dragons, won by the Giants 6-3. After making a phone call to have two taxis pick them up and take them to Kansai International Airport, he went back to his room and took one last hit from two remaining grams of hashish that would last him for a few weeks in Australia. Bringing hashish from Japan to Australia, or to anywhere else for that matter, was no problem at all, as people coming from Japan were never suspected of having drugs and were therefore never searched. He had done it several times before and felt perfectly comfortable doing it again. He put the piece into his right front pants pocket with his keys. Before going through SECURITY CHECK, he would put it behind his glass eye. As for Chie, she had jewelry galore tied up, hooked up, and stuffed up under her Valentino dress because she didn't want to part with it until Mitoko sent them to her along with their other important things.

The taxis came at 9:15. Donovan handed his keys to Tsutomu and said sayōnara to him and Mitoko. Outside the front door, he said, "Ohayō gozaimasu. Minna-san, kirei na o-hana o dōmo arigatō gozaimasu. Kinō no yakyū no shiai wa omoshirokatta ne. Kyojin ga kachimashita ne. Kuwata no ririifu wa yokatta shi Ochiai wa mada umai desu ne. Ē? Masaka Giants no fan dewa arimasen yo. Anchi-Giants desu. Ē? Nattō wa daijōbu da yo. Ē? Kodomo no toki no jiko deshita. Aru shōnen ga nageta ishi ga me ni atattan desu. Sorejā, hoka no shitsumon ni wa mokuyōbi ni kaette kita toki ni kotaemasu." (Good morning. Thanks to everyone who sent the beautiful flowers. Hey, how about the baseball game last night. The Giants pulled it out. Great relief-pitching by Kuwata, and Ochiai is still good. What? No, I'm not a Giants fan. In fact, I'm an anti-Giants fan. Pardon? Yes, I can eat nattō.* What? It happened when I was a kid. Another kid hit me in the eye with a stone. Listen, I'll answer all of your questions when we come back on Thursday.) The hegira of the Woods then began. The great professor led the way, with his fashionable wife showing herself to be a good, traditional wife by walking three steps behind her husband so not to step on his shadow. The triplets followed side by side. Past heaps of presents and piles of flowers, the Wood family walked to the taxis. Everything was going smoothly. Donovan helped Megumi put her suitcase into the trunk.

"Bōringu no bōru demo motte iru no ka, Misa?" (What have you got in here, Misa—bowling balls?)

"Watashi wa Megumi desu yo. Taisetsu na mono bakari ga haitte iru yo. Keisatsu ga kita." (I'm Megumi. Just my important things. Here come the police.)

"Say what?"

Three Metropolitan Police Department police cars pulled up and parked alongside the taxis. Out of the first one stepped the chief of the regional section of the MPD, Kikuji Aoshima.

"Sukoshi o-hanashi o oukagai shitai no desu ga." (There's something we want to talk to you about.)

"O-hanami no arukōru ni yoru hanzai ni tsuite watashi no iken o kikitai no desu ka?" (What is it you want—my opinion about whether cherry-blossom viewing should be outlawed because of all of the alcohol-related injuries?)

"Chigaimasu." (No.)

"Sore nara nan deshō?" (Well, what then?)

---

* fermented soybeans. Mixed with chopped spring onions, hot mustard, soy sauce, and raw egg yolk, nattō is eaten for breakfast, especially by people in the Tōkyō area.

"Hābādo o sotsugyō shita no desu ka?" (Did you graduate from Harvard?)

"Hai." (Yes.)

"Okkusufōdo mo sotsugyō shita no desu ka?" (Did you graduate from Oxford?)

"Hai. Demo dōshite?" (Yes. Why?)

"Kiroku ni nai desu yo." (There are no records.)

"Techigai ja nai ka na. Mō ichido chekku shite kudasai. Sugu ni Ōsutoraria ni kaeranai to ikenain desu. Oyaji no sōshiki ga aru kara." (Well, then there's been some mistake. Check again. Right now, we've got to go to Australia to attend my father's funeral.)

"Shitsumon shitai no desu ga." (We would like to ask you some questions.)

"Muri desu. Jūni-ji yonjūgo-fun no furaito desu node. Mokuyō ni wa modori masu yo." (Forget it. Our flight is at 12:45. I'll talk to you when we come back on Thursday.)

"Dōshitemo ima o-hanashi suru hitsuyō ga arimasu." (I'm afraid you'll have to talk to us now.)

Donovan knew that he had to play the media card to pressure the police into backing down and letting them go. He turned to the television cameras and said, "Keisatsu wa watashi ga hontō ni Hābādo to Okkusu-fōdo daigaku o deta to iu koto o shinjite inai yō da. Karera wa akiraka ni daigaku ni kiroku o toiawasete inai. Moshi shite itara sen kyūhyaku nanajū-san nen ni Hābādo daigaku o, sen kyūhyaku nanajū-roku nen ni Okkusufōdo daigaku o sotsugyō shita to iu koto ga wakaru hazu desu." (The police seem to think that I didn't really graduate from Harvard and Oxford. They obviously didn't ask the universities to go back far enough in the records because, if they had, they would have learned that I graduated from Harvard in 1973 and from Oxford in 1976.) Turning to Chief Aoshima, he added, "Kamera o tsūjite kazoku ya kōshū no menzen de shōmonai koto de iyagarase o suru mae ni, motto chekku o suru beki datta no desu yo. Moshi sōshite itara, watashi ga Hābādo ragubii no wingā datta koto ya, Okkusufōdo kuriketto chiimu no kyaputen datta koto mo wakatte ita deshō. Mokuyōbi ni kishakaiken o hiraite, keisatsu ga ayamareba meiyo kison de hōteki ni uttaeru koto wa yamete oki mashō." (You should have conducted a more thorough check before harassing me with innuendoes in front of my family with television cameras present. If you had, you would have also found that I was a winger on the Harvard rugby team and the captain of the Oxford cricket team. On Thursday, when I give the news conference, I'll accept your apology in return for not suing you for defamation of character.) Turning back to the television cameras, he said, "Karera wa dō iu shinkei o shite irun da. Kare ga yūkaihan o tsukamaeru no o tetsudatta orekai. Karera wa watashi ni iyagarase shitari, watashi no kazoku o kōsoku shitari suru no dewa naku, keisatsukan toshite watashi-tachi o kūkō made esukōto suru beki da. Watashi-tachi wa kinō nakunatta chichi no sōshiki ni shusseki suru tame ni, hikōki ni noranakereba ikenai node shitsurei sasete kudasai." (These guys have got some nerve! So this is the thanks I get for helping them catch a kidnapper. Instead of harassing me and holding us up, they ought to be giving us a police-escort to the airport. Now if you'll please excuse us, we have a flight to catch to attend the funeral of my father, who died yesterday.)

With the media omnipresent, the MPD big brass did not want to make false accusations against a celebrated hero. Perhaps Donovan Wood was right that the universities hadn't checked back far enough in their records. After all, 1973/1976 wasn't exactly yesterday. If he *was* right, then keeping him from attending his father's funeral would add insult to Professor Wood's injury and make the police seem callous on top of incompetent. It was now 8:30 p.m. on Saturday in east-coast America and 12:30 a.m. on Sunday in England. They would have to wait until Monday night Japan-time to conduct the checks. The superintendent general and the deputy superintendent general of the MPD were on the phone with each other trying to decide what to do when the commissioner general of the National Police Agency decided that the false-accusation risk wasn't worth taking and issued orders for Aoshima to let Donovan and his family go to the airport to catch their flight to Australia. Feeling that he had to give a final face-saving directive before telling Donovan that he was free to go, Aoshima had what he thought was a good idea to find out if Donovan was telling the truth about coming back. He asked Donovan to show him his airline ticket.

Donovan's foresight to buy round-trip tickets paid off. It gave him the opportunity to show that the suspicions of the police were wrong. "Keisatsu wa watashi ga Mokuyōbi ni kaeru to iu koto o uso da to omotte iru yō de, kaeri no chiketto o misero to iimasu" (They want to see my ticket because they think I'm lying about coming back on Thursday) he said to the media. Starting with the TBS television camera, he went from one camera to another, holding his ticket directly in front of the lenses for close-ups before disdainfully showing it to Aoshima. Unaware that he was now in the clear, but feeling the scales tilting in his favor, he didn't let up. "Uso o tsuite iru to omotte iru no kai? Uso ja nai yo" (You think I was lying? I don't lie) he snapped at Aoshima. "Kimi wa nanika no hoshō ga hoshii no ka?" (Do you want me to leave something with you as security?) He took his wallet out of his left pants pocket. "Hora, watashi no VISA da." (Here. Take my VISA.) He threw the credit card at the officer. "JCB kādo mo. Tōrokusho mo." (Take my JCB card too. And here's my Alien Registration Card.) Chie whispered "Dame!" (Stop it!) but stopped when jewelry started falling from under her dress. While she was busy picking up the fallen jewelry, Donovan was still busy throwing things. "Untenmenkyoshō mo. Kuruma mo watashitara ii darō. Hora, kuruma no kii da." (Take my driver's license too. Better yet, take my car. Here are the keys.) Forgetting that he had given the keys to his father-in-law, he made the stupidest and most costly mistake of his life. Aoshima, a left-handed first baseman in his baseball-playing days at the perennial high-school powerhouse PL Gakuen, reached out and caught the hashish with his right hand.

It was on the morning of that same day, October 9th, that Seibu department store deliverymen came to Winston's house, and it was on the evening of that same day that the invaders came. Finally in operational control of the massage chair by the time NHK's bilingual *News 7* came on at 7:00, 'Captain' Baldry was watching Donovan throw the hashish again and again in slow motion when, without word of warning from Ground Control, narcotics police raided his house with sniffer dogs. Suspicion by association, not only with the drug-possessor Donovan Wood, but also with the Kuramoto-gumi criminal syndicate, which was, with its affiliate the Yamaguchi-gumi, known to be forming ties with Asian and South American drug cartels, yanked Winston Baldry out of the limelight and into the lemonlight, and his 'record' of having been suspected of trying to smuggle hashish into the country less than two months before was thrown into the spotlight. Sitting there now in his massage chair watching *Sumo Digest,* he was once again happy to be drunk because to be drunk was to be numb. What a month! He finished his beer, opened another bottle, and took a drink. Beer dribbled down onto his Oregon State University Beavers sweatshirt. He watched *maegashira* Kyokudōzan and *komusubi* Kaio draw cheers from the crowd for grappling for fifty seconds, very long for a sumō match, before Kaio used an arm throw and both wrestlers went down at the same time. The five judges came up onto the ring to confer, and Kyokudōzan was ruled the winner on the basis that Kaio's hand touched down first. That meant that Kyokudōzan, having scored an upset, was interviewed. The nicest thing about watching the encapsulated *Sumo Digest* was not having to watch all of the inaction. The second nicest thing was not having to watch the ridiculous interviews.

The interview on *News Station* never happened. So Winston never got the ¥5,000,000. He could have paid for the massage chair on an installment plan, but he wasn't planning to be 'installed' in Japan much longer. George Piper sent him a money order for $3,000 (along with a *USA Today* article about Winston's heroics in Japan), but Japan's inefficient banking system turned trying to cash it into a Kafkaesque nightmare and Winston ended up sending the money order back to George and asking him to wire-transfer the money to his bank account at Sakura Ginkō. Winston could have made money appearing on special TV programs like NTV's ドナバン・ウッドの秘められた人生 (The Secret Life of Donovan Wood) and Fuji TV's 大詐欺師ドナバン・ウッド (Donovan Wood: The Great Impostor), but he couldn't have made much money because parasites were not rewarded in Japan like they were in America. Japanese didn't have Americans' insatiable appetite for dirt-digging exposés, as American Jeff Nichols (known only by his first name in Japan) found out when he came to Japan to promote his fuck-and-tell book about his over-and-done-with relationship with married superstar singer Seiko Matsuda. Jeff would have had much better luck if he had come to Japan and done something nasty like cream Emperor Akihito with a lemon meringue pie and, after a stint in a Japanese jail, gone back to America and joined the likes of Tonya Harding and John Wayne Bobbitt on the talk-show circuit. That sort of option was open to Donovan Wood because Australia had its own versions of *Inside Edition, Oprah Winfrey,* and *Geraldo,* such as *The Clive James Show, Elle Me Feast,* and *Club Buggery;* but even if Donovan had wanted to take that low road, he would have had to finish his own stint in a Japanese jail, the Kōbe Detention Center, where he had now been for one very long month, still sticking to his story that he bought the hashish from an Iranian man who approached him in Tōkyō's Yoyogi Park while he was watching Elvis Presley lookalikes dancing to music blasting from their portable stereos. It wasn't true, but it was more plausible than the story given by the actor of the 26 *Zatoichi Monogatari* (The Story of Blind Masseur Ichi) films, Katsu Shintarō, after he was caught boarding a Tōkyō-bound plane in Hawaii with cocaine stashed in his underwear, i.e. a stranger had given it to him on board and he had no idea what it was. Donovan's story might have been accepted if his credibility hadn't already been shattered and he wasn't considered a pathological liar.

If Winston Baldry had said that the 37 days since he stumbled upon the hanged kidnapper Tomoki Itō were so marvelously uplifting that he felt on top of the world and had, in fact, been singing the Carpenters' song *Top of the World* every morning while taking a shower, he would have been lying through his teeth with a bald-faced lie of his own. The whole hero business and then the whole tarnished-hero business, and the whole business of trying to do his job and get his students interested and involved, and the whole business of dealing with Principle Hirota and Vice Principle Mitsuzuka and the formal faculty-scene, and the whole business of dealing with Rika Koga–Whew! A whole lot of business had been going on. He took another drink. More beer dribbled down onto his OSU Beavers sweatshirt.

Rika was one of the few people whose behavior toward him didn't change after the tarnishment. Winston appreciated that, but he didn't know how big of a Hanshin Tigers fan she was and how much she revered Randy Bass for leading the Tigers to their one and only championship, in 1985, after fifty years of failing. 1985 was the year Rika got married. Thanks mostly to Randy Bass, it was the most blissful year of her life–the only blissful year, to be exact. Her husband, Hirofumi, a salaryman for Sekisui, was also a Hanshin Tigers fan–she wouldn't have married him if he wasn't–and he stood by her and rooted with her (with their cheer horns trumpeting *Popeye the Sailor Man)* until things changed: she got pregnant, had a baby boy, became a mother, and the Tigers went back to their losing ways. The sis-boom-bah, as well as the rah-rah, went out of their relationship. After Rika and the baby, Yūdai, spent the customary one month getting pampered at her parents' house, Hirofumi stayed away from their company apartment as long as possible by drinking and playing *mahjong* with a few of his co-workers who were in the same boat as him. In 1988, Randy Bass was cut by the Hanshin Tigers for going back to the States to be with his seriously ill son and thereby not showing the 'company first, family second' attitude that prevailed among Japanese salarymen, like Hirofumi. Hirofumi was still being a 'good' husband and father by earning a salary for his family, despite coming home drunk every night, playing golf every Sunday, having sex with Rika about once every three months, and hardly ever seeing Yūdai. When Rika asked him if he wanted a divorce, he said no because it would be an embarrassment for him. When Yūdai was old enough to go to kindergarten, Rika was free enough to spend time with housewives who made a hobby out of complaining about their husbands. Finally, she decided to go right ahead and embarrass Hirofumi. For a year after the divorce, she lived with her mother. (Her father left two years before to live with 1,000 people at the Aum Supreme Truth's big complex in Kamikuishikimura in Yamanashi Prefecture.) It wasn't impossible for Rika to get married again but, being a divorcee with a child, it sure wasn't likely. Shortly after she got the office job at Minami Kōbe High School, she and Yūdai moved into a low-rent apartment. She didn't have any plans to move to a nicer place because, chances were, things weren't going to be getting much nicer. A 33-year-old woman in the workplace was facing a wall, and there was writing on the wall that read 'There is only one road, and it doesn't lead to promotion'. Offices in Japan were still men's worlds; homes were still women's worlds. Women generally didn't want to be in men's worlds any more than men wanted to be in women's worlds, but sometimes they had to be because that's where the money was. Before the 1980s, hardly any mothers, young or old, worked outside of the house. By the 1990s, more than half of them were doing so. Almost all of them were married because the divorce rate was still very low (although it was going up). The cards were stacked against them regardless of whether they were married or divorced. Rengō (the Japanese Trade Union Confederation) and Zenrōren (the National Confederation of Trade Unions) didn't do much to help improve the working conditions of men, so they sure as hell didn't do much to help improve the working conditions of women. Moreover, the passage of the Equal Employment Opportunity Law in 1986 didn't really change anything. Married working mothers didn't seem to mind much because there wasn't any such thing as a househusband. Divorced working mothers, without that double income, naturally minded a lot more. For them, spending ¥268,000 on a luxury item like a high-tech massage chair was out of the question. Winston pushed a button to speed up the foot roller and watched Kotonishiki and Kotobeppu throw out fistfuls of salt.

The sumō cards were stacked in favor of *ōzekis* Takanohana, Wakanohana, and Takanonami because they were all in the same stable, the Futagoyama Stable, and wrestlers in the same stable didn't have to fight each other unless they happened to be tied for the lead at the end of their 15th matches. Kotonishiki slapped his *mawashi* before getting down into his charging stance. Winston patted his flabby beer belly, which had become flabbier as it had become beerier. Although he was now wearing his belt one notch looser, he was still not what you would call fat, unless you were talking about the percent of body fat, in which case he would have been much fatter than the sumō wrestlers, who surprisingly had a very low body-fat content, with former *yokozuna* Chiyonofuji taking the high-calorie cake with only 11% body fat. Winston took another drink of beer and watched the two sumō wrestlers slam into each other and maneuver for a hold on the *mawashi*. Kotobeppu's *mawashi* started to come undone, prompting the referee to spare the spectators the sight of a totally nude 178kg (391lb) man by giving the command for both wrestlers to freeze. He then spent thirty seconds tightening Kotobeppu's ten-meter-long *mawashi* before giving the command to unfreeze and resume fighting. At the faculty party six weeks before, Winston wanted to undo Rika Koga's three-meter-long kimono sash and spin her out of it and keep her spinning until she was out of her *kimono* and onto a bed of rice and then roll around with her until that rice had turned into rice cake. She sure looked nice in her kimono. At one point at the party, she was standing next to Shannah Pearl, and it looked like a Japanese cherry tree in full bloom next to a giant cactus. Ikenouchi couldn't help seeing the blossoms, but he was too drunk to see the spines. Shannah reacted to his 'transgression' by grabbing him by his tie and shirt collar, putting him up against the wall, punching him in the stomach, and kicking him in the groin—four moves that were never seen in sumō, but not because sumō wrestlers didn't wear shirts and ties. There were seventy official moves in sumō. Kotonishiki got Kotobeppu in an arm lock and walked him out of the ring.

The main move that Rika had been putting on Winston might have been called the Teachers' Drawers Move, not to be confused with the Teachers' Trousers Move. On the day he went to school with the intention of resigning, October 6th, there was a note in his personal drawer in the plastic teachers' cabinet offering to take him to see Himeji Castle. A week later, there was a replica of a painting of a geisha by Takehisa Yumeji and a note saying that he was her favorite painter. Over the next few weeks, the Teachers' Drawers Move was used again and again. There was a note written on pink stationery inviting him to go to an Elton John concert at Ōsaka Castle; there was an English version of the 30-year-old novel *Kojinteki na Taiken* (A Personal Matter) by Kenzaburō Ōe; there was a piece of homemade cheesecake wrapped in a napkin decorated with hearts; there was an invitation to a J.League soccer game between Gamba Ōsaka and JEF United; there was a tape of alpha music by Takeshi Toyoda; there was an egg-salad sandwich in a plastic container wrapped with a pink furoshiki.* Rika was definitely ready to go, which meant, if making a straight translation into Japanese and considering it from a sexual point of view, that she was ready to come—and indeed she was. A week before, Winston re-connected his phone to make a quick call to Chie Wood at her parents' house and find out how Donovan was doing at the Kōbe Detention Center, and his phone rang as soon as he plugged it in and it was Rika. She told him in her best English that she called only because she wanted to hear his voice. Talking to Rika in English was sort of like talking to a parrot because she repeated practically everything said for her own comprehension before replying. If, for example, Winston had said, "Are you ready to go?" she would have said, "Are you ready to go? Yes, I am." And indeed she would have been. Winston pushed a button to speed up the foot roller and watched *ōzeki* Takanonami throw a fistful of salt hard against his *genkan* door. So it seemed anyway, because something, actually somebody's fist, hit Winston's *genkan* door. It was probably Mrs. Tsujimoto, he thought. Perhaps there had been a phone call for him. Since disconnecting his phone a month before, Junko Teratani, Kenji Maekawa, and a couple of others had gotten a hold of him by calling the Tsujimotos. Nobody had ever called him at such a late hour, though, except once when George Piper, forgetting about the 15-hour time difference, woke up Mrs. Tsujimoto (who proceeded to come over and wake up Winston) at 3:30 a.m. He turned off his massage chair and pushed the PAUSE button on his video remote controller, which didn't do anything because he wasn't watching a video. Then he got up and answered the door.

"Rika."

"Ojama shimasu." (I'm sorry to bother you.)

"Is something wrong?"

"Is somsing rongu? No. Here are persimmons."

"Oh, thank you. Would you like to come in?"

"Would you raiku to come in? Sank you. You smell of garlic."

"Would you like a beer?"

"Would you raiku a biiru? No. I can't drink arukōru. I am arerugii."

"No kidding? I'm allergic to nuts."

They sat down across from each other at Winston's *kotatsu*. By this time, the matches of all four *ōzekis* (Takanonami, Wakanohana, Musashimaru, and Takanohana) were over. They watched the lone *yokozuna*, Akebono, the 64th *yokozuna* and the first foreign one, use his patented *tsuppari* attack and send *maegashira* Daishosho straight out of the ring, bringing *Sumo Digest* to a close.

"Eeeh! Do you raiku sumō, Winston-san?"

"Yes. Do you?"

---

* cloth originally used to wrap bathing things needed at sentōs, but now mostly used to wrap bentōs and other things in.

"Do you? So-so. I raiku bēsubōru. Do you raiku bēsubōru?"

"Of course. It's the great American pastime."

"Where chiimu is your nanbā one raiku?"

"Well, the only major-league team in the American northwest is the Seattle—"

"I raiku Hanshin Tigers. I want present you Hanshin Tigers cap. Dōzo." (Here you are.)

"Rika, this isn't necessary."

"Puriizu."

"Well, OK. Thank you. It fits me perfectly. Are you all right?"

With that Hanshin Tigers cap on, Rika thought he looked exactly like Randy Bass did after the great slugger shaved off his beard in the Gillette commercial. "Are you ōru raito? Yes. Kakkoii. (You look good.) Chotto atsukunattekita." (It became hot.) She took her hand fan out of her bag and fanned herself while gazing dreamily at the lookalike of the great first baseman who led the Hanshin Tigers to the Central League championship in 1985 with a .718 slugging percentage and 22 game-winning hits, and capped off the first of his back-to-back MVP seasons by being named the Japan Series MVP for almost single-handedly beating the Seibu Lions in the Japan Series. "Totemo atsukunattekita" (It became very hot) she said and took off her jacket. She was wearing a pearl necklace above a tight, red sweater. Winston started feeling hot himself. He wiped his forehead with the back of his hand.

"It's beri hotto. Aoide hoshii?" (Do you want me to fan you?)

"Pardon?"

She leaned across the kotatsu and playfully fanned him until he backed away. Then she got up and went over to his side of the kotatsu and kept up the playfulness until he took the fan out of her hand and folded it up and put it on the kotatsu. She was right there. Her hair was touching his shoulder. There was a scent of Chanel No.5. Her breasts were rising with her inhalations. She put her hand upon his shoulder. He looked into her eyes. Her red sweater was like a matador's muleta. Winston 'Bull' Baldry charged. Things started happening fast, much too fast to think about what was happening. They were down on the tatami. He took the Tigers cap off, but she put it right back on. Before he knew it, that cap, and his Salonpas medicated plaster, was all he had on, and she had nothing at all on, not even the pearl necklace. 'Wild' isn't the word; 'hot and heavy' isn't the expression. Man oh man! Mama mia! She was going crazy; he was going wild. Things were happening so fast it was balls-boggling. They had lost all control and were speeding like a runaway train with its big whistle blowing. The neighbors would have had to be deaf not to hear Rika's lovemaking cries of ecstasy ("Bāsu! Bāsu!") as they rolled around on the tatami. Figuring that 'basu' was a Japanese love-making expression, he used it himself. Rika screamed, "Bāsu! Bāsu! Dō shio? Dō shio? Onegai! Basu! Onegai! Daite! Daite! Yatta! Sugoi! Bāsu! Ii yo! Ii yo! Bāsu! Bāsu! Bāsu! Hōmuran! Hōmuran! Gurandosaramu! . . ."

On November 27th, a 13-year-old middle-school student in Aichi Prefecture killed himself and left a suicide note saying he'd had enough of being bullied at school. Media attention to the story, which was filled with details of how he had been forced to get down on all fours and behave like a dog, and so pitifully on and so pathetically forth, got the attention of other victims of bullying, like a 16-year-old high-school student in Aomori Prefecture who hanged himself and left a letter addressing the guilt he felt from being forced to repeatedly steal money from his family to pay the bullies. All of a sudden, there was a chain reaction of suicides of middle-school- and high-school students that made the word 'ijime' (bullying) almost as newsworthy as 'kokusaika' (internationalization). The leftist Nikkyōso (Japan Teachers' Union) and the rightist Mombushō (Ministry of Education) finally agreed on something: there was a problem that needed to be addressed. There was no question that school authorities, especially the teachers, had to sit down and talk, which meant that they had to sit down. Schools across the country started holding meetings to discuss the problem, which meant that the problem was being discussed without really being addressed.

There were many meetings going on after school at Minami Kōbe High School on Thursday, December 8th, the day that Kenzaburō Ōe, the second Japanese to win the Nobel Prize in Literature–the first was Yasunari Kawabata in 1968–gave his speech at the Royal Swedish Academy entitled "Japan, the Ambiguous, and Myself," calling to mind Kawabata's speech "Japan, the Beautiful, and Myself", but calling it to mind in title only because he spoke of being influenced by the Irish poet William Butler Yeats instead of some Japanese writer. Ōe could have made a fortune doing endorsements ("Nike, Coca-Cola, and Myself") if he had played the game instead of doing something as 'disgraceful' as refusing to accept the National Culture Achievement Award from the emperor. December 8th was also the date that the Japanese attacked Pearl Harbor, although Americans remembered Pearl Harbor Day on December 7th. There was a big time difference between Japan and America, as anyone who made or received phone calls between the two countries was aware of, and which Winston had been made more aware of than George Piper when George called him at 10:30 a.m. Piper Time.

It was now 4:45 p.m. on December 8th, Japan Time. All except one of the many meetings going on at Minami Kōbe High School were students' meetings–meetings of the badminton club, the kyūdō* club, the computer club, the basketball club, the English Speaking Society club, the volleyball club, and others. The only non-student meeting going on was the teachers' meeting, at which 19 people, including Shannah Pearl and

* Zen-influenced archery. Emphasis is on form rather than accuracy.

Winston Baldry, were present. Shannah and Winston were not invited to regular teachers' meetings because, as Principal Hirota told Shannah when she claimed that they were being discriminated against, they were not regular teachers. They were invited to this meeting because it was a special meeting–the second special meeting called to discuss the problem of bullying. Statistics showed that bullying had, in actuality, slightly declined, but you never would have known it from the way the media were painting the sumi-e.* They were making it out to be something new, when all that was really new was the wave of copycat suicides. Bullying itself was nothing new. The samurai were more or less glorified big bullies who went around violently hammering back in any of the proverbial nails that stuck out, and their spirits were still to this day roaming around Japan and maintaining conventionality. Individualism was frowned upon and was therefore almost non-existent, because the worst thing for Japanese people was to be frowned upon. Groupism was stamped onto Japanese people's minds like their hankost were stamped onto their documents. Confucius still had Japan by the balls with his ideas of hierarchical order and was still squeezing tightly. Students, as well as salarymen, had the senior/junior mindset, although some salarymen referred to their co-workers in English as their 'member' and said such things as, "I played golf with my member," which made you wonder just how long their 'member' was.

Shannah and Winston came from a different world, where rank, and whatever degree of respect it carried, was determined more by merit than by age. Shannah Pearl was 23 years old and in her first year of teaching. She was an assistant teacher and, as JET teachers were limited to three-year contracts, a temporary one. From an Oriental point of view, that put her far below Masaharu Ikenouchi, for instance, who was 51 years old with 27 years of teaching experience and was third in seniority at Minami Kōbe High School in addition to being a man. If Shannah Pearl had been Japanese, she never would have stood up to Ikenouchi. Of course, if Shannah Pearl had been Japanese, she would not have been Shannah Pearl. Ikenouchi found out the hard way that Pāru-san did not look at things from an Oriental point of view. When the Kōbe District Public Prosecutors Office brought the sexual harassment charges to light, he cowered into the dark and ended up doing something very Japanese in response to the shame. His wife found him dead in their garden after he had drunk a bottle of pesticide. If this had been any time until just a few years before, when suicidal people often killed their families first to spare them the subsequent shame or hardship, Ikenouchi might have 'spared' his wife before doing himself in. Times were changing.

---

* black-ink style of Chinese painting that became popular in Japan in the 14th century.

† personal seals used as signatures for everything from buying/selling land to borrowing books from the library.

Ikenouchi took his life on December 2nd, the day that Verdy Kawasaki won its second straight J.League soccer championship. More poignantly for the faculty at Minami Kōbe High School, it was the day before the first special meeting was held to discuss the problem of bullying and the upsurge in related suicides. Moroseness (the Big M) was understandably present at that meeting, and the Big M would have taken over if the Big P (Pāru-san) hadn't also been there. Shannah made sure that she got her 'two cents' in, which would have been a fraction less than two yen at the rate of exchange then. Language was of course a problem. Everyone at that meeting, except Shannah and Winston, spoke Japanese and, more or less, or rather less and less, English–with the exception of Kenji Maekawa, who was at the high-intermediate level. With Maekawa translating for her, Shannah stood up to speak several times and racked up thirty minutes of preaching time. Had she been Japanese, her behavior would have been completely shocking. As it was, it was *in*completely shocking. She was a *gaijin,* and it was imperfectly understood that *gaijins* played by different social rules. When in Japan, *gaijins* didn't have to do as Japanese did because the spirits of the samurai were only pounding Japanese that didn't play by the rules. *Gaijins* were allowed to play by different rules because it was imperfectly understood that they were playing in an entirely different game. They couldn't get away with breaking laws because laws were laws. Donovan Wood, for example, broke the law and was now paying the price at the Kōbe Detention Center, where he was forced to sit up straight for hours at a time. Ikenouchi also broke the law, if Shannah wanted to be technical about it–and being technical was the only way for her to be. Part of the reason for her assertiveness at the meeting was to project herself as being unfazed by an undercurrent of opinion that she had driven Ikenouchi to his suicide. Another part of the reason was that being assertive was as natural for her as being *un*assertive was for her 17 Japanese counterparts. She believed that victims of bullying should stand up for their rights and not take any shit, and she said so. Shannah Pearl shot straight from the lip.

Japanese never shot straight from the lip. They never shot straight, period. When it came to shooting, they were shotless. When it came to speaking English, they were scared shotless. That was their biggest problem with English. But even when they spoke Japanese, they didn't speak their minds, for doing so would show what they were thinking. Japanese made an art of hiding what they were thinking. Part of the art was not letting their eyes be the mirrors of their souls. The 'act' wasn't performed to hide their true feelings from foreigners; paradoxically, it was performed to hide their true feelings from their fellow Japanese. That's why they couldn't really communicate amongst themselves. That's why they had big problems in matters where communication was vitally important, such as becoming international. Shannah Pearl wasn't really any more international than they were. In many ways, she was as

American as apple pie, but (and this was a big butt) she certainly communicated.

Winston Baldry could not have been said to be big on communication, unless the less common definition of 'intercourse' was erroneously being used. For the past month, his relationship with Rika had been hot, steamy hot. He had never had sex like this before. He had never even imagined sex like this before. If what he used to have once every week or two with Wallis for 13 years was sex, then this was something else. This was hot and heavy, and this was wild. Sex in the afternoon was one thing, but on the kitchen floor—well, that was quite another. He and Wallis never even had sex on the *bedroom* floor. It was always 'had' in bed, always with the lights off, occasionally in the morning, never in the afternoon. With Rika, he was finally able to slip out of the cell in which he had been incarcerated by the Christian influence within his western culture. Perhaps the best thing for Japanese people about the Tokugawa shoguns closing the doors during the Edo Period (1600-1868) was keeping the Puritans and their notions about sex out. There was nothing, absolutely nothing, dirty about sex to Japanese. It was something to be thoroughly enjoyed, and that was that. Comesequently, they didn't have the hangups and the inhibitions. That's why Japanese women were so orgasmic, and that is why, when it came to sex, they were in a league of their own. Japanese men were too often too tired and stressed out from making great cars and great electronic products to make great love, and their wives were generally as disappointed with the men's performances in bed as they were with their performances *out* of bed. So far, Rika was ecstatically satisfied with the big-league performance of Winston, who was wondering how long he could continue performing at that level before his pecker fell off. Rika was pumping him full of testosterone and bringing out the animal in him that he didn't even know was in there. He couldn't help wondering if the Hanshin Tigers baseball cap was his 'Samson's hair'. In any case, he no longer needed Rika's entreaties that he wear the cap during the 'ball game'. In fact, he had been greeting her at the door with it on and thereby giving her an instant shot of Love Potion Number 44 (44 being the number worn by her hero, Randy Bass) and putting her in the mood to 'play ball' as soon as she stepped inside the door. Randy Bass had 134 RBIs (runs batted in) in his stellar season; Winston Baldry, in *his* stellar season, was going at a torrid pace with OBIs (orgasms batted in). He was delivering like he'd never delivered before and like he knew he'd never deliver again, but delivering to Rika was as easy as one, two, three—and those weren't strikes. Her baseball-related cries 'hōmuran' and 'gurandosaramu', and their obvious connection with the baseball cap he wore while 'at bat', seemed like some sort of perversion, but he didn't care. If that cap was doing the trick, then fine. He still hadn't figured out what her most frequent cry 'basu' meant, and she wouldn't tell him. Junko Teratani told him that 'basu' could be the Japanese pronunciation for either 'bus' or 'bath', but neither of those seemed to make any baseball sense. What had been going on for the past month didn't seem to make *any* kind of sense. Sense stayed away from intense heat. In such a heat wave, sense was nowhere in the ball park. Winston and Rika were on fire and needed to be hosed down.

Shannah Pearl needed to be hosed down (or blasted with water balloons) at this second special meeting. She suspected that Maekawa watered down what she said at the first special meeting, and of course he did. So for this, the second special meeting, she came equipped with a written Japanese translation in Roman letters that was translated for her by an Americanized Japanese woman she knew who had lived in America for a few years and spoke good English. It took Pāru-san twenty minutes to read her discourse over the sound of hotrodders going back and forth on the street outside the school. There were six of them, and they were speeding on meta-amphetamines as well as on 400cc motorcycles. To make herself heard over the obnoxious noise of the motorcycles, Shannah had to speak more loudly than usual, and she usually spoke loudly. She said that everybody was to blame—the bullies for being bullies, the victims for being mentally weak, the parents of the bullies and the parents of the victims for being bad parents, and the teachers for being unaware of the problem, not doing anything about it, or being an active part of it. Once again, the Japanese people present gave no inkling about what they were thinking but were shocked. In fact, they were appalled. The reason that so many corporate executives paid off sōkaiya* was because they were so afraid of their shareholders' meetings not going smoothly. Pāru-san was behaving like a *sōkaiya* from a Japanese point of view, and Principle Hirota would have gladly paid her off to sit down and shut up. But Shannah wasn't going to sit down and shut up until she had finished saying everything she had to say, and everything she had to say went beyond the issue of bullying to the issue of the suspension of 17-year-old Fumi Ōmura for her second infraction of the dress code, which specifically stated, among many other things, that underwear must be white. Pāru-san argued that the stringent dress code, over and above the school-uniform requirement, was a denial of the right of freedom of expression and an obstruction to the development of individualism, and she called the underwear checks a throwback to militaristic regimentation.

Winston had no idea what she was saying because she was saying it in Japanese. As far as he was concerned, which wasn't very far, she was just making noise, like the hotrodders outside who had opened the school gate and were now hotrodding around the school grounds on their Kawasaki Zephers, the motorcycle of choice for younger hotrodders, with the older hotrodders still preferring the old Honda CBXs. Miyajima-san, the gateman and caretaker, had gone home for the day.

---

* racketeers who hold a minimum number of shares in a company or corporation and extort money by threatening to disrupt shareholders' meetings. In decline after the revision of the Commercial Code in 1982, there were still about 1,200 in 1994.

The three office ladies still there, one of whom was Rika Koga, were not in decision-making positions and therefore didn't do anything. The leader of the hotrodders was Masato Ishikawa, an 18-year-old ruffian from a more permissive high school at which he was a truant. The son of a *yakuza* in the Yamaguchi-gumi syndicate, Masato happened to be the boyfriend of Fumi Ōmura, the girl suspended from Minami Kōbe High School for wearing pink panties in violation of the dress code. Like his five hotrodding companions and virtually all truants, Masato was a chapatsu.* Winston wasn't in the mood to hear Shannah rambling on in Japanese at this meeting any more than he was in the mood to listen to her rambling on in English at the previous meeting. In fact, he was much less in the mood because of the nonsense that Rika had laid on him. The day before, there was a note from Rika in his drawer that said, "I think I and Winston-san maked a baby." Winston knew a little bit about making a baby because he and Wallis had tried earnestly to make one. He knew, for instance, that it took at least six weeks after sex to ascertain if a woman is pregnant. As it had been only one month since he and Rika had sex for the first time, exactly one month to be exact, what in the hell was she doing sounding the alarm? So she was about ten days late for her period and was always, so she said, very regular—so what? That didn't mean anything. How could it, when he and Wallis had tried everything and didn't have any luck? He shot blanks—that's the way their doctor put it. So Rika *couldn't* be pregnant. Stranger things had happened, though, and strangeness was already in the picture with the self-shocking sexual performance of Winston 'Bull' Baldry, Taurus of Corvallis. Could his spermatozoa have suddenly become able to put down their heads and charge? Were they having a career month with all of them wearing little baseball caps? It was only at Rika's insistence that he started using condoms, and he didn't see any need to worry on the five occasions when those too-tight Japanese condoms broke and all he had on were the rims. With or without condoms, he probably came inside her ten times. But so what? His sperm was too weak. So why was she bothering him with this ridiculous talk about *maybe* being pregnant? There were no maybes about it! He had gotten up on the wrong side of the *futon* that morning. Ordinarily, he didn't speak up at meetings. His presence was hardly ever known, much less heard. The only thing he said at the previous meeting was that he was sorry to disappoint them but he wasn't going to grow his beard back to play Santa Claus at the school Christmas party slated for December 20th, an idea first suggested by Rika. He did, however, agree to play Santa Claus at the party with a fake beard. Sitting there now, he didn't feel like letting out a jolly 'Ho ho ho'. He felt more like letting loose with a rotten tomato and yelling, "Take that, Shannah!" So he spoke up.

"Shannah, that may all be fine and well, but—"

"But what?"

---

* literally 'brown hair', but used to refer to young people who dye their hair brown.

"What are you trying to prove?"

"I'm expressing my opinion?"

"Why don't you express it somewhere else so we can get this meeting over with?"

"Oh, I get it. You don't care about making the world better; you just want to go home and hide in your hole. So why don't you? Go ahead and leave."

"I will."

And he did. He shut the door behind him and went into the teachers' lounge to get his winter coat. It hadn't snowed yet and wouldn't for a while, but it was definitely winter-coat weather. People were keeping a supply of oil to pump into their room heaters. Yakiimo* trucks were cruising around slowly with their rhythmical recording ("Yakiimo, yakiimo, yakiimo . . .") coming from loud speakers. Hot-pot dishes, like oden,† were often on dinner tables. Year-end parties were already going on. (There would be no year-end party at Minami Kōbe High School this year because of the death of Ikenouchi-san.) The coming year, 1995, would be the Year of the Wild Boar in the eto,‡ so many people were putting a cute drawing of a wild boar on the New Year's cards they would be sending out. The number of New Year's cards people sent out depended upon their social positions, which meant that wives of guys in high social positions had to spend a lot more time addressing and signing the cards because that job was the women's job. Chie Wood, for instance, sent out 600 New Year's cards at the end of 1993 (the Year of the Chicken) for *this* year, 1994 (the Year of the Dog), because of the high standing of her husband, who was born in the Year of the Rat. Winston Baldry was planning to send out only about ten Christmas/New Year's cards and perhaps some calendars showing Japanese gardens, Japanese temples, or something else Japanesey. He had already received about thirty rolled-up promotional calendars from various businesses and would soon have so many that he would be able to wallpaper his entire house and thereby increase the insulation. On a sunny winter day, it was colder inside a traditional Japanese house than outside it. Winston had been wearing a stocking hat inside his house when he wasn't wearing his Hanshin Tigers baseball cap (during which time he usually wasn't wearing anything else). When Rika wasn't there, he wore thermal long underwear, heavy wool socks, a sweat suit, and a robe. Maekawa had recommended going to Bali during the winter break from December 23rd to January 8th, and he was seriously thinking about going.

---

* baked sweet potatoes.

† hotchpotch of Japanese radishes, eggs, fish cakes, potatoes, and devil's root.

‡ ancient, cyclical Chinese zodiacal system involving twelve animals, which are in the following order: rat, cow, tiger, rabbit, dragon, snake, horse, sheep, monkey, chicken, dog, and wild boar.

Winston had also become cold personality-wise. Even when he wasn't listening to alpha music on his Walkman, he kept the headphones on to make people think that he *was* listening to music. He didn't want people coming up and talking to him, whether they wanted to practice their English or not. When children said 'Haro' to him, he no longer said 'Hello' back because he knew that they would then laugh about it with their friends, and they were always with their friends because they would never say 'Haro' or anything else to a *gaijin* if they were alone. It was much more like harassment than a greeting, and he'd had enough of it. He'd had enough of Japan in general and was already counting the days until he'd go back home to Corvallis. The hotrodders roared past the window of the teachers' lounge while he was putting on his coat and muffler. Habitually checking his teacher's drawer, he found a draft of a speech in a plastic binder that Yū Yanagisawa, a third-year student, was going to give on January 14th at a speech contest sponsored by the Kansai International Friendship Association. Winston had been helping Yū with his speech, titled "Internationalization is not Westernization", by correcting his grammar and, more importantly, serving as his pronunciation coach so Yū could deliver his memorized five-minute speech with good enough pronunciation to hopefully beat the many other memorizers in what amounted to a memorization contest. A member of the English Speaking Society club at school, Yū elucidated becoming international in his speech by metaphorically referring to a tiny seed that grows into a blossoming plum tree. Winston was reading the sentence 'We must open ourself widely in order to receive deeply the seed' when Rika came into the room.

"Hi, Rika. How are you?"

"How are you? I'm fine, thanks. And you?"

"Not so good. Listen, Rika, I'm leaving Japan after my contract ends in March. I'm only going to be here for 101 more days."

"I wish you were leaving today," blurted Shannah Pearl, who stormed into the room like the 46 samurai (known as the 47 Rōnin) stormed into the home of Kira Yoshinaka in 1703 and killed the high lord in revenge for the death of their lord, Asano Naganori. Winston could have used a samurai sword right there and then because he was definitely at bay. "You've had an attitude ever since you were hailed as a hero and Hirota nominated you for Teacher of the Month," Shannah snapped. Winston made no reply. He put Yū's speech into his knapsack and took out his headphones.

"Are you blaming me for that bastard killing himself?"

"No."

"I didn't force him to drink a bottle of pesticide."

"Nobody's saying you did."

"They're all thinking it."

"Maybe they are, but when did you start caring what anybody thinks?"

"Hey, I'm not here to try to win a popularity contest."

"Obviously not."

"Get a life, Baldry. You're living in a virtual-reality world with your headphones and your alpha music. You've got your head in the sand. I think you're paranoid."

"I don't care what you think, and I don't care to *hear* what you think. Please leave me alone."

"This is the teachers' lounge. I've got a right to be here. If you don't like it, you can leave."

"I will."

And he did. He put his headphones on and switched on his Walkman. With his knapsack on his back, he went out to the reception area and exclaimed "Holy moly!" One of the hotrodders drove his motorcycle right into the school and right up into the lobby. It was Masato Ishikawa. Like his companions revving up their bikes outside the entrance, he had a perforated soft-drink can in his muffler to raise the sound to an ear-splitting level that could have been surpassed only by having a sawed-off muffler. High on paint thinner as well as speeding on meta-amphetamines, he stopped in the middle of the lobby and revved his Kawasaki Zepher up full power. The faculty and many of the students came quickly to see what in the hell was going on and were shocked to see what in the hell was going on. Shannah Pearl knew only one scornful Japanese word and used it. "Baka!" (Fool!) she shouted and then took to her heels because Masato came at her on his bike and chased her around the periphery of the lobby. When he got alongside her, he kicked her into the wall and knocked her down. "Hey, kid, what do you think you're doing?" Winston shouted and likewise took to *his* heels. Everybody else just stood and watched the hoodlum chasing the geography teacher on his 400cc bike because they didn't know what else to do. Masato kicked out at Winston, but lost control of his bike. He hit the wall and went down. "Somebody call the police!" Winston shouted, but none of the spectators, which is what everybody had become, were prepared to make a move to the phones in the office for fear that Masato would set his sights on *them*. Everybody was looking at Principal Hirota because he was first in command, then looking at Vice Principal Mitsuzuka because he was second in command, then looking back at the ruffian, who was back on his feet with his sights re-set on the *gaijin*. One of the big reasons that Japanese are initially off balance with *gaijins* (over and above having English-phobia) is because they find *gaijins* unpredictable. Japanese culture, with its social rules on top of social rules, makes behavior so trite that what's prophetic is often pathetic. To Japanese, *gaijins* are sort of like wild-west cowboys coming into their cozy, little Japanese saloons. Winston Baldry wasn't wearing a Smith and Wesson holster packed with Colt .45 six-shooters; he was wearing Panasonic headphones plugged into a Sony Walkman. *The Lone Ranger Theme Song,* less well known as Rossini's *Willam Tell Overture,* wasn't playing on the Walkman. What was playing was Takashi Toyoda's alpha-wave synthesizer music, which was as inappropriate at the moment as it would have been for Gene Autrey to be singing

Happy Trails To You. In the lobby of Minami Kōbe High School, there was no sign saying 'Happy Trail', and if there had been one, Winston wouldn't have taken it because he wouldn't have seen it. He was focused on the hoodlum, who was not a patron in that cultural saloon and didn't grow up watching cowboy movies starring the likes of John Wayne, Gary Cooper, Alan Ladd, and Audie Murphy. Masato wasn't the least bit off balance about being in this showdown with a *gaijin*. He didn't think twice. He didn't even think once. He just charged. "Calm down," is all Winston had time to say before Masato threw a right roundhouse that only grazed Winston's right earphone because he ducked. Masato went sailing into a notice board that had Christmas decorations on it and a notice about the upcoming Christmas party at which Winston would play Santa Claus. He fell down hard on top of the notice board and cracked two ribs. Winston backed away. He had been in only one fight in his life, when he was 12 years old, and he lost that one. He was no match for this kid. This kid was tough. He *looked* tough. He wore a scowl like Princess Kiko (Kiko-chan) wore a smile. It wouldn't be true to say that he never smiled, but it would be true to say that he smiled about as often as his rebellious girlfriend, Fumi, complied with the dress code by wearing white underwear. Winston's only chance, if he had one, was to keep his cool, because this kid was reckless, but Takashi Toyoda might as well have turned into Ozzy Osbourne. Winston pulled off his knapsack while backing away farther and, because four meters of the five-meter-long cord for the headphones were wrapped up, his Walkman got lifted out of the knapsack. Before he knew it, Masato was back on his feet and charging at him like a raging bull, yelling "Koroshite yaru!" (I'll kill you!) "Somebody call the police!" shouted Shannah Pearl, who would have called the police herself if she had known what to say in addition to what number to call. "How about some help!" 'El Winston' shouted, but he didn't get anyone to come into the ring and play the part of a banderillero. If his Hanshin Tigers baseball cap had been within reach, he would have put it on and put the Samson's Hair Theory to the test. Just trying to keep himself from getting hurt, he crouched into a boxing stance and looked like the great bare-knuckle champion Jim Jeffries or, rather, as Jim Jeffries might have looked if he had fought wearing a muffler draped over a long winter coat and had huge head-phones with a Walkman dangling down behind his back at waist level. The Walkman wasn't just dangling—it was swinging. That distracted Masato like a matador's waving muleta distracts a bull. He missed with another wild roundhouse and slammed headfirst into the doorjamb of the teachers' lounge. He got back up on his feet with a front tooth missing. Blood was streaming down his chin and dripping onto his sweatshirt and onto the floor. Still backing away, Winston finally took off his headphone set and let it (and his Walkman) fall, then took off his muffler and his coat. Nobody expected him to keep taking things off until he was down to a pair of Everlast boxing trunks, but as the 'Corvallis Kid' seemed to be handling himself pretty well in the 'ring', that would have been much less surprising than if he had stripped down to nipple tassels and a G-string. Three days before, Yasuei Yakushiji won a hard-fought split decision over the power-punching Jōichiro 'Ōsaka Joe' Tatsuyoshi in their WBC bantamweight unification fight, but Yakushiji had to do a lot of counterpunching, in addition to a lot of ducking, to win that fight. Masato was already bleeding almost as badly as Tatsuyoshi was, and Winston hadn't yet thrown a punch. A few students at 'ringside' would nevertheless later report that he put on an amazing display of jabs, hooks, and uppercuts. One student would even say that he did the 'Ali Shuffle'. The only shuffling Winston was doing, however, was because he was wearing slippers, which was another disadvantage he had. Masato was wearing hard boots that were good for kicking somebody's teeth in. Seeing his own blood made Masato pause for a moment. During that moment, Winston positioned himself behind the overturned motorcycle that was now silent after having idled for a minute. Masato spat out some blood and charged again with reckless abandon, but he slipped on some blood, stepped on the Walkman, slipped on the muffler, slid on the coat, and tumbled headlong into the motorcycle, hitting his face against the footstep and breaking his nose. Desperate, he reached under the motorcycle seat and grabbed a small knife, the kind with the two-piece cover that flips down into a handle, and he snapped it open. His companions were no longer outside. They left as soon as they saw three police cars show up. Masato saw a policeman rush in and take off his shoes to step into slippers. Brandishing the knife, Masato got the people near the stairs to do like the Red Sea allegedly did for Moses, and he ran up the stairs to the third floor of the three-story building.

Some of the club meetings that had been in progress on the third floor were still in progress because the members couldn't tell the difference between the noise coming from outside and the noise coming from down in the lobby. The members of the kendō* club, for instance, were still doing their thing in room 304. Two members, Kazunari Anai and Haruo Takenaka, were in full *kendō* gear with their men† on. They were practicing their footwork for a jumping attack. Kazunari had a shinai‡ with a long handle-grip because he was better at in-close attacking, whereas Haruo's *shinai* had a shorter handle-grip because he was better at outside attacking. While two policemen in slippers were systematically checking the rooms on the second floor, Masato burst into the sweat-smelling room with knife in hand. All he wanted to do was get to the window and jump out, but none of the *kendō* club members knew that. Kazunari happened to be standing between Masato and the window. He

---

* Zen-influenced style of fencing based on samurai swordfighting. The sport consists of ten grades.

† kendō headgear.

‡ kendō sword. Made of four sections of bamboo, its length and weight are determined by one's age rather than one's size.

reacted by swinging his *shinai* up with both hands on the handle-grip and then swinging it down on top of Masato's head with the yell *'Men!'* As Masato wasn't wearing a *men,* or any other headgear, it would have been more appropriate if Kazunari had yelled 'Atama!' (Head!) Feeling an awful knotting of what was going to be an awfully big knot, Masato lashed at Kazunari and slashed his kote.* Haruo swung his shinai down on Masato's knife-hand with 'Kote!' instead of 'Te!' (Hand!) and fractured the hapless hoodlum's wrist, knocking the knife out of his hand. Not wanting to stay long enough for Kazunari to swing his *shinai* down again and turn this into a version of *kendō* Ping Pong, Masato picked up the knife with his good left hand and dashed out of the room and into the next room, room 305, which had a sign saying 'ESS' on the outside of the door.

All 16 members of the English Speaking Society were present for their weekly meeting, which meant that they had, as they would have said, 'full member'. That was one of many Japanese-English (Japlish) expressions that made the users think they were speaking English when, in fact, they were speaking Japanese. Yū Yanagisawa, the kid that Winston had been helping for the speech contest, was one of the 'full member' and one of only two boys in the ESS club. High-school students interested in studying the international language were mostly and foremostly girls. Boys were by and large (and by and small) in boys' clubs, i.e. sports clubs, if they weren't clubless (but groupful) cigarette-smoking *chapatsus.* Boys in ESS clubs were generally considered sissies and deserving of being dealt with like the evil sorcerer Jafar dealt with Aladdin in the then very popular Disney animated movie *Aladdin,* which the ESS club did a rendition of six weeks before at the school culture festival with Yū playing Aladdin, despite the fact that he looked like a monkey and was therefore better suited to play Aladdin's pet monkey, Abu.

The ESS club's usual props and posters were set up or taped up to show English words for parts of the body, articles of clothing, fruits and vegetables, animals, colors, countries, and so on. There was a big cardboard prop of Big Bird, as *Sesame Street* was very popular in Japan with children and many ESS members. Several *Sesame Street* books were in a big box with other children's books, such as those of Dr. Seuss. The *New Horizon* series, popular with Japanese English teachers, was there, along with many of the old and older textbooks (updated with colored photos) that were popular with *gaijin* English teachers: *Expressways, East-West, Streamline, Interchange, Side by Side, Coast to Coast, Person to Person,* and *On Course.* A shoe box was full of cassette tapes to help them with their listening comprehension. The tape for Book One of the *Side by Side* series by Molinsky & Bliss (two of the most famous English-textbook people, along with

---

* kendō gloves, which extend up to the forearms.

Hartley & Viney, Helgesen, and Richards) was in a Sony tape player that had a counter on it. The leader of the ESS club, third-year student Kumiyo Iwami, was operating the tape player while the other 15 students were listening to check their listening comprehension. It was the Reading Section at the end of Part 3, and it was going peacefully like this:

The Jones family is in the park today. The sun is shining and the birds are singing. It's a beautiful day!

Mr. Jones is reading the newspaper. Mrs. Jones is listening to the radio. Sally and Patty Jones are studying. And Tommy Jones is playing the guitar.

The Jones family is very happy today. It's a beautiful day and they're in the park.

It was right then that battered and bloodied Masato stormed into the 'park' wielding his knife. Everybody froze. Mr. Jones stopped reading the newspaper. Mrs. Jones stopped listening to the radio. Sally and Patty Jones stopped studying. Tommy Jones stopped playing the guitar. The birds stopped singing. The sun stopped shining. It was no longer a beautiful day. It was a frightful day. Masato hated every subject in school, but he hated English the mostest. For him, it was the worstest. So this was just as much of a nightmare for him as it was for the ESS members and the Joneses. He put his hands to his throbbing head like it was going to implode. All around him was English, English, and more English, and it was all Greek to him. The tape was still rolling, but the location had changed from "In the Park" to "In the Yard", and now it was not the Joneses but the Smiths.

The Smith family is at home in the yard today. The sun is shining and the birds are singing. It's a beautiful day!

Mr. Smith is planting flowers. Mrs. Smith is drinking lemonade and reading a book. Mary and Billy Smith are playing with the dog. And Sam Smith is sleeping.

Masato looked as terrified as the woman on the bridge in Edvard Munch's painting *The Scream*. He let out a scream that Edgar Allan Poe would have found inspiring. He slashed Big Bird on his way to the tape player. (The Smith family is very happy today.) He grabbed the tape player with both hands (It's a beautiful day and they're at home in the yard.) and flung it with a running start and all of his might at the window that ceased to be a window any longer. He kicked out the remaining pieces of glass at the bottom and punched out the pieces at the top. Then he jumped up onto the window sill and looked down. One of the police cars was parked twenty feet below. The tape player was lying on the far side of the police car, and Sam Jones would have had to have been in a coma to still be sleeping. "Tomare!" (Stop!) shouted a policeman who came into the room. Masato jumped . . . and landed on his feet on top of the police car, but then fell backward onto the long, cylindrical, red light and broke his back. Unable to move, he lay paralyzed on top of the police car and was taken that way very slowly, with the red light flashing, to the wild, black-and-blue yonder, where there was a hospital.

The Southern Cross was beaming in a star-studded sky. Waves were washing in so calmly that the loudest sound was a soft crackling of little stones rolling together on the shoreline. He was all alone on the beach as far as his eyes could see, except for somebody about seventy yards away who was sleeping or perhaps passed out. Quite a few tourists had done more than their fair share of New Year's Eve partying. Many of them, especially a group of Britons, were drunkenly out and loudly about with their party horns and bottle rockets until 1:30 or 2:00. Shortly after he was finally able to fall asleep, he was awakened by loud love-making of two German lesbians in the next bungalow. They were really going at it, and they kept really going at it. Assuming that it would be a while before it was quiet enough to go back to sleep, he slipped out from under his mosquito net and went outside barefooted, wearing only boxer shorts and a T-shirt. His bungalow was about fifty yards from the water— just a hop, skip, and a splashing jump. It wasn't as easy as that one two wet three, however, because of the stoniness of the black sand of Lovi-na Beach. Winston had taken Maekawa's advice after all. On December 23rd, a national holiday because it was the emperor's birthday, he took an eight-hour flight on Garuda airlines, only the second flight of his life, and disembarked with his Samsonite suitcase in Denpasar, Bali. Sitting there on the beach at three o'clock in the morning, he was amazed at how many stars he could see. He couldn't remember seeing any stars in Japan. Perhaps it was because he never looked up, or perhaps he never looked up because there was nothing to see. There was too much light pollution. 90% of Japan's 125 million people were packed into areas totaling 10% of the country's surface area. Those neatly packed people didn't see the light pollution any more than they saw the air pollution. When you're in it, you're deep in it; when you're out of it, you're way out of it. Winston was way out of it. He was 3,500 miles out of Japan, but that still didn't seem far enough away from Rika Koga.

How it happened was a mystery. He and Wallis had given it his best shot, but his best shot wasn't any good because he shot blanks. Was he to believe that he now shot live bullets? Well, he certainly seemed to have a new gun or, to use a more appropriate metaphor, a new baseball bat. Babe Baldry, the Louisville Slugger, was told in no uncertain terms on December 20th that a urine test confirmed that he had driven in a baby and there was absolutely no doubt about him being the father because she hadn't had sex with anybody else. OK OK—so his 'Rawlings' balls had somehow gotten some sort of shock treatment and now produced a higher count of spermatozoa that could swim well and maybe even do the butterfly. OK OK—so he'd gotten her pregnant. If 'her' had been Wallis, he would have called for a celebration. As it was, he called for an abortion. Rika was not against having an abortion per se. She was pro-choice in a land where the pro-choicers didn't have to be united because abortion wasn't even an issue. Japan had the lowest birthrate in the world, and a major reason for that was that it had the world's highest abortion rate. As many as two million abortions were performed a year. There would have been a lot fewer if birth-control pills were available, but the Pill was banned by the Health and Welfare Ministry because the ministry, especially its Central Pharmaceutical Affairs Council, functioned for the health and welfare of the Japan Medical Association and its legions of doctors who made small fortunes performing abortions. Rika knew that Winston was not going to marry her because he made that as clear as Commodore Matthew Perry made it when he arrived with his 'friendly' armada of black ships in 1853 to 'negotiate' a treaty of commercial friendship. 99% of Japanese women in Rika's position would have gone ahead and had an abortion, but Rika wanted to wait a few more weeks to make her decision because in a few more weeks it could be known whether it was a boy or a girl. It all boiled down to the gender factor. If it was a girl, she would go ahead and have an abortion, but if it was a boy, she would not. It had nothing to do with Confucianism; it had everything to do with Bassism. If it was a boy, she would name him Randy, Randy Koga, and raise him to become a power-hitting, left-handed-batting first baseman for the Hanshin Tigers. And if her dream would not come true and he should happen to become a blatant homosexual with a preference for classical ballet–well, perish the thought! All Winston could do was hope that it was a girl and then spend the rest of his life feeling guilty about the abortion, which he figured was better than spending the rest of his life feeling guilty about being a neglectful father to his son Randy.

It was at the Christmas party at Minami Kōbe High School on December 22nd that Winston finally figured out the Randy Bass connection. Dressed up as Santa Claus, fake beard and all, he was approached by the science teacher, Fujita-san, who said, "Bāsu ni nita iru ne" (You look like Bass) and answered Winston as best he could in English when Winston asked, "What is basu?" So he had been just a medium through which Rika had been having sex with her baseball idol. That was all fine even if it wasn't all well, but he felt foolish for having been conned into wearing that Hanshin Tigers baseball cap during sex. After being enlightened by Fujita-san, he felt like taking Rika over his red trousers and giving her a whacking with his black Santa Claus belt for being so whacky. He couldn't get out of Japan and away from her perverse fixation fast enough. He would have left sooner if he hadn't promised to play Santa Claus at the Christmas party, for he was suspended from teaching on December 12th, pending a police investigation of the fight he had with Masato Ishikawa. The authorities found it hard to believe that Winston's fighting was purely defensive, as Masato ended up with a broken nose, a black eye, a detached retina, a cut below his eye requiring 16 stitches, a fat lip, a knocked-out tooth, a concussion, a separated shoulder, a broken wrist, two broken ribs, and a broken back. The broken back and perhaps a couple of other injuries were attributed to the fall onto the police car, but that still left quite a few unexplained attributions. The *kendōists* in the *kendō* club didn't want to admit inflicting any of the injuries because *kendō* was a Zen-influenced gentleman's sport and certainly not a sport in which you struck someone not wearing protective wear. Contradictory accounts instilled doubt in Winston's claim that he did nothing more than duck and sidestep. Many people affirmed Winston's claim, but there were too many conflicting reports to give it credence. Shannah Pearl's affirmation didn't carry any weight because it was just a case of one *gaijin* supporting another. Second-year student Teruo Nonaka, who was the one who said that Winston did the Ali Shuffle, was joined by several boys in saying that Winston put on a boxing clinic and should have been a pro. A few boys even wanted to start a boxing club with Winston as their coach. The media painted the already-famous Winston Baldry pugilistically and bullyistically by running headlines like ウインストン、生徒をノックアウト (Winston KOs Student) and ボールドリー教諭、18歳の少年に重傷を負わせる (Teacher Baldry Maims 18-year-old Student). The Juvenile Law prohibited the publication of Masato Ishikawa's name because he was a minor charged with a crime—the crime being trespassing. There was no law prohibiting the publication of Winston Baldry's name, though, and his name became mud. Some reports made him seem to be just one step below serial murderer Tsutomu Miyazaki, who brutally murdered four girls in 1988 and 1989. Under pressure from the Ministry of Education, Principal Hirota, who supported Winston's contention that he did nothing more than duck and sidestep (but admitted when pressed that he couldn't be absolutely sure because the action was so fast and furious), felt he had no other choice than to suspend Winston temporarily until his name was unmuddified and he was cleared of any wrongdoing. Previous allegations about drugs were rehashed and rehashished along with an alleged connection to the Kuramoto-gumi criminal syndicate. The alleged *yakuza* connection probably saved Winston's life because Masato Ishikawa's father, Kōichi Ishikawa, was a member of the Yamaguchi-gumi, making Winston and Kōichi sort of like brothers.

Japan felt so far away, not just in terms of distance. A lot had to do with the pace and the way it seems to affect one's perception of time. Balinese time seemed to pass much more slowly than Japanese time. There was nowhere in the world where time seemed to pass as fast as it did in Japan. This isn't true for tourists visiting Japan because of the uniqueness of the Japan Experience. It usually takes about three months for the novelty to wear off, as foreign English teachers find out. Then they're either high on Japan or down on Japan, with being down on Japan far and away the norm. People who stay high on Japan still get out and about and have the kinds of experiences that put markers in their memories, but people who get down on Japan burrow in with their negativity and, when it's finally all over, their Japan Experience is mainly and yenly a big blur. Japanese were neither high nor down on Japan, but they might as well have been down on it for the amount of new experiences they had. They lived according to the book, so their lives didn't make for good reading. The formula-stories of their lives were pagey because of the longevity factor, but most of the pages were empty and almost all of the footnotes were Ibid. Young people would be old before they knew it, and then perhaps they'd really know it. Buddhist timelessness had been consumed by consumerism. Nirvana would have been a suitable name for a shopping paradise like Tōkyō's Akihabara or Waikiki's Kalakaua Avenue. Japanese were economic animals through and through, all of the way down to their brand-name souls. Zen Buddhism was still deep down in their culture but nowhere in their cerebrums. The lights had gone out on enlightenment because it didn't have anything to do with the materialism that went shopping-bag-holding hand in shopping-bag-holding hand with the miraculous economic prosperity. Zen was out; Yen was in. Everything had a price tag. Japanese were on the move and the pace was fast. They couldn't slow down because they didn't know how to slow down. The only kind of kōan* they could have focused on would have been something like 'What is the sound of one mobile phone ringing?' Buddha might as well have been the name of a car–a Toyota Buddha or a Nissan Buddha–with a Navigator pointing the way on that one-lane fast-lane they were speedliving on. If Buddha had been brought up in this society as a shinjinrui,† he might not have turned around and gone against the flow. He might have been a frequent rider on the bullet train, sitting there in a smoking car in a blue salaryman's suit, talking on a mobile phone with his appointment book open and an eye on the clock. Japanese lived by their Casio and Citizen clocks that had them running up and down escalators and pushing the CLOSE button inside elevators so the automatic door would close one second sooner. Time was money. Money was flowing. Time was flying.

Winston had been in that rat race for four and a half months. It probably would have taken him about that long to completely unwind. This was certainly better than nothing, though. It was his ninth night in Bali. He spent one night in Ubud at a place on Monkey Forest Road, then took a bemo‡ north to Lovina Beach, where he had been wiling away the days doing a pretty good imitation of a zombie–just sitting in a bamboo chair on his tiled front porch and staring out at the sea. His bungalow was in a new complex of bungalows in Kalibukbuk that had a big lawn and enough enclosure to keep away the massage ladies and the guys hawking dolphin-spotting trips. It cost him US$23 a day to stay there. Actually, it cost him 50,000 rupiahs a day, but he was still thinking in terms of American dollars–that is, when he was thinking at all. His brain was still frazzled from going haywire on the day after he arrived at

---

* puzzling question for Zen Buddhist trainees to reflect upon.

† literally 'new humans', but used to refer to the young people that grew up in prosperity and were on the shallow side of a huge generation gap.

‡ Indonesian mini-bus.

Lovina Beach. It was December 25th, Christmas Day. He went out for breakfast and, feeling like an omelette–that is, feeling like eating one–ordered an omelette from the menu that was listed as Magic Mushroom Omelette. He knew that magic mushrooms, more technically known as psilocybin, are hallucinogenic mushrooms, but he figured that the 'Magic' of Magic Mushroom Omelette was like the 'Super' of Super Submarine Sandwich. Not for one second did he consider the possibility that the Magic Mushroom Omelette might be filled with what Balinese called oong.* He was back at his bungalow, back in his bamboo chair, back staring out at the sea when he was suddenly struck by the way the clouds were making sunlight sweep back and forth across the lawn and by the many different shades of green in the grass, the bushes, and the trees. He felt charged with energy. His senses were heightened. His mind was activated. All of a sudden, he was in GRIN MODE. He was thinking about Donovan Wood's big charade and he couldn't stop grinning. The plight of 'Professor' Wood was too much! Unable to contain himself, he went into his bungalow and exploded into laughter. He dropped down to his knees, laughing his ass off. Holding his stomach, he rolled around on the floor and howled until a bluish swallowtail butterfly that had followed him inside caught his attention because it was leaving trails of blue as it fluttered (and buttered) about. Things were getting wierd. Something was very wrong. His heart was racing; he could feel it pounding. He thought that he was having a heart attack, and that's exactly what he told the Dutch couple staying at the next bungalow then. Emergency cries for help caused a scene that continued as Winston, now talking to God (who was talking back to him), was carried out to the road and laid on a straw mat in the back of a *bemo* that sped off to make the ten-kilometer trip to the main hospital in Singaraja. The driver made a quick stop at a warung† on the way to the hospital to buy some Garam cigarettes, and when he got back to the *bemo,* his 'dying' passenger was gone. Overcome with paranoia, Winston ran inland on a narrow road past thatched-roof houses and then rice fields. A mangy barking dog sent him headlong off on a path and into a forest. He climbed a banyan tree and was soon joined by several macaque monkeys. Although they're fairly big, macaques are basically harmless, unless they get angry for some reason, such as somebody being in their territory. Still, Winston's encroachment would have been tolerated if they hadn't smelled fear in this unTarzan of a person that was up in one of their trees and fearfully going up higher. Before long, he was too far out on a limb. The branch broke and he fell to the ground. A hard hit on the head knocked him unconscious. A large group of macaques took

---

* The magic mushrooms grow during the rainy season, which is from October to March.

† simple Indonesian eatery.

turns pissing on him until he was found by an old woman cutting down coconuts.

Winston still had a bump on his head from the fall from the tree seven days before, but he no longer needed the crutch he had used because of a sprained ankle. He lay down on his back in the black sand and put his hands under his head. There were so many stars that it would have been scary for someone who had never been far enough away from light pollution. Aside from the twinkling lights of the stars and the faint light of a fishing boat, there were no lights at all. It was so peaceful, and so very quiet. The only thing he could hear was the soft rolling of the stones. It sure was nice to be out of Japan with its incessant train announcements both on and off the trains, ubiquitous muzak in shops and stores, grocery-store guys shouting out for your attention like they had stalls out on the street, ladies in campaign trucks saying the candidates' names over and over, campaigners with microphones giving speeches, collection-basket groups outside train stations yelling their never-ending 'Onegaishimasu' (Please), right-wingers' trucks blasting fascistic fanaticism in the hearts of cities, newspaper-collection trucks cruising around side streets early in the morning with their loudspeakers blaring their repetitive recordings, automatic beep-beep-beeps of trucks backing up, tour-guide girls blowing whistles while the tour buses are backing up, continuous recordings of "Migi ni magarimasu/Hidari ni magarimasu" (Turning right/Turning left) of trucks waiting to turn, beeping of traffic signals that have turned green, hotrodders roaring around late at night and in the wee hours of the morning, slow-moving *yakiimo* trucks with loud speakers bellowing out the taped 'Yakiimo', people on old bicycles applying squeaky brakes that should have been oiled years ago, mobile phones ringing and people talking loudly on them no matter where they are, coffee-shop people yelling "Irasshai" (Welcome) and "Arigatō gozaimashita" (Thank you) when customers come and go, school children and boisterous drunks on trains, spoiled children shouting and jumping on train seats and restaurant chairs, clanking coming from pachinko parlors, people showing up at your *genkan* and hollering "Suimasen", piano-playing of next-door neighbors whose telephones you could even hear ringing because of the rabbit-hutch houses, stray cats in heat that sound like babies crying, and the barking of nervous dogs kept in much-too-small pens. On January 8th, he'd be going back to the noise pollution of Japan, but until then he'd keep on basking in the peacefulness.

He had been going to the bungalow-complex's restaurant for a fruit-salad breakfast and a nasi-goreng* lunch. The rest of the day, he had been sitting in his bamboo chair on his tiled front porch until just before dusk, mosquito time, when he put on socks and long pants and headed out to drink large Bintang beers at a couple of little outdoor seaside

---

* Indonesian fried rice.

cafés from where he could watch sunsets that threw color all of the way across to the other side of the sky. A shooting star shot by Omega Centauri. He sat up and brushed away the sand on his back. With a stone, he wrote the initials WC in the sand between his legs. Clarke was Wallis's maiden name. Was she the only one for him? It was common to think such thoughts, but also ridiculous. Even if she were one in a million, which she realistically wasn't, there would be thousands of others. The Japanese expression 'Hoshi no kazu hodo onna wa irun da' (There are as many women as there are stars) is often expressed in English as 'There are many fish in the sea'. There were probably thousands of starry (and maybe even fishy) Japanese ladies that Winston could have been happy with. There may have been hundreds in Kōbe alone. But Rika Koga wasn't one of them.

Out in the water, ten or twelve feet from him, was a dead fish. At least he thought it was a dead fish. He'd seen quite a few dead fish in the past week, some floating in the water, most washed up on the sand. He tossed stones at it mindlessly. Finally, he hit it and heard a sound that cast doubt about it being a fish, unless it was a kind of fish that could have been appropriately named 'clangfish'. He stood up and took a few tentative steps out as the tide was on the ebb. When the tide washed in over his ankles, he saw that it was a bottle. "Oh, it's just a bottle," he said to himself. He turned around to go back but decided to do the environmentally-friendly thing and take it out of the water. Doing so, he saw that there was something inside it. He took it back to his bungalow. The lesbians had stopped going at it and were now quiet. He turned on the light. There was a folded piece of yellowish paper inside the bottle. He twisted off the cap and used a pen to pull out the paper. It was slightly torn in a couple of places, so he unfolded it carefully. Then he read what was written on it: "This is a chain-message in a bottle, started on July 22nd, 1982 by Wallis Baldry of 633 Sunnyside Street in Corvallis, Oregon, USA, wishing whosoever may find it happiness. If you wish to participate, please contact the last person on the list and also the person who lives farthest away from where you live. Then add your name to the list, put it back into the bottle, being sure that the cork seals it well, and throw it back into the sea."

He felt weak. He had to sit down. This couldn't be happening. Things like this don't happen. What were the chances? Somebody must be playing a joke on him. But how could anyone have known that he would be out there at the exact time that he *was* out there? Besides, he knew Wallis's handwriting and this was definitely Wallis's handwriting. Could he be dreaming? Well, he didn't need to pinch himself, not with so many mosquitos about. Perhaps he was having a delayed after-effect of the magic mushrooms he ate a week before. Perhaps he was going to start tripping his brains out again. Perish *that* thought! A few mosquito bites later, he was back under his mosquito net. He sat there stunned with the letter before him. He tried to think, which wasn't easy. The last thing he knew, the bottle was on the southwestern coast of Australia. Currents of the Indian Ocean would have naturally taken it north. It couldn't have gotten swept east through the Timor Sea because it would have kept going east, probably through the Torres Strait, and then back down along the eastern coast of Australia. So it must have gotten swept west and then gotten taken by a crosscurrent that sent it between either Sumatra and Java or Java and Bali. He sat there for almost an hour trying to make sense of what had happened. Unless God, with whom he conversed just a week before, had an almighty hand in this, or unless Wallis was communicating with him from beyond the grave or, rather, beyond where half of her ashes were scattered at Kinkakuji Temple, this had to be the mother, the holy mother, the holy moly mother of all coincidences. The lesbians in the next bungalow deserved a big thank-you (along with a big double-dildo) for getting him to go out there. He slipped back out from under his mosquito net and got a pen and a piece of paper. He jotted down the name and address of the last person on the list (Chelsia Kotkin of Fremantle, Australia) and the name and address of the person who lived fartherst away (Lucrecia Mosquera of Esmeraldas, Equador). Then he added his name and his Corvallis address to the chain-message list. He was going to fulfill Wallis's wishes right now. He folded the paper along its creases, put it back into the bottle, and twisted the cap on tightly. Seconds later, he was outside, carrying the bottle with both hands. He walked straight out into the sea and started swimming when the water was up to his neck. He was very bad at swimming, but he could do the back float and propel himself by kicking his legs. In that way, he went farther and farther out into the Bali Sea until a current carried him out and away and up and down on waves that were getting bigger. All around him was water. All above him were stars. Two shooting stars crisscrossed. He brought the bottle to his lips and kissed it, then let it go. He couldn't tell directions by the stars, but he knew about the oceans' currents. The bottle was heading east, in the direction of New Guinea. He swam alongside it for a while, but got hit by a wave and swallowed water. "Goodbye, Wallis," he shouted and swallowed more water.

Chelsea Kotkin lived near the Swan River in 'Freo', as she and other locals called Fremantle. Some of her friends called her 'Crocodile' Kotkin, which she didn't like. She had been bitten by 'crocs' many times, but never badly enough to need so much as a Band-Aid because all of the 'bites' occurred in the nursery of the Fremantle Crocodile Farm, where she took care of baby crocodiles that could fit in the palm of her hand. She certainly didn't sign her name Chelsea 'Crocodile' Kotkin on the travel articles she wrote as a freelance travel-writer. She had tried Chelsea A. Kotkin, C.A. Kotkin, C. Anne Kotkin, and was now back to Chelsea A. Kotkin, having decided not to try Chelsea Anne K. She had gotten articles published in newspapers and magazines, but they were all small, budget publications and didn't pay much. That's why she worked at the crocodile farm. It was her latest in a long line of jobs, as she had a habit of quitting as soon as she'd saved enough money to travel and get more ideas for travel-writing. Her dream was to become a regular travel-columnist for a big newspaper like the *Sydney Morning Herald* or the *West Australian*. Then she could get travel-allowance in addition to regular pay. But the big newspapers had their own staff-writers doing the travel-writing, so she would first have to carve out a name for herself with big-name magazines, and the glossier the better. She had a large ideas-file and was forever sending query letters to big-league editors, but commissions were seldom given to non-established freelancers for ideas. The best that she could do was submit completed articles, but that required time for traveling, not to mention money. Writers' Project Grants and other grants had been denied to her time and time again. Those denials brought as much disappointment as did the rejection-slips that locked her in obscurity, where she felt she didn't belong, not with her track record of published articles that she kept a running count of (now 16) and was quick to quote. The problem was that her portfolio didn't carry any weight, at least not on the scales of the big players, and if her submissions weren't sent along with an SASE (self-addressed, stamped envelope), they not only registered a big, fat zero, but also ended up in the big, fat editor's big, fat waste basket. Nevertheless, Chelsea believed that it was just a matter of time before she moved up to the big leagues. Freelancing was a tough business, and if you were going to let letdowns let you down, then you'd better get into another business. She wasn't going to give up. She believed that her star was rising. She believed that she was going to be moving up-market. Through all of the writing and re-writing, through all of the searching and researching, through all of the query letters and submissions, through all of the disappointments and frustrations, she still believed. All she had to do, she told herself, was keep on plugging away and keep on gathering ideas. She gathered one idea at Rous Head Harbor on October 25th, when she found a message in a bottle.

Well, it was sort of a travel story. That bottle had done a fair bit of knocking around in the past twelve years. It was found off two oceans, on three continents, and in four countries. Before throwing the bottle back into the sea, Chelsea made photocopies of the chain-message and took many photographs of the bottle, both in and out of water. "A Bottle For All Oceans" is the title she thought might be catchy. Through international directory assistance, she got the number of a Baldry, Winston Baldry, listed at the Corvallis, Oregon address. She made the call and was told by one of the three ladies renting Winston's house that Wallis had died several months before and Winston was presently teaching in Japan. Chelsea was very sad to learn of Wallis Baldry's death because interviewing her was the only way she figured she could get enough information to put together a really good article, especially a really good attention-grabbing beginning. So she put that idea on the back burner and moved to the front burner an idea about snorkeling off Malaysia's Perhentian Islands. Two and a half months later, on January 11th, when the article about snorkeling was on the back burner and she was working on an article about a ride on the Ghan train in Australia, she received a picture-postcard of a Balinese legong dancer from a man who said that he found the chain-message in the bottle, and that man's name was Winston Baldry. Hmm. That name rang a bell. She checked her file about that chain-message story and a lot of bells started ringing. When most of the ringing had stopped, she started thinking. At first, she thought that it was some kind of a joke, but she thought about it some more. The more she thought about it, the more wishful her thinking became, because if it were true, it was big, really big. Maybe this Winston Baldry was vacationing in Bali and happened to find the bottle that his wife threw into the sea off the Oregon coast twelve and a half years before. Stranger things have happened—not many, though. There was only one way to find out if it was true. She made another phone call to Winston Baldry's residence in America and got his phone number in Japan. Upon making the call, she received a "Moshi moshi" (Hello) from the party at the other end, who was none other than Winston Baldry.

Saved by the crew of a small squid boat a mile out in the Sea of Bali at dawn on New Year's Day, Winston was alive and back in Japan. He was back in his massage chair with a bottle of Asahi Super Dry beer when the phone call came from Australia. He told the caller that yes, it was true, that yes, it was really true, that yes, it was really really true, and that no, he wasn't interested in being interviewed. Chelsea didn't hear that No. That is, she didn't really really hear it. She was too excited about this stranger-than-fiction truth. This was one big story. This was her ticket. Her boat had come in. She was going to sail to the top of the journalistic world. She wasn't even going to bother sending query letters. To hell with that! She was going to go and get this story and put it together and let the fat cats fight over it. All they were going to get was First Rights because she was going to retain the right to take it further and much further, further being serialization in big foreign publications and much further being Hollywood. This story had all of the ingredients for a great love story. That's the way she would slant it. A wedding photo of Winston and Wallis was a must, as were a couple of later photos of them happily together. Interviews with Winston were essential. But wait a minute—did he say 'No'? "Did you say 'No'?" she said and went 16 right 16 into her professional 16 background with the 16 track record of 16 published articles and 16 found herself 16 saying, "Hello. Hello. Hello."

Chelsea A. Kotkin wouldn't, couldn't, and knew that, as a professional journalist, she shouldn't take 'No' for an answer. A face-to-face meeting with Winston Baldry was what was needed to turn that 'No' into a 'Yes'. She quit her crocodiley job and spent a couple of days getting some money together. Then she took a flight to Japan.

January 16th was a national holiday in 1995 because the previous day, Coming-of-Age Day, fell on a Sunday. In the past year, 2.06 million people came of age, i.e. turned 20 years old, thereby earning the right to smoke and drink. That wasn't very many, relatively speaking. Japan was an aging society. There were almost as many elderly women with violet hair as there were high-schoolers with brown hair. 15% of the population was now over 65. It was projected that it would reach 32% by 2050. That was going to be a problem from the standpoint (and bedridden point) of taxation. In the 1980s, there was serious talk about dealing with this impending problem in a way that was typically Japanese: export the elderly. It made perfectly good business sense, as less social-security money would be needed for the keep of the 'silver citizens' due to the power of the yen. The plan stopped being seriously talked about because it was seen in the eyes of the world as carrying business a little too far. Japan did not want to be seen in a bad light in the eyes of the world because that would be bad for business. That's why Japan's prime ministers were forever apologizing for insensitive remarks made by cabinet ministers that pissed off foreign countries like China and South Korea and well-established foreign associations like the Jewish lobby and the NAACP that were capable of putting a hole in Japan's pocketbook through a boycott. Japan's 'silver citizens' had no political organization to represent them and demand sensitivity. They could have had greater strength in numbers than Sōka Gakkai,* but all they had was numbers, ever-increasing numbers. Without any political clout, the government didn't see any electoral need to make promises about improving their quality of life. Old people had been sitting on the shelf for too long. That was what made them negligible. They didn't get off the shelf to go shopping. Their only significant contribution to Japan Inc. was purchasing medicines that their doctors handed out to them like candy. Unimportant as consumers, they were unimportant period,

---

* cult-like lay-Buddhist organization. Based on the Nichiren sect, it is led by Daisaku Ikeda (66 years old in 1994), arguably the most powerful man in Japan because of his ability to deliver the electoral votes of the organization's eight million people.

so unimportant that they could be thought of as commodities for exportation. They were the ones whose hard work produced the economic miracle that young people were caught up in, but the young people were essentially saying to them, "Thank you very much for coming in, and be sure to shut the door on your way out." 'Out with the old, in with the young' could have been used as a variation on Setsubun.* Yes, Japan was an aging society, but it was a young people's culture. Youth was packaged like a product and labeled FRESH. Kids were as spoiled rotten as fresh can get. With their trend-following materialism that centered around being kakkoii,† teenagers and young adults constituted a collosal market. In the 1980s, the marketeers targeted college students; in the 1990s, high-school students were also being targeted because many of them too had part-time jobs and were just as fashion-conscious and even more capricious. The 2.06 million people that had come of age in the past year were in the prime of youth and therefore at the heart of the economic matter, and on Valentine's Day and White Day,‡ that was a chocolate heart. The emphasis on youth had a bounceback effect in which people from 15 to 25 were defining the culture. Their values were taking low-culture to astounding depths that had turned The Land of Wa, a country once so rich in culture, into the most superficial society in the history of the world. A big reason that these voracious, young, economic animals had so much money to spend was that they didn't have more than one sibling to share the amount that their mothers could allocate for allowance and their relatives could dish out for otoshidama.§

A very big reason for Japan's world's lowest birthrate was that abortion was so commonplace. Rika Koga put another notch on a doctor's abortion-room wall the day before, January 15th, after finding out that she was carrying a girl. So that matter was taken care of. There wasn't going to be a Randy Koga. Rika would have to live knowing that she would never see 'Randy' hit a sayonara hōmā** and stand on the pedestal for the hero-of-the-game interview. That was going to be tough. She really had her hopes up. Over and above that, actually under and below that, she'd gotten dumped and it hurt. Winston didn't want to hurt

---

* traditional celebration of the coming of spring. Celebrated in the first week of the coldest month (February) because of adherence to the ancient Chinese lunar calendar, people throw soybeans outside their homes at sunset and shout, "Oni wa soto! Fuku wa uchi!" (Out with demons! In with good luck!)

† 'cool' in the teenage sense of the word.

‡ March 14th. One month after Valentine's Day (on which girls and ladies give chocolates to boys and men), White Day is the day for guys to reciprocate.

§ New Year's gift money from parents, grandparents, and other relatives. The collective average in 1995 was ¥27,000.

** game-ending home run.

Rika. She was a little nutty with her fantasy, but there's a little bit of Walter Mitty in all of us. Elvis impersonators are besieged with women wanting to make burning love to the 'King', especially if the lookalikes are good at gyrating their hips and singing *Love Me Tender*. Rika was no nuttier than those nutty women. Randy Bass was *her* king, her King of Swing. Long swing the King! Winston Baldry wasn't well-hung, but he was well-swung, whatever *that* meant. Who knew what anything meant in this farcical fiasco? It had been a wild roller coaster ride. But now that ride was over, and Winston wasn't going to give Rika the ticket for another ride. He offered to fork out the ¥70,000 for the abortion, but she didn't want his money. What she wanted were his genitals. She wouldn't have minded being left high and dry, but it was tough being left low and wet. The heart of the matter was not her heart at all but her clitoris. With time, she would come to appreciate what she'd had, but right now she was very unappreciative. She threw the ¥35,000 in Winston's face when he insisted that they at least 'go Dutch'. It had been an emotional, trying couple of days for both of them, and it was going to continue being awkward seeing each other at school. Rika was scorned. But that was Rika's problem. It sure as hell wasn't Winston's problem. His problem, as he saw it, was how to get through seven more weeks at Minami Kōbe High School teaching students who didn't know which end of the world was up and didn't care because world geography didn't have anything to do with being *kakkoii*. One of the only students who seemed to care was Yū Yanagisawa, the kid he coached for the speech contest on January 14th, just two days before.

Yū did quite well on his memorized five-minute speech "Internationalization is not Westernization". Unfortunately, he sprayed two of the judges with spittle in the middle of his speech, and those two judges, both westerners, penalized him so severely that he was put out of the running. At a special conference, the two sprayed judges told the surprised three other judges, none of whom were westerners, that, in addition to presenting a speech in a natural manner with good pronunciation, it should be presented in such a way that listeners not be made to feel that they need umbrellas. Poor Yū had never been so disappointed in his whole life. He broke down and cried like high-school baseball players often do on TV when their teams bow out of the national tournament. Actually, it was much worse than that. It was pathetic. Yū may have been traumatized. But that was Yū's problem. It sure as hell wasn't Winston's problem. Winston's problem was going to end in 51 days. At least he could count the days until the end of his 'confinement'. That was more than Donovan Wood could do in his cell at the Kōbe Detention Center. The disgraced 'professor' still hadn't had his day in court and had no idea how long they were going to keep him locked up. Whenever Winston thought about Donovan's plight, he didn't know whether to have another laughing fit or break down and cry. Chie broke down and cried when Winston phoned her at her parents' home three days before. Apparently, the prosecutors were going to ask for seven years on the fraud charge. What an unfine mess Donovan had gotten himself into! But that was Donovan's problem. It sure as hell wasn't Winston's problem. Winston may have felt cooped up, but it was nothing compared to what Donovan was so poignantly feeling.

At 10:00 p.m. on this January 16th, Winston was staggering home on a thin layer of snow. It snowed the day before over most of Honshū and all of Hokkaidō. Snow that stayed on the ground had become something of a rarity in Kansai* in recent years and was rarely enough to build the standard Japanese two-snowball snowman. A few years before, a government official justified keeping American ski-equipment companies from penetrating the Japanese market by arguing that Japanese snow is different than American snow, but it seemed the same to Winston as he staggered home from the *okonomiyaki* restaurant Tanuki. He hadn't been there in a long time, so the woman, Shinohara-san, said "Hisashiburi desu ne" (It's been a long time) before adding "Yaketa!" (You have a suntan!) The salubrious effects derived from two weeks in Bali were going to fade much faster than his suntan–that was for sure. In fact, they had already faded and seemed to have done so as quickly as the beer he was going to piss out as soon as he got home. He certainly could have thought of better ways of going than from Bali to abortion, even though that was the way he had been hoping to go. He didn't want that guilt weighing upon his shoulders, not when it involved feeling responsible about helping out with child support. Sure, he had been selfish, but he did not, could not, see any other way to be. His field of vision was narrow because he had blinders on, but within that field, it was, as far as he could see, all cut and dried. He believed, not wholeheartedly, but much more than halfheartedly (about seven-eighths-heartedly) that the right thing to do, or at least the best thing to do, was done. That didn't make it something he could feel good about, but it did make it something he could feel not quite so badly about. The night before, he called Rika several times to show his concern about how she was doing after the abortion, but he kept hanging up because he didn't like talking to telephone-answering machines. On the afternoon of *this* day, the day after the abortion, he went to her apartment in Higashi Nada Ward to show his concern but was rebuffed. They both knew that if he had been wearing his Hanshin Tigers baseball cap, she would have pulled him inside, locked the door behind him, and had him rebuffed (in the sense of renuded) faster than she could say the popular children's tongue-twister 'irohanihoheto'. But he was wearing a wool stocking cap, the same stocking cap he was wearing now as he staggered home with his shoulders shrugged and his hands in his coat pockets.

The day before, temperatures dropped below zero centigrade, to -1°C, for the first time that winter. Minus one degree centigrade (31°F)

---

* the area in and around Ōsaka, Kōbe, and Kyōto, which has a more cultural connotation than the same area also known as Kinki.

does not seem very cold to people accustomed to central heating, but Japanese houses didn't have central heating to get accustomed to. The traditional wooden houses, originally built with summer in mind, could get as cold inside as it got outside–colder, in fact, on sunny days. There were two main ways besides having sex to generate enough heat between your *futons* at night: (1) using an electric blanket and (2) going straight to bed after taking a hot bath. Winston had been using both of those ways. Care had to be taken because, in addition to the common cold, there was a Type A Hong Kong Flu epidemic going on that would end up claiming the lives of 1,244 people nationwide, most of whom were elderly. Damn it was cold–as cold as a witch's tit, as he heard 'Spike' Gallagher refer to the cold when they were in eighth grade. Well, Winston didn't know about witches' tits, but he sure knew about Rika's. He sure knew about her pussy too and would have liked nothing better than another wide-open invitation. He was missing their romps as badly as she was. It had been six weeks since the last time they had sex. Staggering home, he was thinking about how much he would have liked to go to bat in Rika's batter's box just one more time.

'Just one more time' is what the construction-company bosses essentially started saying and re-saying in January with their self-destructing and reconstructing minds set on using up their entire budget allocations by April 1st. The road that Winston was walking along was in the process of being one-more-timed. Road construction was, in fact, going on right outside his house–not now, of course, because it was ten o'clock at night. Jackhammers would be blasting away again at nine o'clock the next morning, though. Winston was looking forward to the road construction getting done so he could have some peace and quiet on the weekends. What he was looking forward to most of all right now was getting home and pissing. "Holy moly, I've got to take a leak!" he said to himself. He reached under the lowest button of his coat and squeezed his dick to hold back the piss that seemed to be making his tonsils float. Looking up while squeezing tightly, he saw a woman standing in front of him.

"Are you Winston Baldry?"

"Yes. Who are you?"

"Chelsia Kotkin. We spoke on the phone five nights ago."

"I thought you were in Australia."

"I was."

"So what are you doing here in Japan?"

"I'm hoping that I can change your–Are you all right?"

"I've got to take a leak."

"Well, don't let me stop you. This is your house, isn't it? The woman at the bookstore next door said it was. At least, I think that's what she said. I'd really appreciate it if you'd invite me in. I've been standing out here in the cold for more than an hour."

"OK, but only until you get warmed up. Holy moly, I've got to get to the toilet fast before it starts coming out of my ears!"

Chelsea followed Winston inside and followed his lead of stepping out of shoes and into slippers. Winston turned on the lights and switched on the *kotatsu*. While heading for the toilet, he told Chelsea to grab a *zabuton* and sit herself down at the *kotatsu*. When he came back a few minutes later with an empty bladder, Chelsea was hiding something in the hollow between her crossed legs. Winston turned on the room heater and sat down across from her. After some small talk, Chelsea got back to the point.

"Winston, getting back to the reason I'm here–this story is really big. With the right person to tell it, you could become a celebrity."

"No, thank you. I was a celebrity here in Japan just three months ago and I don't ever want to be a celebrity again."

"I'm talking big money, Winston. You could name your price on the talk-show circuit. I'm the catalyst that can make it all happen. I've been published 16 times. I think I can swing a serialization-deal with Rupert Murdoch. Then we can talk to Steven Spielberg. This story has Hollywood written all over it. I envision Harrison Ford playing you and Nicole Kidman playing Wallis."

"Have you warmed up enough yet?"

"I contacted a few of the people who found the bottle. Did you know that it was found in the belly of a shark? That adds a nice touch to the story."

"I think you'd better leave. I have to teach tomorrow and I want to do a little preparation before *Sumo Digest* comes on."

"I can come back tomorrow."

"You don't give up, do you?"

"I'm a journalist. Journalists have to be tough. But I can be sensitive too, and I can understand that you're still grieving over the loss of your wife, Nicole."

"Wallis."

"Sorry. Winston, I came all of the way up here from Australia."

"I told you 'No' the other night."

"I'll give you a cut of the screen rights."

"I'm not interested in getting rich."

"So do it for humanitarian reasons. This is a story that can warm the hearts of millions."

There was a soft click, then another one. Chelsea looked at the small tape recorder she was hiding. Something was wrong with it. It was going from forward to reverse, back to forward, back to reverse, and so on. She tried tapping it and shaking it before switching it off with a louder switch-off click that Winston was very familiar with.

"You're taping our conversation!"

"Well, what am I supposed to do? You won't let me interview you."

"I don't know what you're *supposed* to do, but I'll tell you what you're *going* to do. You're going to get out of my house, and my life, right now."

"Can't we–"

"RIGHT NOW!"

"I can't. My sock's caught on something."
Chelsea's sock was caught on a hook-clip attached to the *kotatsu* cord. Winston had to get under the *kotatsu* to do the unhooking. Finally able to get out and up, she straightened out her sock while standing on one leg but lost her balance. Reaching out to steady herself against the shōji,* she put her hand (and arm) through the shōjigami.† She saw no need to apologize to any great degree from her paper-thin point of view because it was only paper, and paper was cheap, even if colored, which this door-paper wasn't. Her last apology came as she stood outside the *genkan* and saw Winston vanish sideways behind the sliding door.

Winston grabbed a beer out of the beer case he kept near the *genkan* and headed back to the living room, which would be harder to keep warm now that there was a huge tear in one of the *shōji*. There was no need to refrigerate his beers because his house was like one big refrigerator. In fact, if it got any colder, he would have to put his beers into the refrigerator so they wouldn't freeze. He took a swig of beer and saw upon lowering the bottle that the red light was flashing on his room heater. He took out the empty canister and carried it out to the *genkan* area, where he pumped more oil into it. Since mid-November, he had been keeping the heater within arm's reach so he could turn it on half an hour before getting up and have the room tolerably warm by then. Two alarm clocks had become a necessity. After putting a full canister of oil into the heater and turning it on, he directed his attention back to the beer and took a swig on his way to the *furo* to re-heat three-day-old water. He had half the bottle drunk by the time he finished laying out his *futons* with the electric blanket in between. After setting his alarm clocks, one for 6:45 and one for 7:15, he plopped down in his massage chair to massage Chelsea Kotkin out of his nerves and Rika Koga out of his nuts. It had not been a nice, long weekend, but it had been a long one with the extra day off and the extra abortion on. Tomorrow he'd be back teaching world geography at Minami Kōbe High School. It wasn't going to be easy teaching with a hangover, but he knew from experience that it wouldn't be much more difficult than teaching without one. He pushed the button to make the rollers roll up and down his upper back and soon fell sound asleep. He woke up at 12:30, an hour after *Sumo Digest* was over. While taking a piss, he remembered that the gas to the *furo* was still on. The water was much too hot to get into, too hot to even reach in and pull out the stopper to let some water out so that cold water could be added. With the *furo* top on, he figured that the water would be just about right in the morning. Fortunately, he had warm *futons* to get in between. He called it a night and went to bed.

He woke up at five o'clock and had to take a piss. He hated getting out of the warmth of his *futon* to piss, just as people camping out in the

---

* sliding door with paper that is inside a wooden frame.

† paper used in shōji.

cold hate getting out of their sleeping bags to do so. He lay there for a while, trying to exert mind over bladder, but a full bladder is powerful matter. An hour earlier, he definitely would have gotten up; an hour later, he probably would have waited it out. Wetting the futon was an option, but not a real consideration. His first alarm wouldn't sound for an hour and 45 minutes. He wanted an hour and 45 minutes more sleep, but he didn't want to take the steps in the cold to make it possible. After half an hour, he decided to get up, leaving only the courage to muster. After three false starts, he finally made his move and slipped out, taking care that his top *futon* remain in place so that no heat would escape. At his TOTO urinal, he power-pissed to his bladder's content. When he finally finished, he started shaking himself. All of a sudden, there was a flash of white light at the window and a spooky, loud gurgle with a bizarre, upward and downward push. Then, with the sound of deafening rolling thunder, came intense, violent, sideways shaking that filled him with 'I'm going to die' horror as he bounced off the walls and fell to the floor with the house crashing down on top of him. Buried in the rubble with the toilet door on top of him, he was stunned. What had just happened? Whatever it was, he was alive. That much was clear. That much was a relief. It must have been a bomb, he thought while crawling out of the rubble.

There were no lights at all, except a faint illumination of a full moon. He stood in the darkness. Destruction was all around him. He ran his hand through his hair and felt the thick wetness of blood. Where in the world was he? For that matter, *who* in the world was he? He didn't have a clue. A bang on the head had given him total amnesia. There he was, with one slipper on and his pecker out. He put his pecker back in. Everything was so still, so silent, and so very eerie. The silent stillness was suddenly obliterated with a panic-filled explosion of screaming and shouting as people seemed to simultaneously recover from their initial shock at least enough to understand that this nightmare was real. "Tasukete!" (Help!) cried out people trapped in the rubble of collapsed houses. Those who had been able to free themselves, but couldn't find family members, shouted out names and listened for faint voices. "Eri-chan! Eri-chan!" screamed a woman near Winston. A man ran by with a top *futon* over him. There was a piercing howl of a dog. The air was thick with choking, eye-burning dust. The smell of gas was everywhere. Fires were breaking out. Massive destruction extended as far as Winston could see in the increasing light of the rising sun.

The twenty-second-long, 7.2-magnitude temblor, which would become known a week later as 'Hanshin Daishinsai' (the Great Hanshin Earthquake) struck at 5:46 a.m. About 3,300 people died immediately. 2,000 or so were buried alive. Buildings still up highlighted the magnitude of what was down. Even utility poles and power lines were down. Rubble was everywhere. Here and there, people were stumbling in piles of roof tiles and broken wood and calling out names. "Kanai o tasuke dashite kudasai!" (Please help me get my wife out!) an elderly man pleaded while tugging on Winston's arm. The man led him to a pile of rubble in which they could hear groaning. Winston took off his pajama top and wrapped it around his bare foot, then helped the man remove debris for an hour until they pulled out his wife. "Dōmo arigatō gozaimashita" (Thank you very much) the man said again and again while sobbing. SDF (Self-Defense Force) reconnaissance helicopters flew overhead and observed the extent of the shocking destruction. 'Shocking' is too soft of a word for the perceptions of those who were deep down in the thick of it. BOOM BOOM BOOM came one loud explosion after another as isolated, windswept fires, fueled by wood, leaking gas, and flammable substances like paint-thinner stored in the synthetic-shoe factories, spread and created a crisis on top of a crisis while government officials at all levels demonstrated complete lack of leadership by passing the buck up and down and back and forth and creating a crisis-management crisis that delayed deployment of the SDF for rescue operations. Some people rushed in to give a helping hand, but the number of people rushing to get in was nothing compared to the number of people rushing to get out. Many for whom it was already too late stood by powerlessly and watched everything they had go up in smoke. The few volunteers were overwhelmed with the awareness that almost every house that was down had at least one person buried under its rubble. There was no time to waste digging out dead people, so they had to listen for voices, and they had to listen carefully because most of the muffled voices were faint. "Okaasan! Okaasan!" (Mommy! Mommy!) Winston heard a trapped child calling out.

Prime Minister Tomiichi Murayama studied the situation and awaited recommendations, while Defense Agency Director General Tokuichi Tamazawa worried about martial law vs. civil law implications and wondered if the massive destruction and mounting death toll constituted a 'genuine emergency' that would thereby justify sending in the SDF without the customary formal request from the prefectural governor. At 10:00 a.m., more than four hours after the killer earthquake, the governor of Hyōgo Prefecture, Tokitami Kaihara, was persuaded to make the formal request for the deployment of the SDF. The SDF then proceeded to demonstrate ineptness in mobilization, which further delayed deployment. By 11:30 a.m., when Ōsaka Gas finally got around to shutting off the gas that was feeding the fires, Winston had dug out six people, four of them alive. He was covered with blood from falls on unstable debris containing splintered wood and broken glass. Completely exhausted after another rolling fall, he crawled to a spot under a broken water pipe and let the water flow into his mouth and onto his bruised and bloodied face. A man wearing a burned hanten* with the cotton stuffing coming out helped him get up and walked him over to a fallen vending machine. "Daijōbu?" (Are you all right?) the man said as he sat Winston down on

---

* thick, half-length, cotton robe.

the vending machine, but Winston made no reply. The man took off his *hanten* and put it on Winston, then went back to do more volunteer-rescue work. Winston spat out blood and looked over at an elderly man in dirty long underwear sitting stoically in front of a collapsed house and drinking sake from a 1.8-liter bottle. A few university students who had rushed in from their dormitory to do volunteer work came over and said to Winston, "Koko wa abunai yo!" (Hey, it's dangerous here!) Winston allowed himself to be helped up and escorted away, but the elderly fellow refused to leave, saying, "Kore wa watashi no ie desu. Zutto koko ni sunde irun ya. Doko ni mo ikanai." (This is my home. I've lived here all my life. I'm not leaving.) Winston walked slowly, dripping blood in his footsteps. His mind, focused on nothing more than the next step he was taking, was without fear of dying. An old woman was kneeling in front of a leaning four-story apartment building and praying for it to fall on her. Winston grabbed her by the arm and dragged her several steps without breaking his stride or even fixing his eyes on her. Television camera crews circling in helicopters filmed hundreds of fires that were not fought with aerial firefighting, with the reason being that many people trapped in rubble might drown. So many people trapped in rubble burned to death, and the fires kept spreading. A mass exodus was going on. Many people left messages on wooden boards saying where they would be taking refuge. Tens of thousands of people were already at places serving (without service) as evacuation shelters. Many were in need of medical treatment, which would not be coming from the Japan International Cooperation Agency's relief team of 500 doctors because the JICA said that this disaster did not apply to them since it was not abroad. The Health and Welfare Mininstry rejected first-aid medical groups as being unnecessary. Foreign doctors were not allowed to come in and help out on the basis that they didn't have Japanese doctors' licenses. Foreign offers of help were repeatedly turned down because officials didn't want Japan to seem to be a third-world country that couldn't take care of its own problems. Swiss rescue dogs would have been helpful in finding trapped people, but the Swiss govenment was told thanks but no thanks. The first two days are crucial in getting trapped victims out, but the people buried alive in Kōbe were going to lose the battle against time because of delays. Meanwhile, fire fighters and SDF rescue workers were stuck in horrendous traffic jams because no route was blocked off for emergency passage.

Government officials could not have demonstrated more indecisiveness if they had been trying to. The fiasco laid bare the biggest defect in the Japanese educational system, a system that placed so much emphasis on rote-learning and groupism that it stifled development of free, individualistic thinking. The high-ranking government officials weren't stupid people. They could pass examinations with the best of them and had, in fact, done so, which is how they got into top-notch universities like Tōkyō University that paved their way to officialdom. What they couldn't do was make big decisions on their own without having to resort to precedents or refer to policy manuals. This was a major crisis. Decisions needed to be made, and they needed to be made fast. Real leadership needed to be demonstrated, but there wasn't going to be any because there weren't any real leaders. Taking charge was frowned upon in Japanese society. Group-oriented Japan functioned, and generally functioned quite well, without real leadership. Decisions were reached by consensus in order to maintain harmony within the group. That took time. Sometimes it took a long time. Sometimes it seemed to take forever. But that's the way it was done. They couldn't do it any other way. There was talk about instilling individualistic free-thinking into the educational system, but that would stay in the talking stage because the educators themselves would have to be re-edu-cated, and the powerful Nikkyōso (Japan Teachers' Union) wasn't going to go for that. About 10,000 boys and girls had been returning as kikokushijos* a year. Some of them had picked up a little assertiveness and an ability to think for themselves. For that, they experienced discrimination for having lost their Japaneseness. There are definitely times when other peoples could do with a little Japaneseness. There are also times when Japanese could do with a little less of it. This was one of those times. It would take the government one whole week to designate this a "severe disaster" instead of an "ordinary disaster" and thereby justify special financial assistance.

Things weren't getting better; they were getting worse. The worst of the worse was in Nagata Ward, where Winston was now walking . . . past a dead woman, a burned truck, a child carrying a stuffed animal, burning debris, a car sticking out of a pile of rubble, the smell of burning syn-thetic rubber, another loud explosion, a woman retrieving her butsudan,† a man removing roof tiles and calling out for his mother. With the eye-stinging haze blocking the sun, Winston had no directional guide, and he wasn't really getting anywhere because he kept having to veer this way and turn that way on narrow streets blocked by collapsed houses and toppled buildings. By 5:30, when it was starting to get dark, he had gotten no farther than Komagabayashi Park in Nagata Ward.

A group of about seventy Vietnamese had gathered in the park. Except for the children, almost all of them came to Japan as 'boat people'. Being refugees was not something new for them. They were bundled up and huddled around a bonfire. About 250,000 people were now shivering in school gymnasiums, churches, athletic fields, parks, and other places that served as evacuation shelters. These Vietnam-ese at least had heat. They also had food. One of the guys had killed a lame dog, and it was being boiled. Back in Vietnam, they used to eat dog often. They used to eat cat too, and even rat. They knew how to

---

* children returning from school abroad, usually because their fathers were transferred overseas.

† Buddhist family altar, which is traditionally passed on to the eldest son.

survive. A girl returning with a load of wood to keep the fire going saw Winston sitting beneath a tree. A couple of minutes later, a young man with a flashlight came over and assisted him to the warmth of the bonfire. Space was made for him to squeeze in and sit on a turned-over beer crate. A woman washed the dried blood off his face and cleaned the cuts on his feet. When asked in English where he was from, he said that he didn't know. "Ông ta hoãng hôn" (He's in shock) a man said and put an end to the special attention the newcomer had been receiving. Everybody there was in shock to some degree, and they all knew that if this westerner lost his wife or even his whole family in the earthquake, he wasn't such a special case. Except for one woman weeping too much to do anything else, the women were busy making dog noodle soup, something the makers of Campbell's never considered selling in the can. Winston ate a bowl of the soup. He would have asked for seconds, but there weren't any seconds to be had, and there certainly wasn't any dessert. Winston's favorite dessert was apple pie à la mode, but he couldn't have said so. His amnesia was as total as total amnesia can get. He stared into the fire with the others until he fell asleep.

It was light when he woke up. The fire was still going and the women were up and working. This was going to be their home for a while and they were going to make the best of it. It wasn't bright and early only because it wasn't bright. The smoky, dusty haze was too thick to let in brightness. Winston was given a breakfast of cat noodle soup made with the meat of a black cat, believed to have medicinal value. Then he set off—not on his way, because he didn't have a way. He had no idea where he was going; he was just going. He had to sit down after a couple of minutes because he was out of energy. For half an hour, he sat near a flattened house that had a bouquet of flowers set in its rubble. His eyes felt better from having had them closed during sleep, but his throat was sore. He vomited and began to feel a little better, good enough to resume walking anyway. He walked north to the JR and Hankyū tracks and then headed east. The tracks gave him a direction to go so he wouldn't be walking around in circles. No trains were running. Trains coming toward Kōbe from Ōsaka went only as far as Nishinomiya–about 14 miles from where he was now walking.

Fires had raged throughout the night. Many fresh fires broke out and were still breaking out. The sky was filled with gray smoke. 2,500 people were confirmed dead, with 'confirmed' being the operative word because about 5,000 were *actually* dead. The number of people in evacuation shelters was 220,000 and climbing. Food was on their minds because it wasn't in their stomachs, but it took the Food Agency seven hours to decide to send rice after the request was finally made. Many of the people in the shelters needed medical treatment but were turned away by hospitals because there was no room, not to mention no gas, electricity, or water. The water shortage was going to cause hygienic problems, and things were already getting unsanitary with germs and viruses moving about. Winston was probably better off walking. He walked past a derailed train, a collapsed condominium, and a gutted building, and kept on walking, following the train tracks. Within an hour, he was in Hyōgo Ward. The second half of Hyōgo Ward and the first half of Chūō Ward were not nearly so bad, but that didn't mean that things were getting better. There were gaps, just as a ravaged area could have one block relatively OK and the next one completely destroyed. Areas hit with the full force of the 7.2-magnitude temblor extended past Kōbe and Ashiya and into Nishinomiya. Winston crossed into Chūō Ward at 2:30. He saw some SDF rescue workers there in their khaki uniforms. Two of them were carrying a blanket-covered corpse on a stretcher. He went up hard-hit Tor Road in the Sannomiya district hoping to find something, anything, to eat. Without a yen on him, he needed a handout. Some people were taking advantage of the situation and selling food for two or three times the normal price, but they were far outnumbered by charitable people giving food away. People were waiting in long lines, and they were waiting patiently. Throughout the disaster-stricken areas, nobody was looting or rioting—a strong statement about the integrity of the Japanese. Winston waited in three long lines that proved to be too long for the amount of food available. Finally, he gave up and wandered off—in the direction of Kaikyō Jiin Mosque.

The 60-year-old mosque, undamaged by air raids during World War Two, survived the Great Hanshin Earthquake with minimal damage. It was the place of worship for the 100 or so Muslims living in Kōbe, half of whom were students from several countries. About forty Muslims were now there as evacuees. A Bangladeshi student was on his way back there with a bag of rice when Winston came along. "Welcome, my friend," he said to the man he thought was a fellow Muslim going to the mosque for refuge, and he opened the door for him. Inside the mosque, a purification ceremony was going on for an Algerian student killed by the temblor. After recitations from the *Koran* were finished, attention was turned to the new evacuee. As neither the imam* nor the managing director recalled ever seeing him before, he was asked what country he was from, and in a raspy voice caused by inflammation of the throat, he answered that he didn't know. The Bangladeshi student who let him in said that he heard the man say 'Holy moly' upon entering and asked if 'Moly' was a reference to Allah in any of their mother tongues. Nobody had ever heard of it, but that didn't mean that 'Holy moly' wasn't an expression like 'God is great' in some other language. A Malaysian man stepped forward and said, "Praise be to Allah," and Winston said, "Holy moly." That was enough to have him Islamically welcomed and washed in preparation for a dinner of halal† meat curry and rice.

---

* Muslim priest.

† strict Koranic food guidelines pertaining to cleanliness, from slaughter to storage to preparation.

Water supply had been shut off, but the mosque had its own well from which they could draw water to purify their faces, hands, and legs before their regular five-times-a-day prayers. For the final prayer session of the day, Winston was given a cloth to kneel on. Doing as the others did, he prostrated himself, but doing as the others did not, he fell asleep and snored. He awoke shortly after the early-morning prayer session and was given tea and bread. A few of the students left to stay in undamaged apartments of friends. One of them said to Winston before leaving, "Peace be with you. Salaam. Holy moly." Winston went out after them. He walked down to destroyed Hankyū Sannomiya Station and headed east along the Hanshin Railway tracks. The tracks ran along the elevated Hanshin Expressway. Cleanup operations were just starting. Big, orange cranes were picking things up and pulling things out. Swiss rescue dogs were finally allowed in (after going through quarantine), as the government stopped being too proud to accept foreign help, at least non-human foreign help. Foreign doctors would not be allowed in for another five days to help out at evacuation shelters, where many among the now 300,000 people were sick and/or suffering from post-traumatic stress disorder. The Swiss rescue dogs arrived before Prime Minister Murayama, who was occupied with various formalities. (Crown Prince Hironomiya and Crown Princess Masako went ahead with their planned diplomatic trip abroad, as formality had precedence over humanity.) Thirty fresh fires informally started that morning, and strong winds were fanning the fires and making firefighting difficult. Water was in very short supply, and long lines of people were waiting with the hope of getting some. Winston was dehydrated but kept walking. Sorely but surely, the total amnesiac walked slowly through totally destroyed and badly damaged areas. In parts of Nada Ward, where one-third of the country's sake breweries were located, there was a strong smell of sake. Winston found a big, unexploded bottle of Hakutsuru sake and sat down with it near a charred, upside-down truck to quench his thirst. Some time later, the now totally drunk total amnesiac was swervely but surely back on his feet and staggering along the train tracks. By nightfall, he was staggering in Higashi-Nada Ward with vomit all over the front of him. He had just kicked a UCC coffee can past a yellow bulldozer when a man coming toward him grabbed him by the shoulders and pulled him aside. The man's face was hidden behind a surgical mask, dark sunglasses, and a stocking cap pulled down low. The man took off the sunglasses and lowered the mask. He had a sunken left eye.

"Winston! What a sorry sight you are! I know I'm not much to look at myself. My friggin' glass eye popped out in the quake. The whole jail house came down. I found the guard's handgun on my way out. I'll use it if I have to. I'm not going back to rotting in jail. I'm a friggin' fugitive, mate. Listen, I got a hold of Chie from a public phone. She came to meet me yesterday and again a little while ago. We're getting smuggled out of the country tonight. You've got to come with us. Seismologists are talking about another big one hitting. Winston, do you hear what I'm saying?"

"Is my name Winston?"

"What! You've got amnesia? Yeah, your name is Winston Hun. You're a direct descendent of Attila the Hun and the tenth husband of Zsa Zsa Gabor. I could have a lot of fun with a guy suffering from amnesia, but there will be time for that later, I hope. I've got to keep moving to make it on time. Come along with me, mate."

Through a short chain of connections that started with a Chinese friend of Donovan's who ran a restaurant in Kōbe's Chinatown, a member of the criminal syndicate Snakehead had been contacted. Based in Hong Kong, Snakehead, which had ties to the Yamaguchi-gumi, routinely smuggled mainland Chinese into Japan on fishing boats. Very rarely were they asked to smuggle people out of Japan. It was a whole lot easier getting people out of Japan than getting people in, and with the Maritime Safety Agency in complete disarray in Kōbe, it was considered as easy as one two three million. That was yen, and that was for all five of them—¥600,000 a head. Chie didn't have that kind of cash at her immediate disposal, so she hocked her jewelry–all of it. There was a Chinese cargo ship leaving Kōbe Port at 8:30 after two days of suspended operations due to heavy damage. The deal was that they'd be put on board, smuggled into Hong Kong, and given forged passports, another Snakehead specialty. Chie worked everything out with a Chinese mobster named Jong-bong 'Johnny' Wong and explained how things stood when she met Donovan the evening before at his hiding place near destroyed Ashiya Station. After receiving the final phone call on the morning of this day at her parents' home in Amagasaki, the Wood minutewomen took the Hankyū train as far as it went, to Nishinomiya-Kitaguchi Station. Then they put on surgical masks and walked straight into the hazy, nightmarish scene of flattened houses, toppled and leaning buildings, broken glass and wood, roaring fires, smoldering ashes, firetrucks and firefighters, cranes and bulldozers, cleanup crews, SDF rescue workers, news crews, collapsed sections of the Hanshin Expressway, demolished trucks and cars, fallen expressway pillars, exposed iron reinforcing rods, broken cement, makeshift outdoor shops, long lines of hungry people, and people bringing in relief supplies.

Thousands of people from near and far were coming in with instant noodles, mineral water, and other provisions for the victims. Throughout Japan, people by the millions were generously donating money to help out. The empathy and the solidarity showed Japanese groupism at its very best. The difference between the Wood women and the thousands of community-spirited people coming in was that *their* knapsacks and carts were loaded with things intended only for *them*. On their way to meet Johnny Wong, they stopped at Donovan's hiding place, and Chie told him to meet them at 7:00 one block north of Mikage High School in Higashi-Nada Ward, which was housing 2,500 evacuees. It was 6:30

when Donovan ran into Winston, and he was on schedule. He showed up with Winston and said that the drunken amnesiac would be going too. Wong demanded another ¥600,000 for Winston, which created a problem because Chie had only ¥250,000 left on her. It didn't look good for Winston until Donovan remembered what *he* had on *him*.

"How about if I give you a gun instead, Mr. Wong?"

"What type gun you have?"

"The very best. And you must know how hard it is to get a good gun in Japan."

"Let me see."

Donovan handed him the gun. Wong shined a flashlight on it. It was a New Nanbu .38. "It's loaded," Donovan cautioned. Wong put the gun into his coat pocket. "Follow me," he said.

They followed Wong 1,631 steps—according to Wong's pedometer. He always had his pedometer clipped to him, except when he was sleeping. He would have kept it on when he slept if he had been known to sleep-walk. Wong liked to keep track of his steps, most of which, like this particular business transaction, were indirectly to the bank. He walked briskly now as he always did. The others, especially Donovan, who was assisting the now hiccuping Winston, had to make efforts to keep up with him. They arrived at a pier in southern Higashi-Nada Ward. All of them, except Wong, stepped down into a motorboat and crouched between the seats. The driver put a black tarp over them, then started the motor and drove half a mile out to a small, anchored, unlit fishing boat. Two men on board pulled up their belongings first and then helped them up and in. They huddled in the engine room and rocked back and forth on the waves, waiting nervously for the cargo ship to take off. Finally it did. One man pulled anchor; the other turned on the engine. The fishing boat moved slowly with its light off, following the lights of the big ship. About three miles out, the big ship's motor was turned off and the crew waited to receive the six stowaways.

Safely on board, they looked out at the faint lights of the fires burning in Kōbe.

"Otōsan, hontō ni–" (Dad, is it really true that–)

"You'd better get used to speaking English, Mari."

"I'm Misa. Well, is it really true we're going to live in a condominium near Sydney Harbor?"

Megumi and Mari were also wanting to know if it was really true. Donovan looked at Chie. She was looking him straight into his good eye. Undamaged Port Tower was disappearing from sight. "Yeah, it's true," he said and saw three jumps for joy. Then he pulled Chie aside.

"What else did you have to tell them to get them to come, Chie?"

"Only one more thing—that we're going to have a Mercedes Benz."

"It's going to be a used one."

"I'm happy."

"I'm glad you're happy."

Winston turned away from the couple in each other's arms. He looked down and watched the ship cutting through the water. One of the Chinese crew members came over and offered him a Tsingtao beer. Winston thanked him. The man also gave him a bag of mixed nuts to go with it. Winston thanked him again.

Epilogue

After leaving Winston Baldry's home on the night of January 16th, Chelsea Kotkin went to her hotel in Kōbe's Chūō Ward and lived to write an article about her firsthand experience of the Great Hanshin Earthquake, which was her 17th published article. After sending the article from Japan, she headed to the USA to get information about Wallis Baldry, and she was steered by the three ladies renting the Baldrys' home to a few people, including George and Adele Piper, who had been trying desperately, like several worried others, to obtain information about Winston from the American Embassy in Tōkyō. On January 28th, 14 people were still listed as missing, and Winston was one of them. He recovered from amnesia on January 30th while staying at the seedy Chungking Mansion on the Kowloon side of Hong Kong. Not wanting to go back to a cold winter, he took up Donovan on an invitation to come to Australia and stayed with the Woods for six weeks at a lovely condominium near Sydney Harbor that they bought outright. He was reading a magazine in early March and came across Chelsea A. Kotkin's 18th published article, titled "A Bottle For All Oceans". The article caused a great sensation Down Under, and a bar owner in Sydney offered A$100,000 for the bottle. The size of the offer made the story newsworthy enough for the Associated Press and Reuters. Fishing boats in waters between Indonesia and Hawaii doubled up as search boats. *Time* magazine ran a condensed version of C.A. Kotkin's article, giving her another big journalistic boost and turning Winston Baldry into a celebrity. C.A. Kotkin sold the screen rights in March of 1997 for US$2,000,000. The role of Wallis Baldry went to Sharon Stone, after being turned down by Winona Ryder because the script called for a sexually explicit love-scene during the Baldrys' honeymoon in the Caribbean. John Travolta, cast as Winston, said in a *Playboy* interview that it was his most challenging role to date. The $20,000,000 production of *Wallis and Winston,* completed in April of 1998, is slated to be released, for promotional reasons, as soon as the bottle is found, and Paramount Pictures is now offering a $2,000,000 finder's fee. As for the real Winston Baldry, he dropped out of sight shortly after the *Time* magazine article and took with him his and Wallis's entire savings, which was substantial because of 13 years of no expenses that fell under the category TRAVEL. There is, however, a "Winston Watch" homepage at www.winstonwatch.com that keeps tabs on his most recent alleged sightings, which have ranged from rollerblading in New York City's Central Park to playing roulette at the MGM Grand Hotel in Las Vegas. No "Donovan Watch" home page needs to be set up because he seldom strays far from their condominium, where he does translation work and things that fall under the category LEISURE in his soundproof room. Barred like her husband from ever returning to Japan, Chie Wood manages a boutique in the Queen Victoria Building. She can sometimes be seen driving a used Mercedes Benz. Misa, Mari, and Megumi have become very pretty, young ladies and spend much more time with their boyfriends than on their homework. Donovan still can't tell which one is which.

The author with his best friend (and wife)

Also by Jim Riva

The *Champion of Reason* by Jim Riva. Published by Soaring Sparrow Press. Set in the superficial city of Addleton, where religion reigns over science and people merely exist instead of really live, *The Champion of Reason*, written by the author of *The Geographer*, is a philosophical comedy, a scathing satire, and a rock-'n'-roll adventure of one man's heroic efforts to stand up against folly and battle for truth, justice, and the rational way.

For information: http://www.jimriva-ssp.com

EXCERPTS FROM *THE CHAMPION OF REASON*

"Why isn't there a superhero to fight foolishness?"–seven-year-old Jolly Wagner to Jake of Jake's Rock 'n' Roll Show

CHAMP OF REASON STRIKES AGAIN!–front-page headline in the *Addleton Aether*

"I'll be a whole lot better when they catch that Champion of Reason outlaw. This town won't be safe while he's at large."–socialite Constance 'the Duchess' Mazur to her daughter Jennifer

"The fellow you are referring to ought to be called the Champion of *Treason*. His boring harangues are blasphemous and un-American. But we have more pressing things to worry about than some goofball who likes to dress up in an asinine costume and gets his jollies giving stupid speeches and then running away like a sissy."–Mayor Yaroborough at a special press conference

SWASHBUCKLER RIDES HORSEBACK! DRAMATIC RIDE THROUGH CITY STREETS–banner headline in the *Addleton Aether*

"I'm not preaching, I'm teaching. There are a lot of people telling you to believe this or believe that. I'm not telling you to believe *any*thing. All I'm saying is, 'Be reasonable.'"–The Champion of Reason to the students in the seventh-period science class at L. Ron Hubbard High

"I tell you, the evildoer who calls himself the Champion of Reason is the Antichrist. And if you don't denounce him, you'll go to Hell."–Father Ralph Ryan to his Sunday catechism class

"Undercover cops are going to be all over the place."–Chief of Police Lyle Verdon to Mayor Yaroborough

"Superheroes can't quit."–retired Albert Mavis to Jake Leander

"Oyez, oyez, hear ye, hear ye: $53,000 reward for bringing in the Champion of Reason alive!"–city clerk and part-time town crier, Emile Yassky

"I'm issuing orders right here and now for you to instruct your men to shoot the bastard on sight, and to shoot to kill."–Mayor Yaroborough to Chief of Police Lyle Verdon

"Do you have the situation under control, or am I gonna have to declare Addleton in a state of emergency?"–Governor Montgomery Marsluf to Mayor Yaroborough

Dear Reader,

    I self-published *The Geographer* and *The Champion of Reason* under the name Soaring Sparrow Press, and I don't see any reason to make pretenses to the contrary. I decided to self-publish my books without even trying to get them published by a publishing company because I didn't want to put my books (not to mention the lion's share of the profits) into the hands of somebody else, especially since the Internet has created a whole new ball game for self-publishers. Through a homepage on the Internet, I can display both the front and back covers of my books and, more importantly for discerning readers, provide large sections of reviews of the books instead of just presenting the usual 'dazzling', 'sizzling', and 'spellbinding' extractions used in blurbs. If you can't find my books at a book store near you, you can order them through Amazon.com. I hope that you enjoy my books and consider them well worth the money.

Sincerely,
Jim Riva

For Information: http://www.jimriva-ssp.com